CATWAD

ME, THREE!

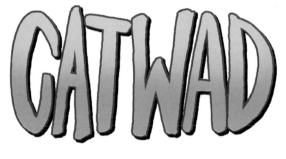

FOR DEBRA DORFMAN

THANKS TO KRISTEN LECLERC, MICHAEL PETRANEK,
KATIE FITCH, AND DAVID SAYLOR.

ISBN 978-1-338-61628-6

10 9 8 7 6 5 4 3 2 1   20 21 22 23 24

Printed in the U.S.A.   40

First edition, April 2020

Edited by Michael Petranek
Book design by Katie Fitch

ME, THREE!

Jim Benton

AN IMPRINT OF
■SCHOLASTIC

BEDTIME

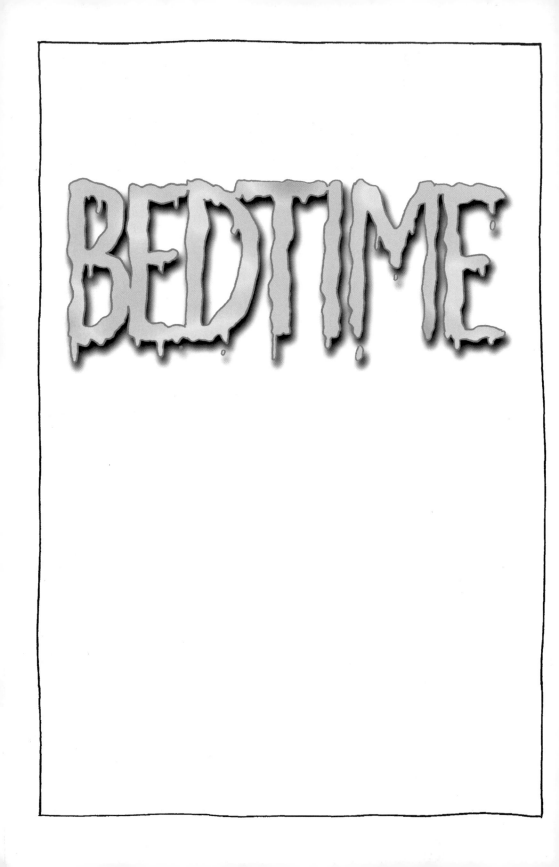

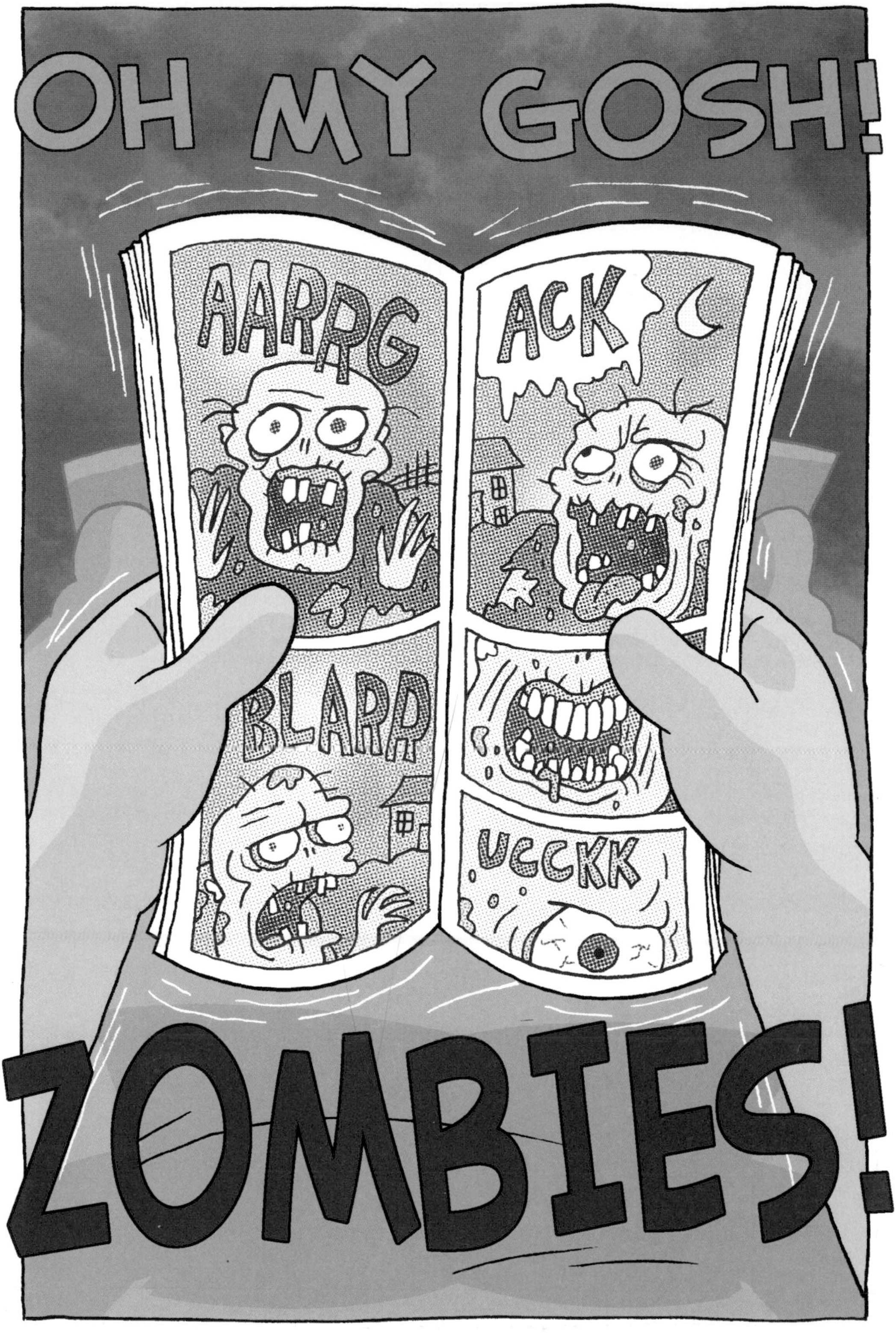
OH MY GOSH!
AARRG
ACK
BLARR
UCCKK
ZOMBIES!

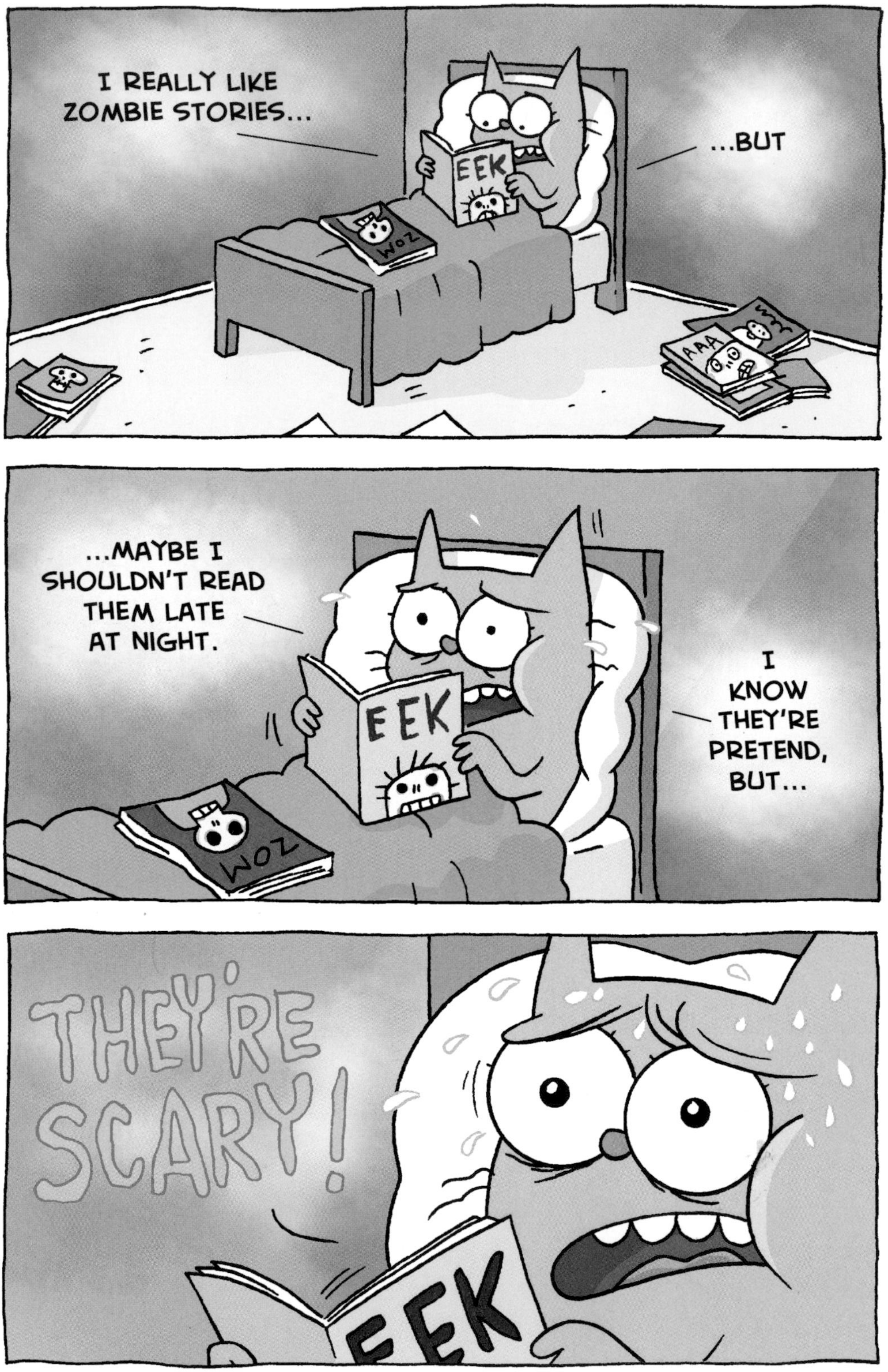
I REALLY LIKE ZOMBIE STORIES...
EEK
WOZ
...BUT
AAA
...MAYBE I SHOULDN'T READ THEM LATE AT NIGHT.
EEK
WOZ
I KNOW THEY'RE PRETEND, BUT...
THEY'RE SCARY!
EEK

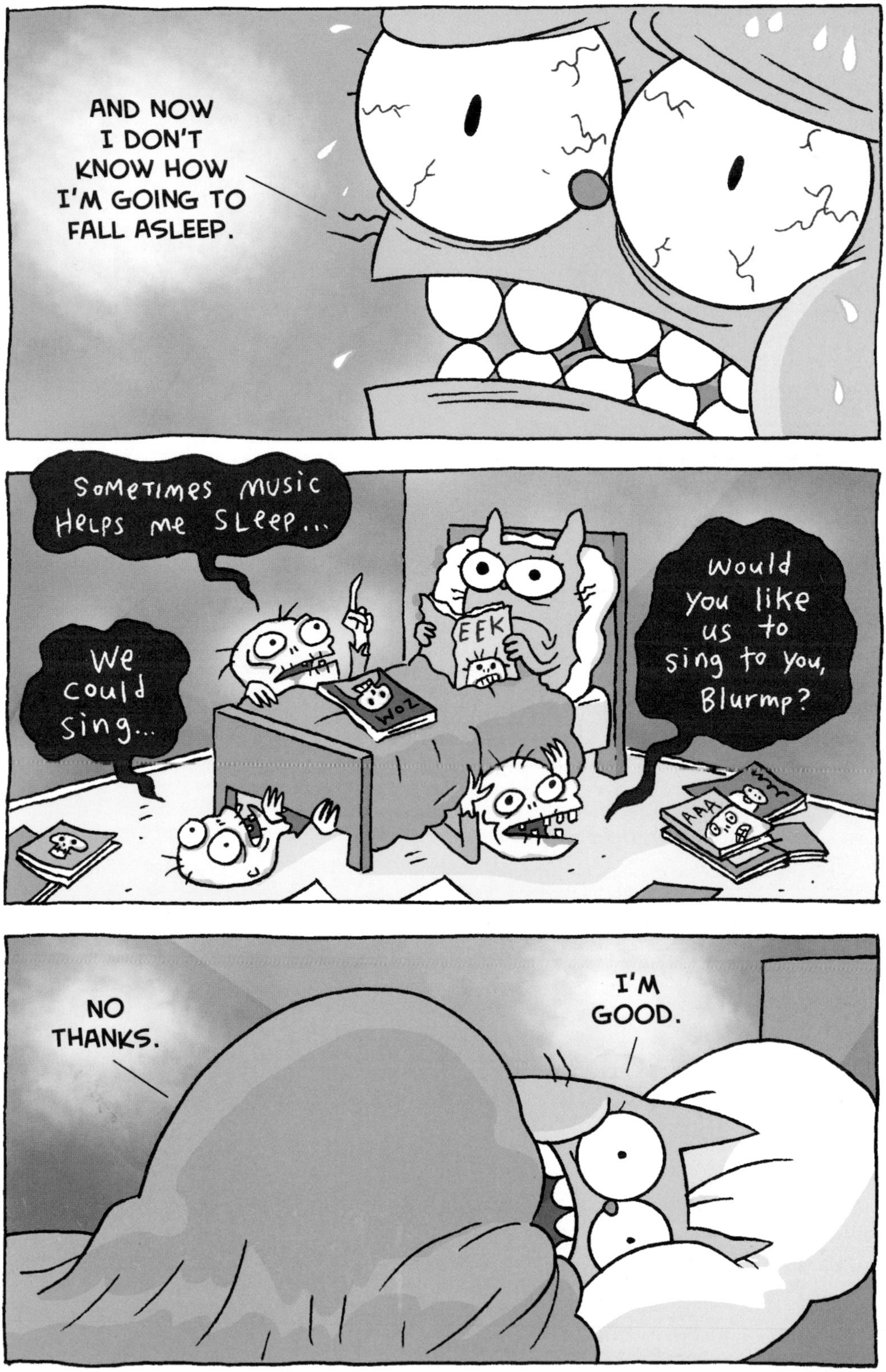
AND NOW I DON'T KNOW HOW I'M GOING TO FALL ASLEEP.
SomeTimes music Helps me SLeep...
We could sing...
Would you like us to sing to you, Blurmp?
EEK
WOZ
AAA
NO THANKS.
I'M GOOD.

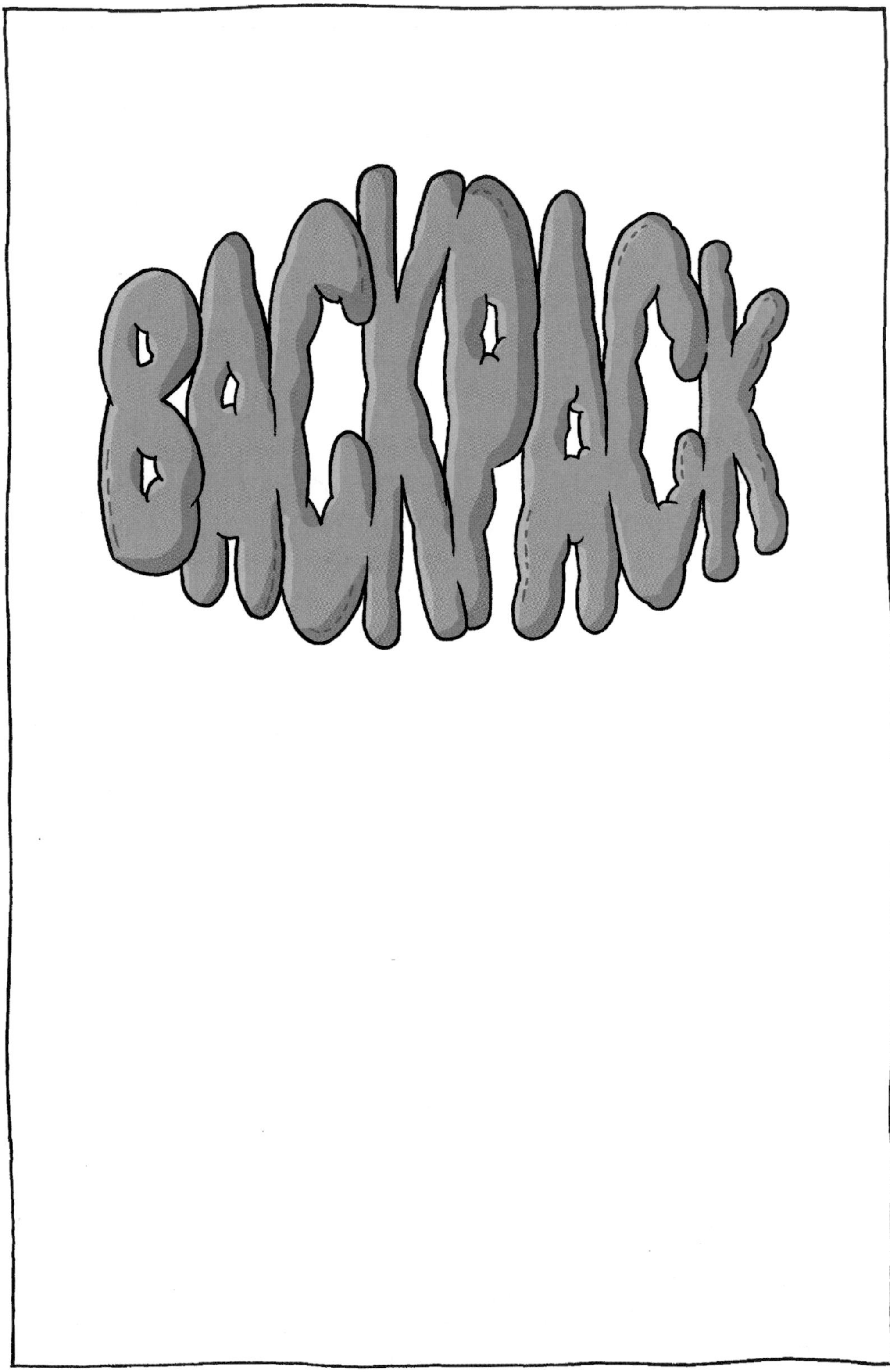
BACKPACK

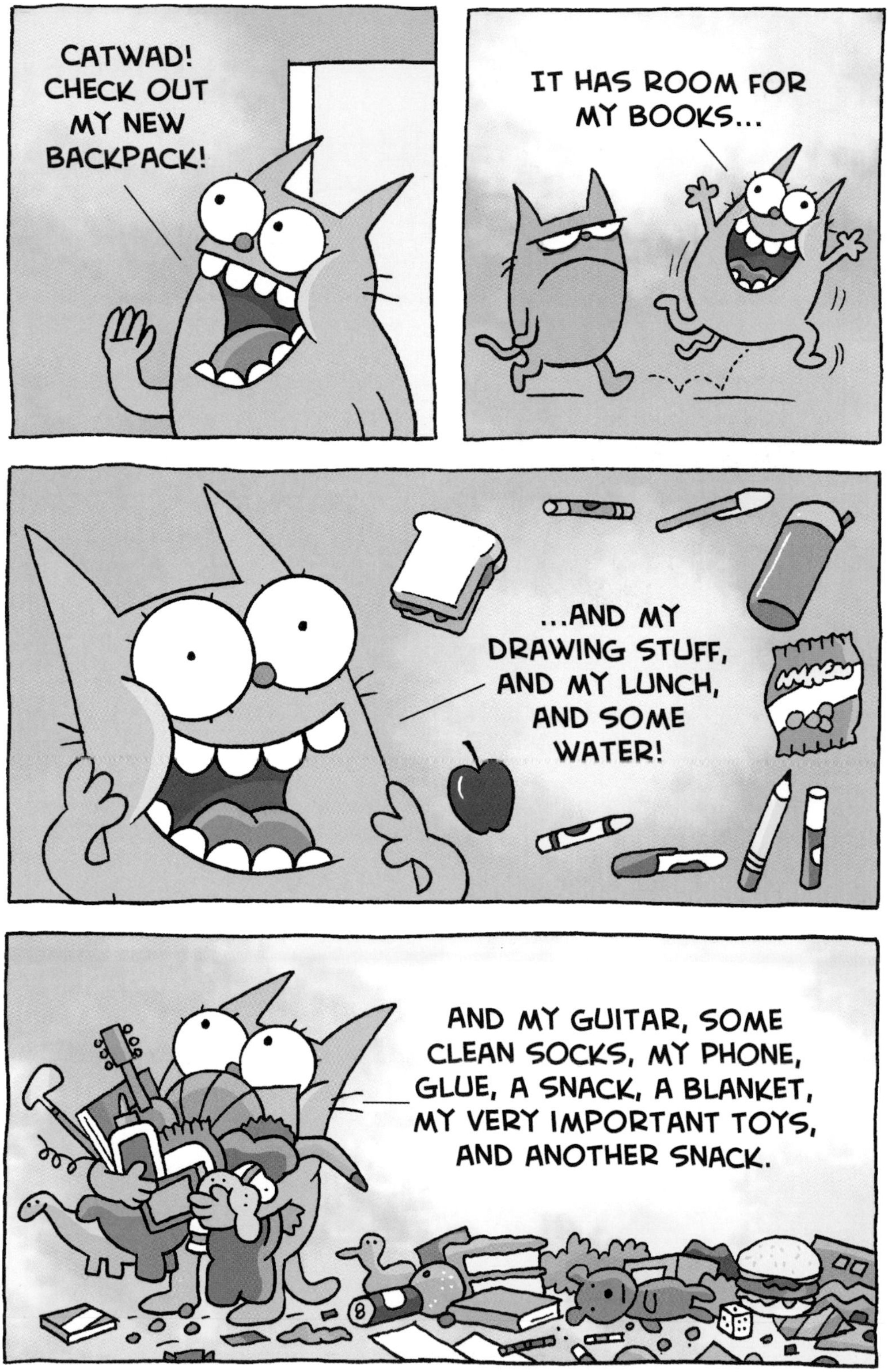
CATWAD! CHECK OUT MY NEW BACKPACK!
IT HAS ROOM FOR MY BOOKS...
...AND MY DRAWING STUFF, AND MY LUNCH, AND SOME WATER!
AND MY GUITAR, SOME CLEAN SOCKS, MY PHONE, GLUE, A SNACK, A BLANKET, MY VERY IMPORTANT TOYS, AND ANOTHER SNACK.

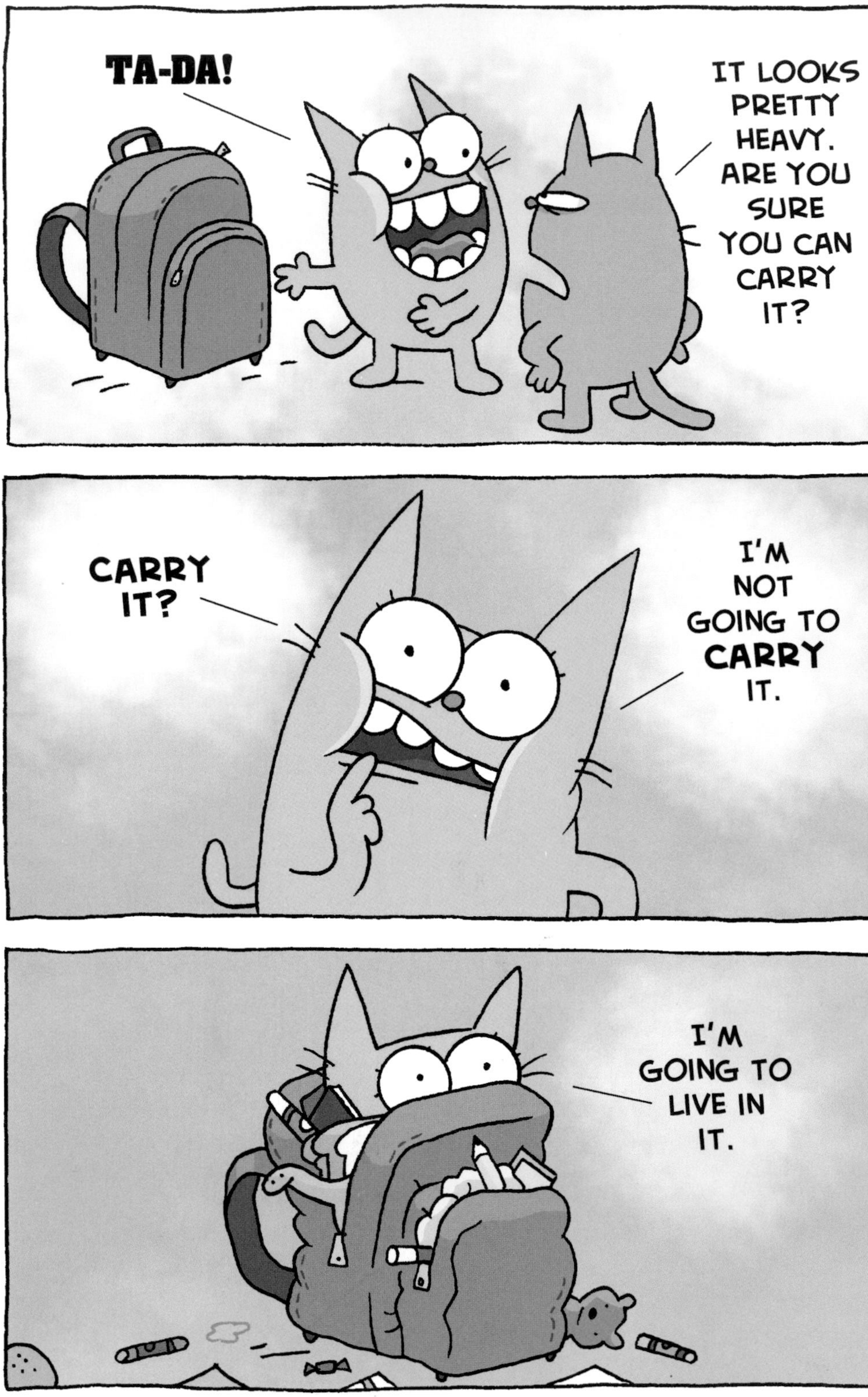
TA-DA!
IT LOOKS PRETTY HEAVY. ARE YOU SURE YOU CAN CARRY IT?
CARRY IT?
I'M NOT GOING TO CARRY IT.
I'M GOING TO LIVE IN IT.

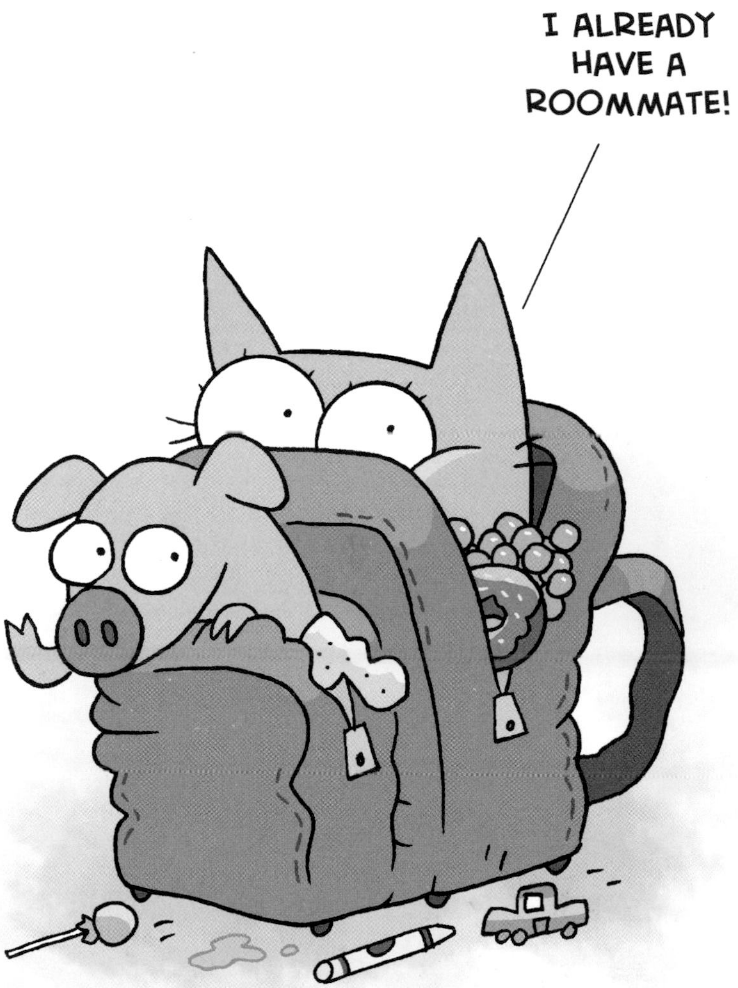
I ALREADY HAVE A ROOMMATE!

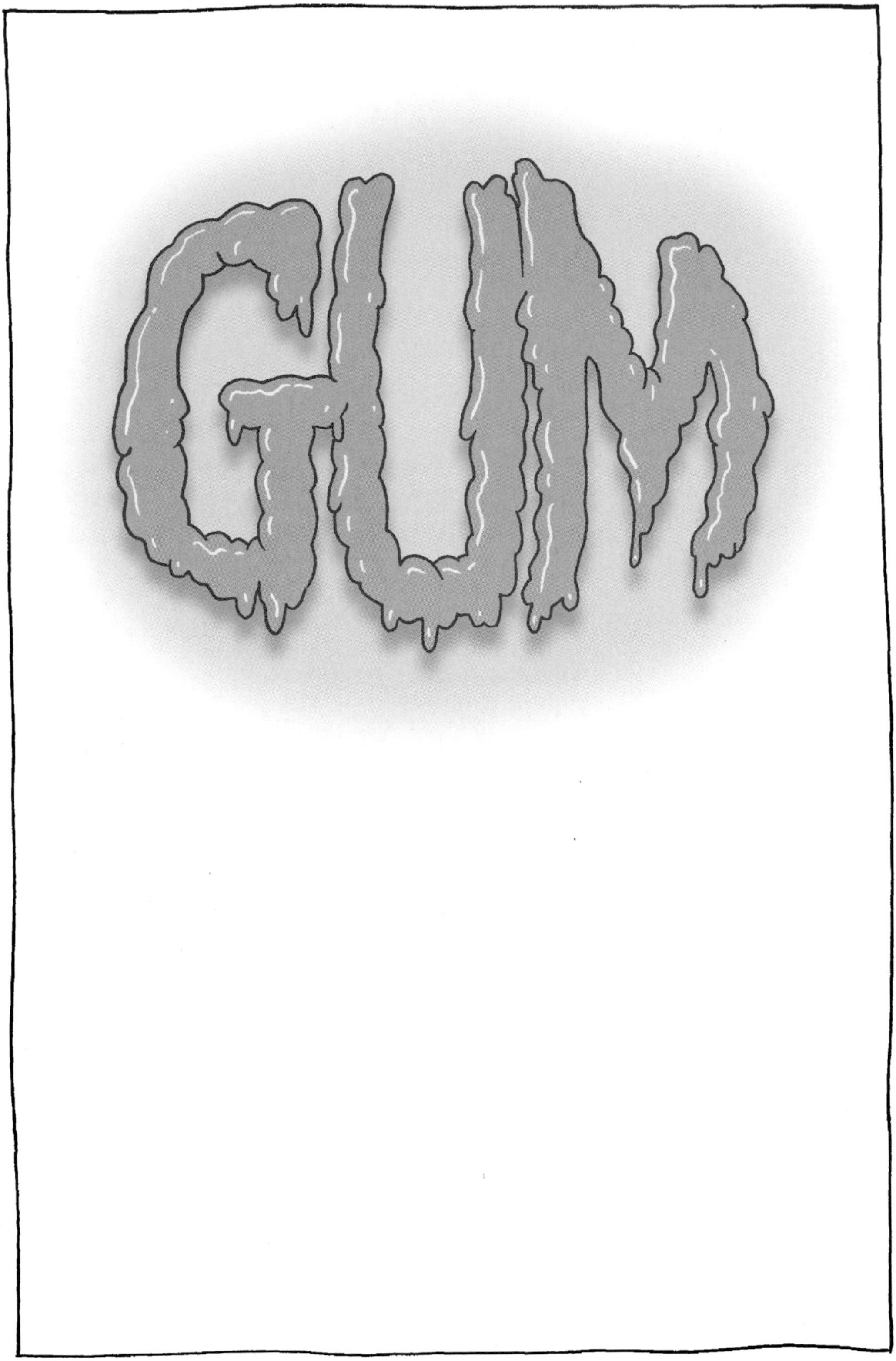
GUM

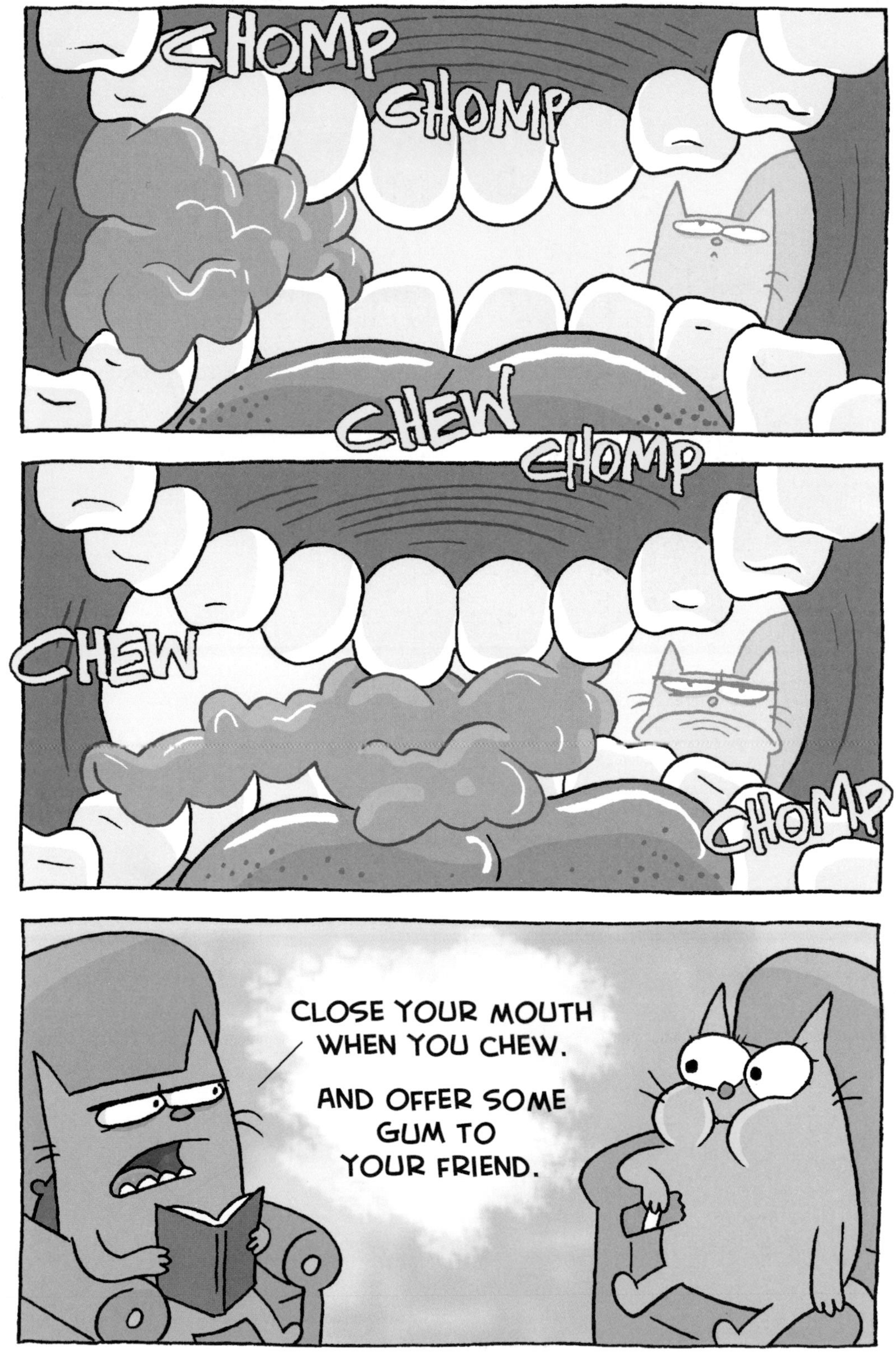
CHOMP
CHOMP
CHEW
CHOMP
CHEW
CHOMP
CLOSE YOUR MOUTH WHEN YOU CHEW.
AND OFFER SOME GUM TO YOUR FRIEND.

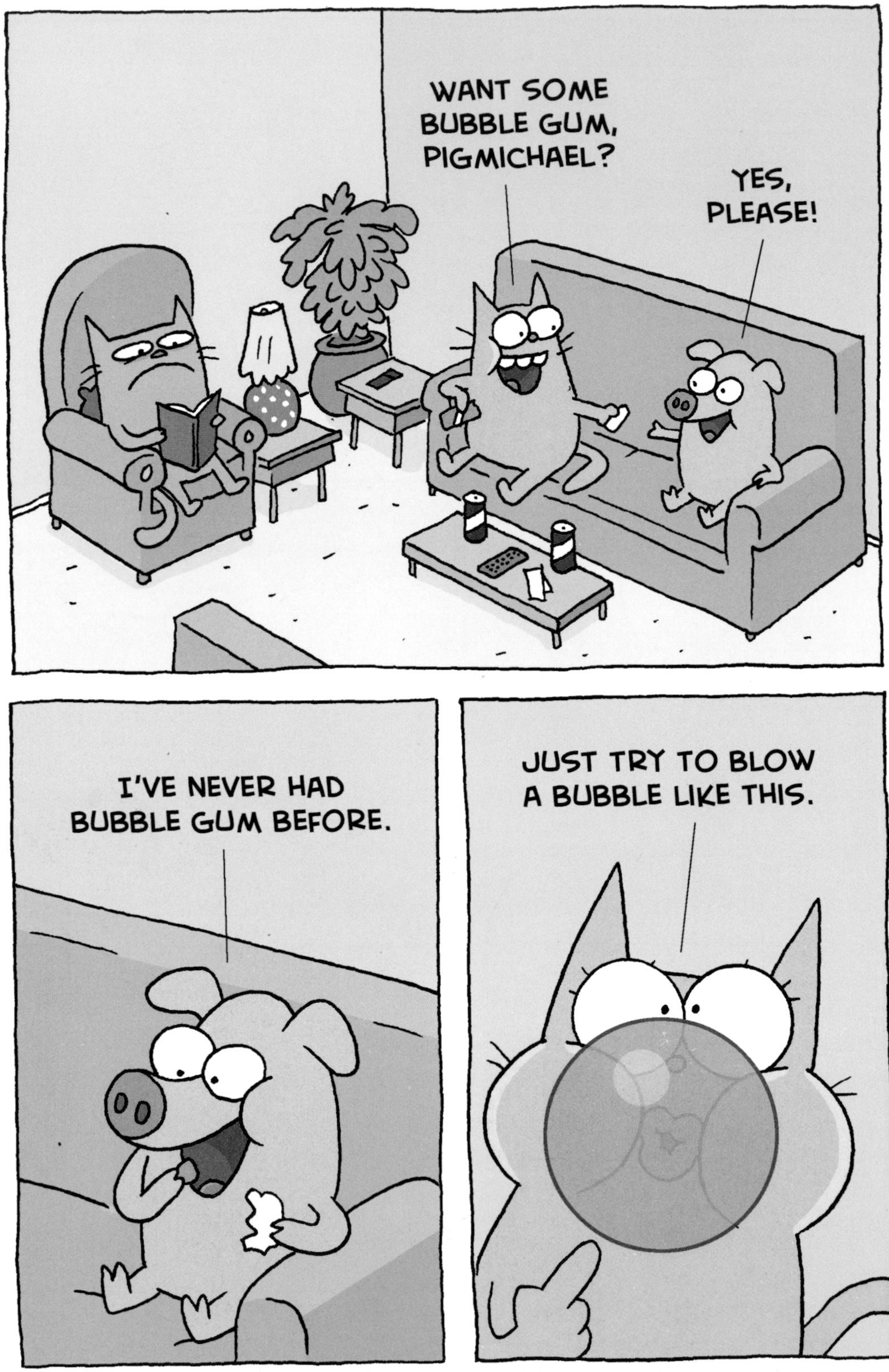
WANT SOME BUBBLE GUM, PIGMICHAEL?
YES, PLEASE!
I'VE NEVER HAD BUBBLE GUM BEFORE.
JUST TRY TO BLOW A BUBBLE LIKE THIS.

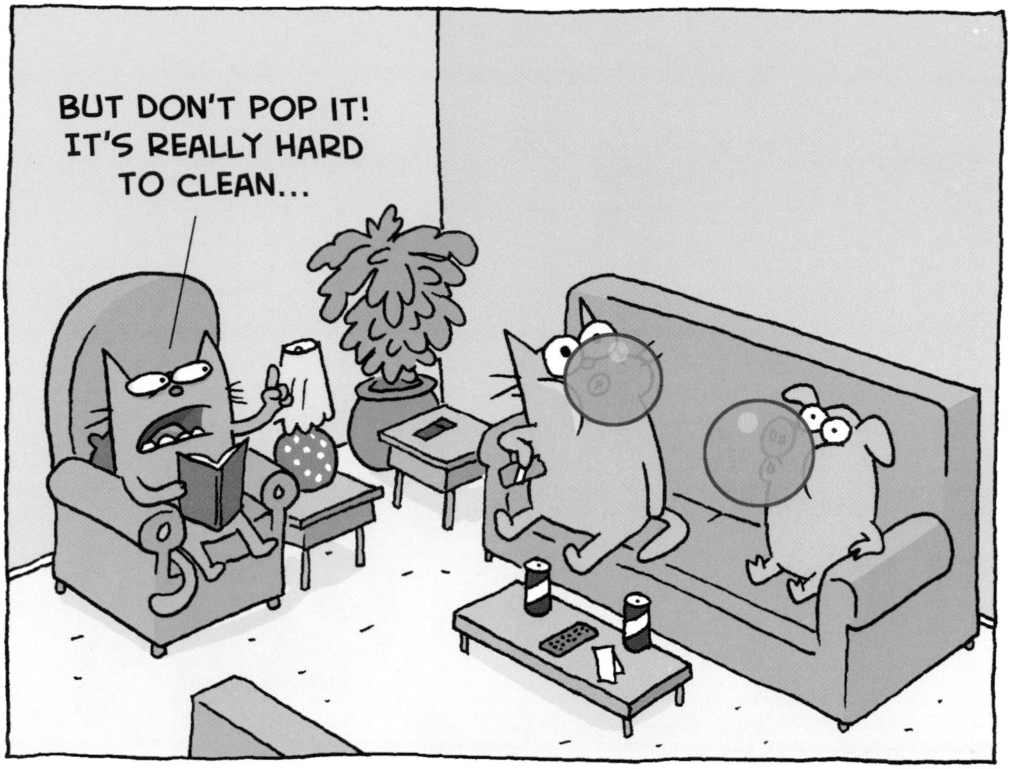
BUT DON'T POP IT! IT'S REALLY HARD TO CLEAN...

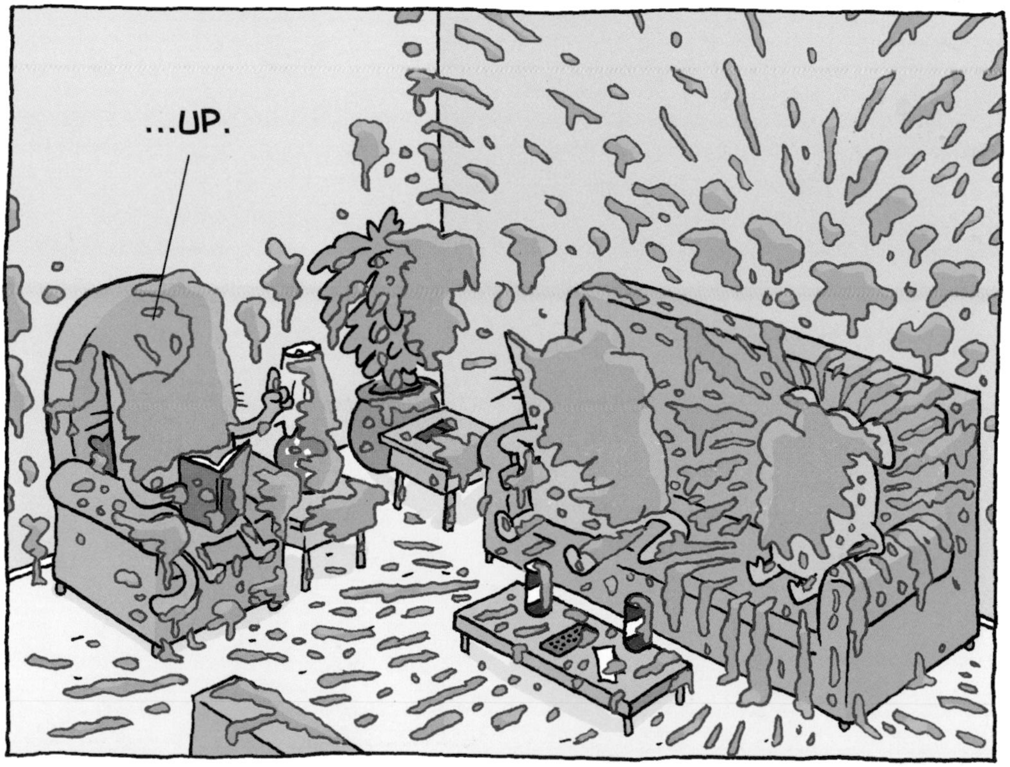
...UP.

The Ocean

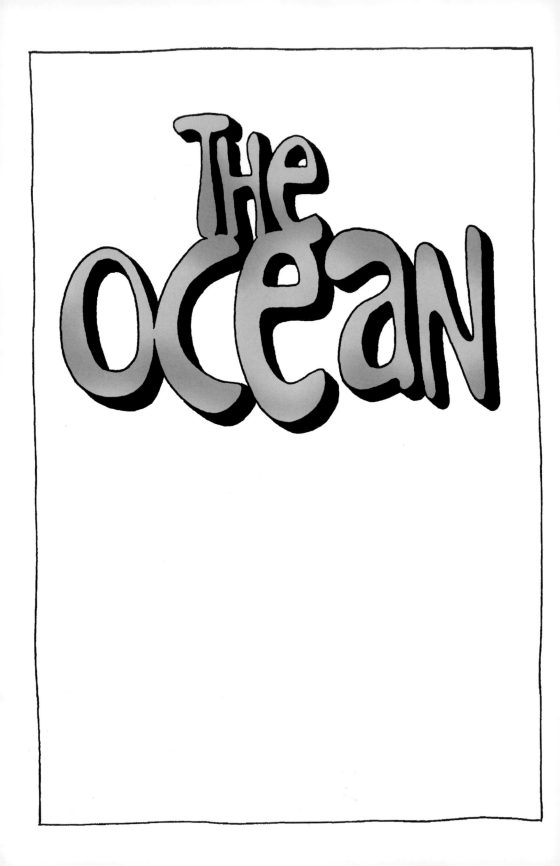

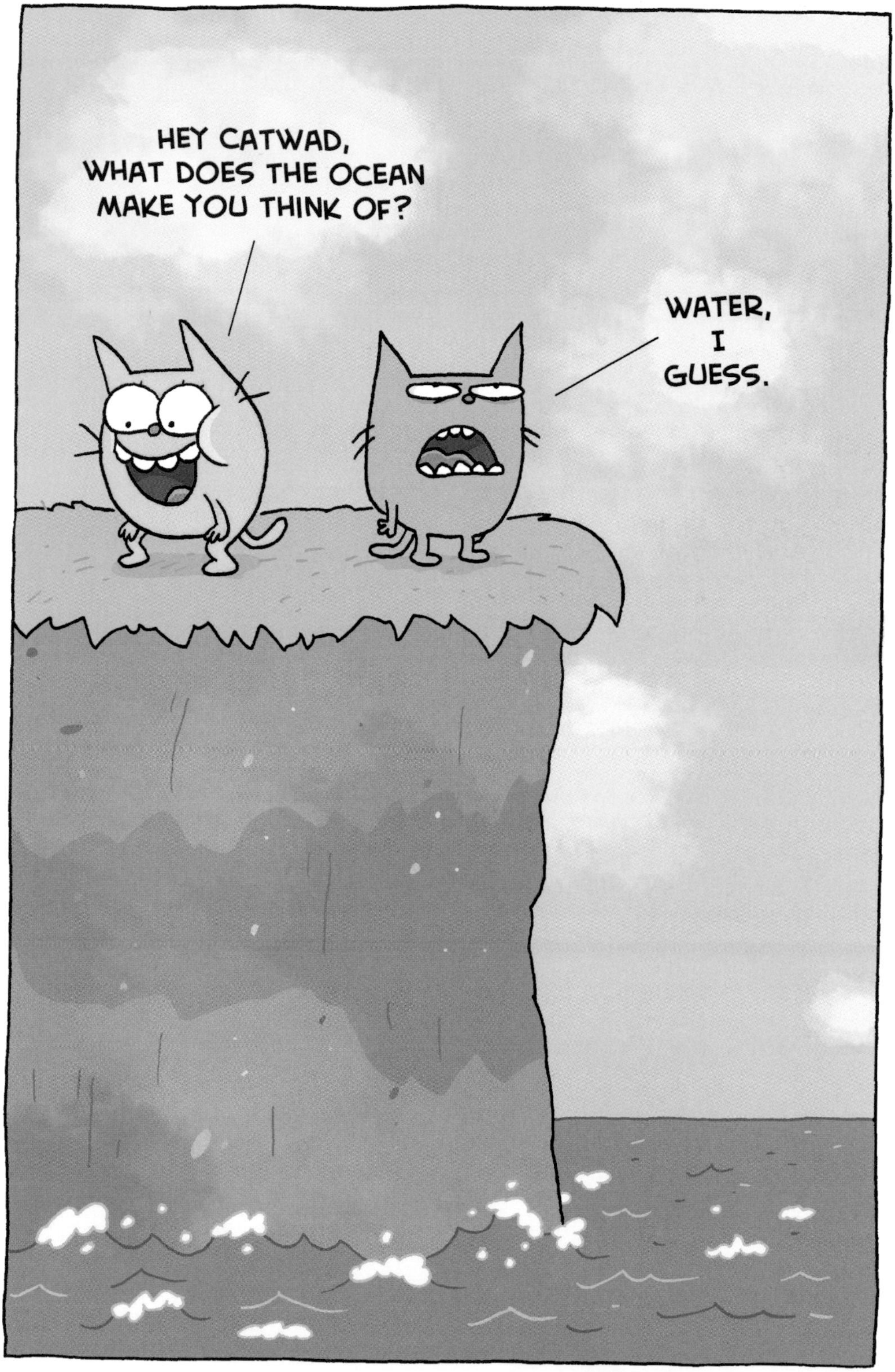
HEY CATWAD,
WHAT DOES THE OCEAN
MAKE YOU THINK OF?
WATER,
I
GUESS.

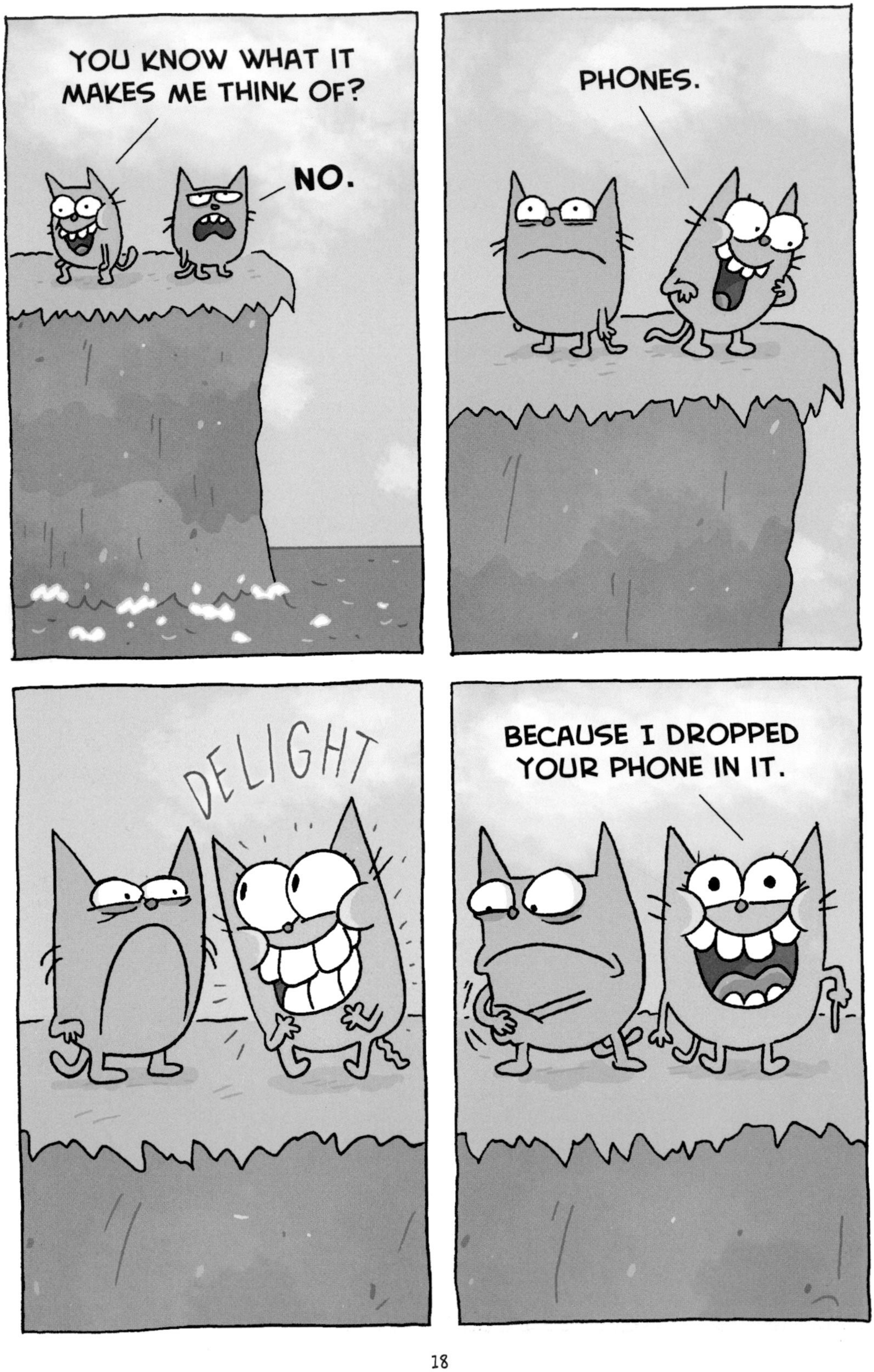
YOU KNOW WHAT IT MAKES ME THINK OF?
NO.
PHONES.
DELIGHT
BECAUSE I DROPPED YOUR PHONE IN IT.

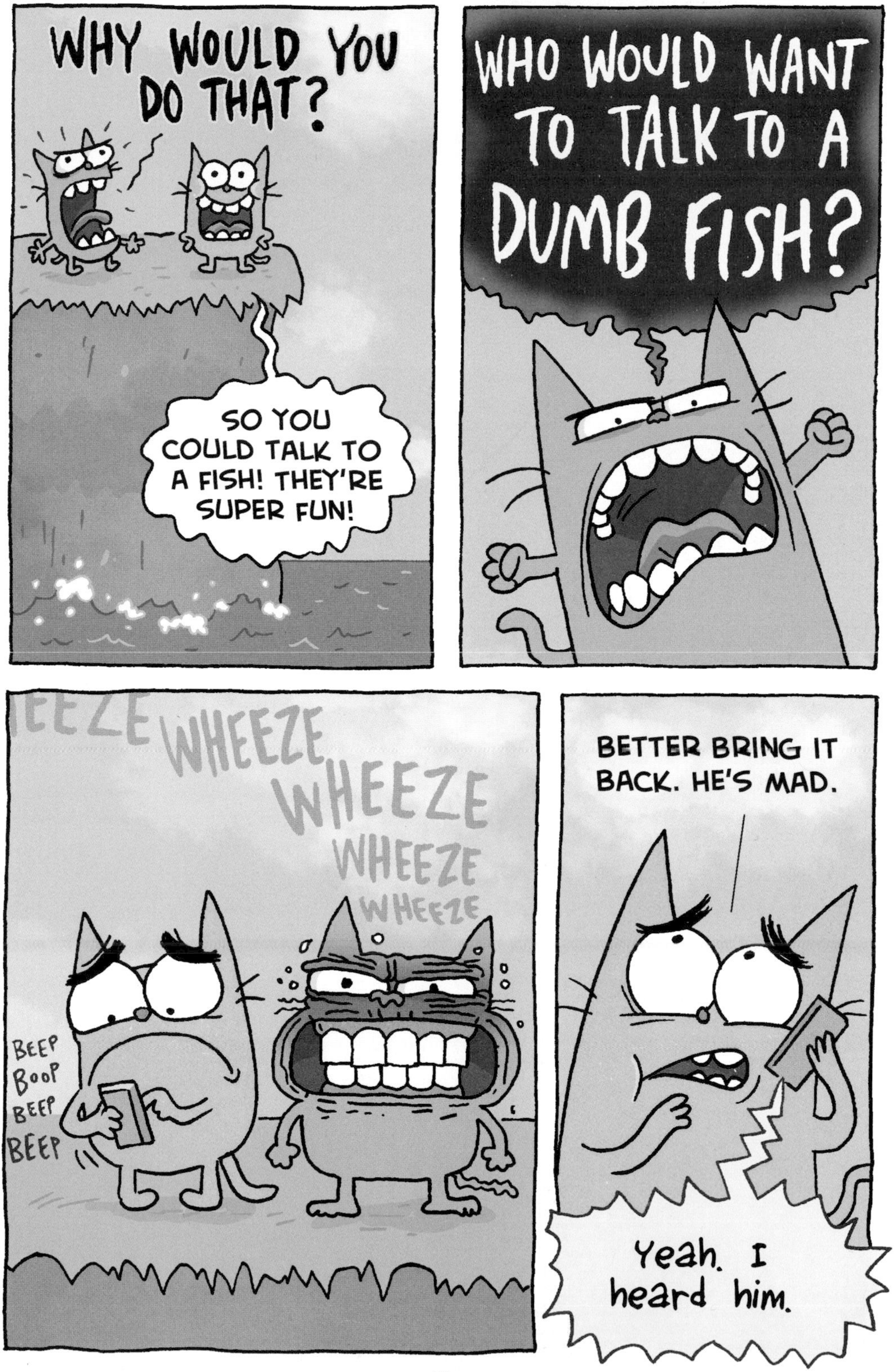
WHY WOULD YOU DO THAT?
SO YOU COULD TALK TO A FISH! THEY'RE SUPER FUN!
WHO WOULD WANT TO TALK TO A DUMB FISH?
WHEEZE
WHEEZE
WHEEZE
WHEEZE
BEEP BOOP BEEP BEEP
BETTER BRING IT BACK. HE'S MAD.
Yeah. I heard him.

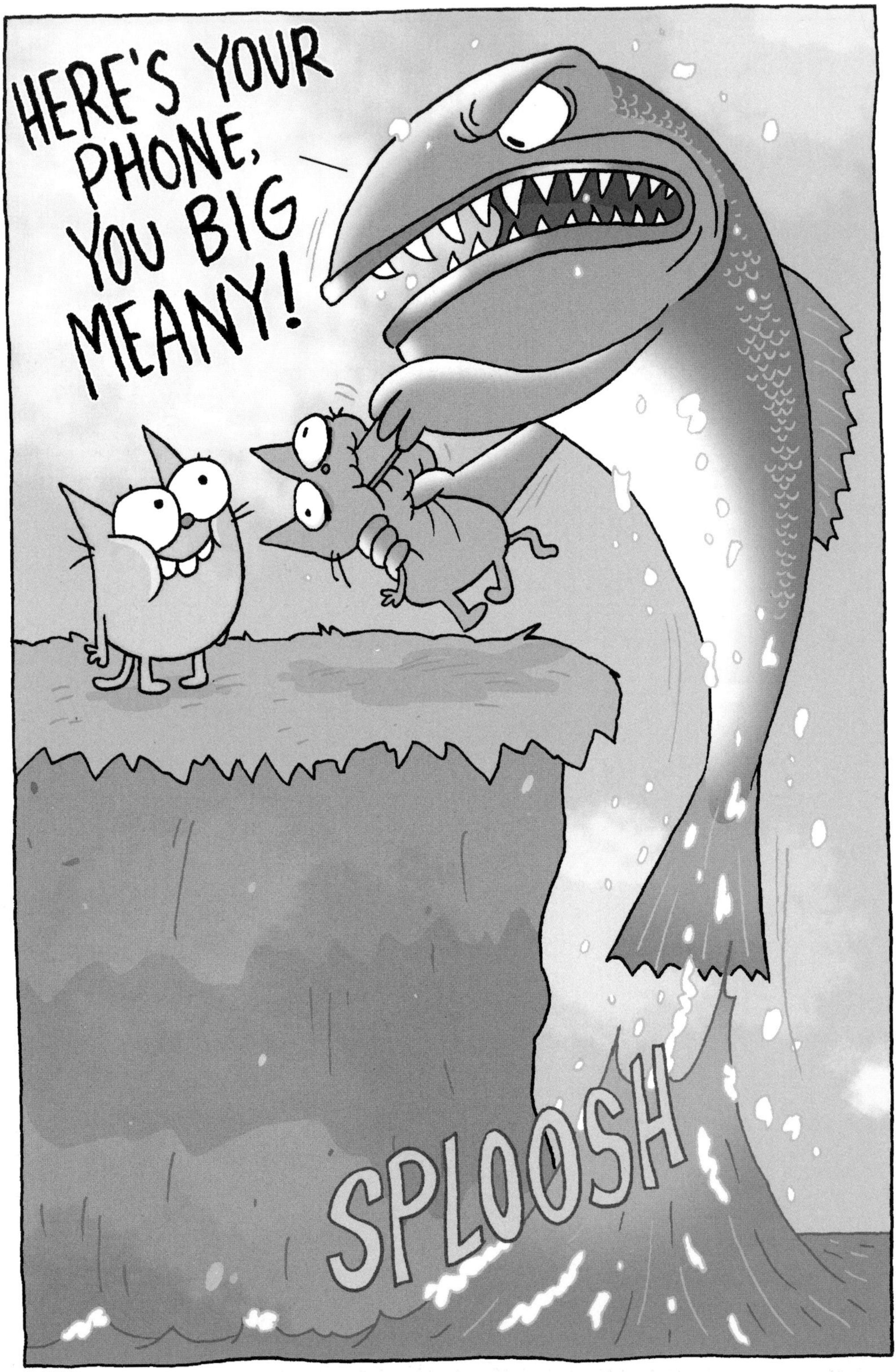
HERE'S YOUR PHONE, YOU BIG MEANY!
SPLOOSH

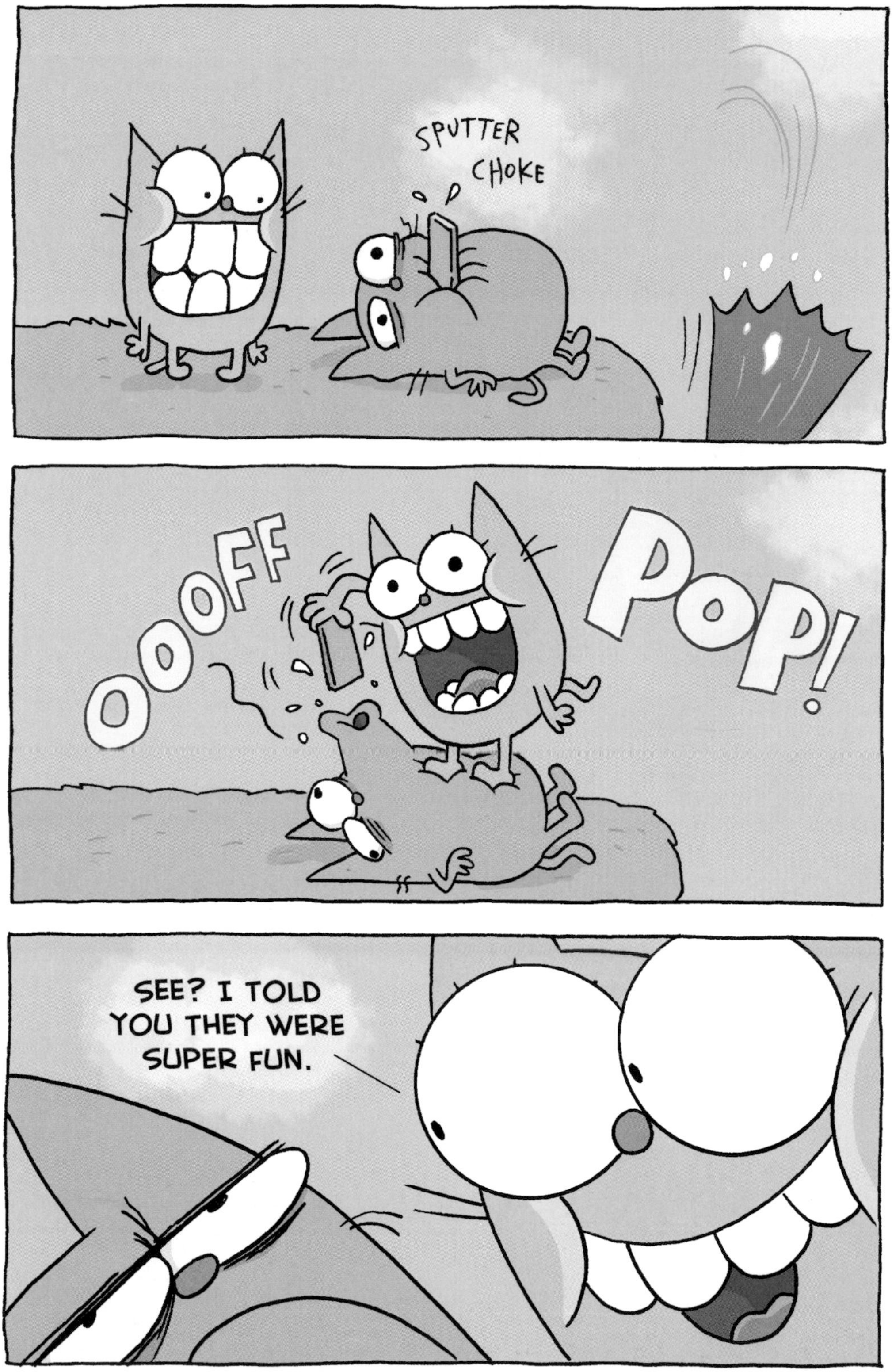
SPUTTER
CHOKE
OOOFF
POP!
SEE? I TOLD YOU THEY WERE SUPER FUN.

KICKBOXER

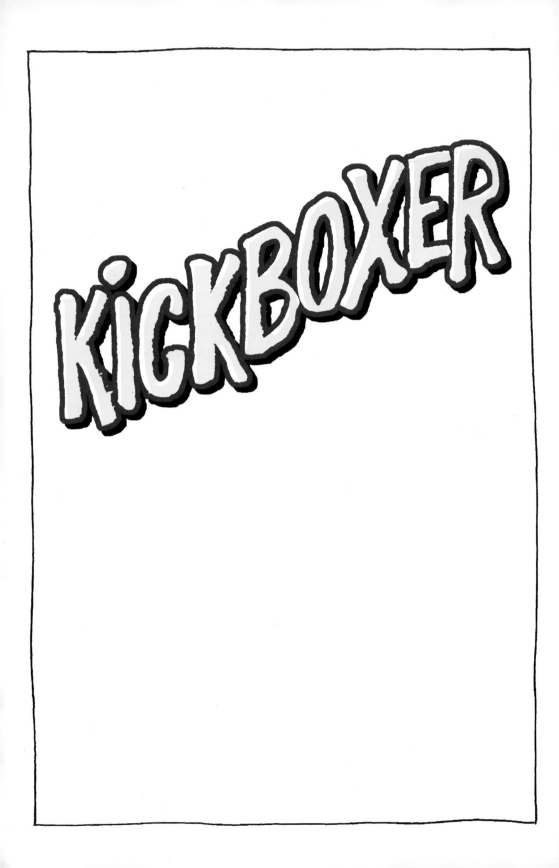

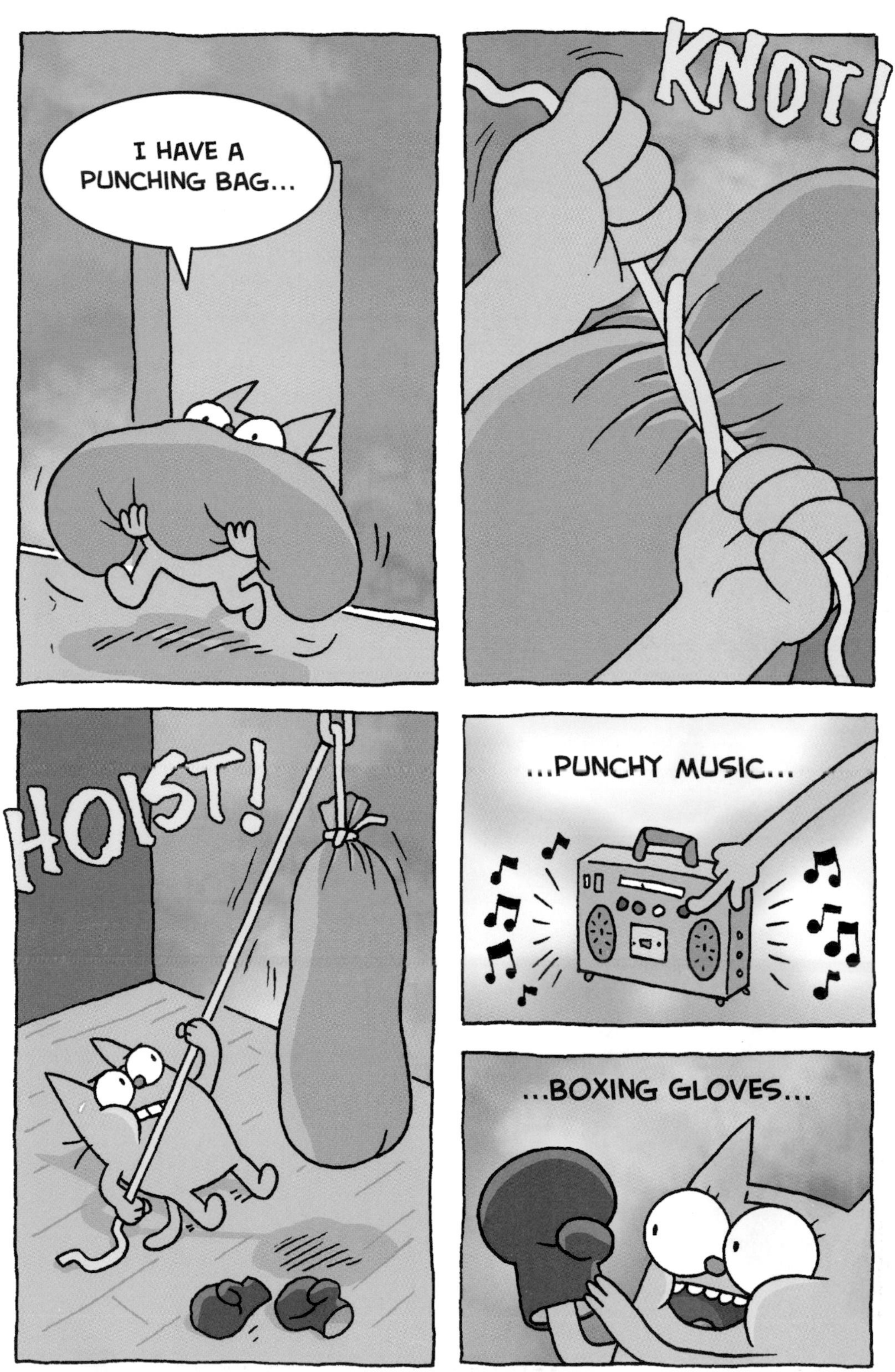
I HAVE A PUNCHING BAG...
KNOT!
HOIST!
...PUNCHY MUSIC...
...BOXING GLOVES...

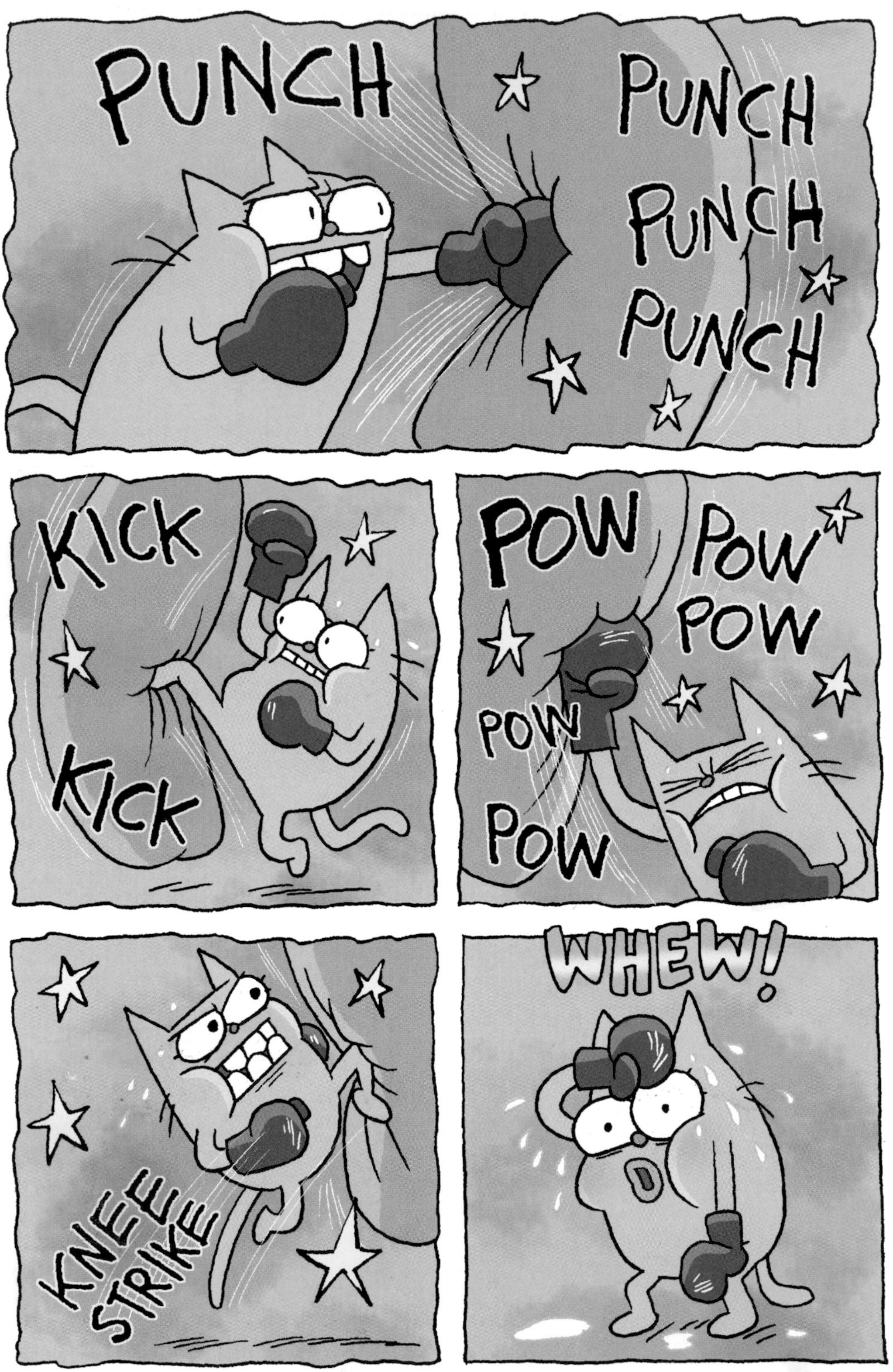
PUNCH
PUNCH
PUNCH
PUNCH
KICK
KICK
POW
POW
POW
POW
POW
KNEE STRIKE
WHEW!

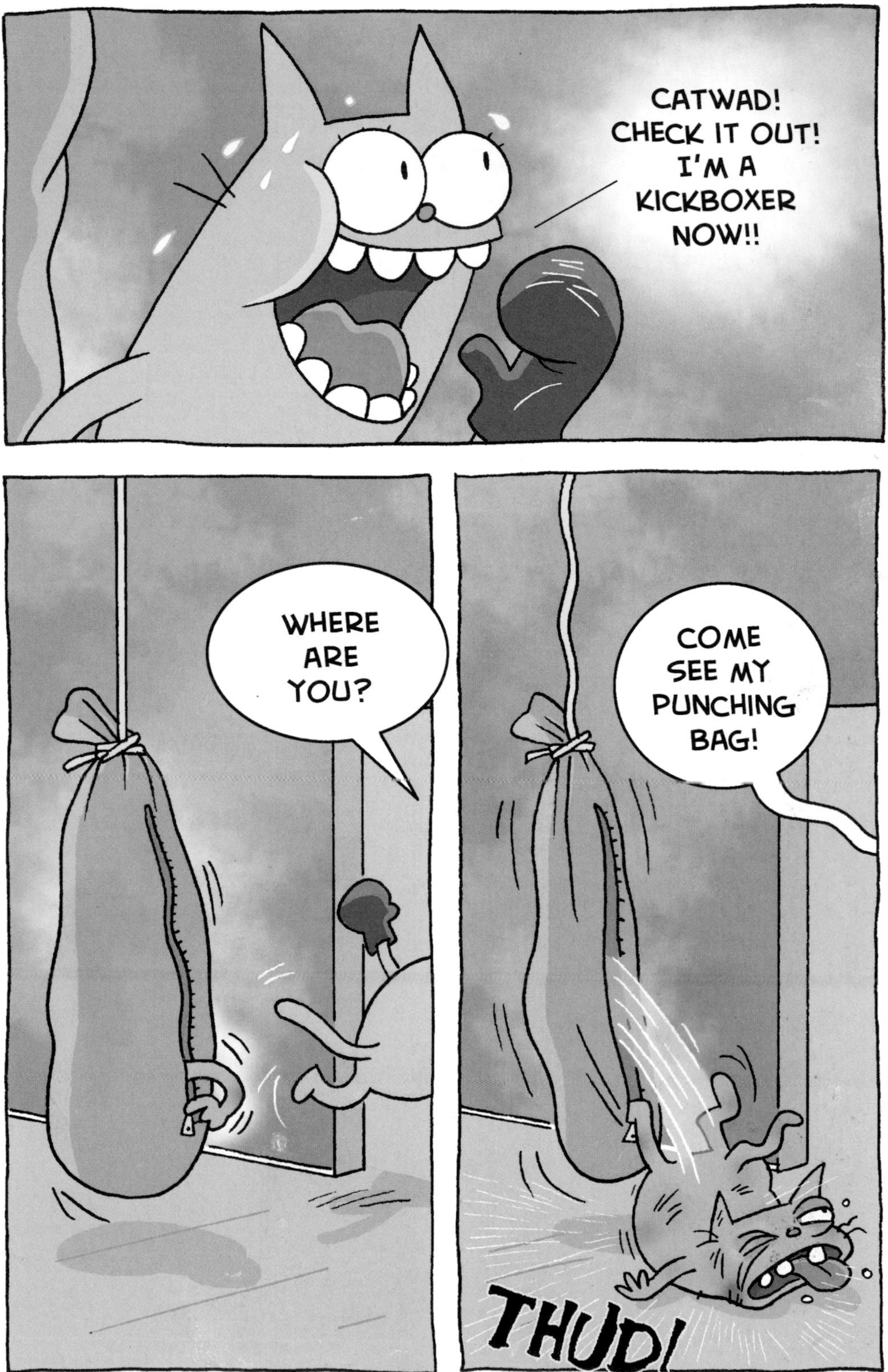
CATWAD! CHECK IT OUT! I'M A KICKBOXER NOW!!
WHERE ARE YOU?
COME SEE MY PUNCHING BAG!
THUD!

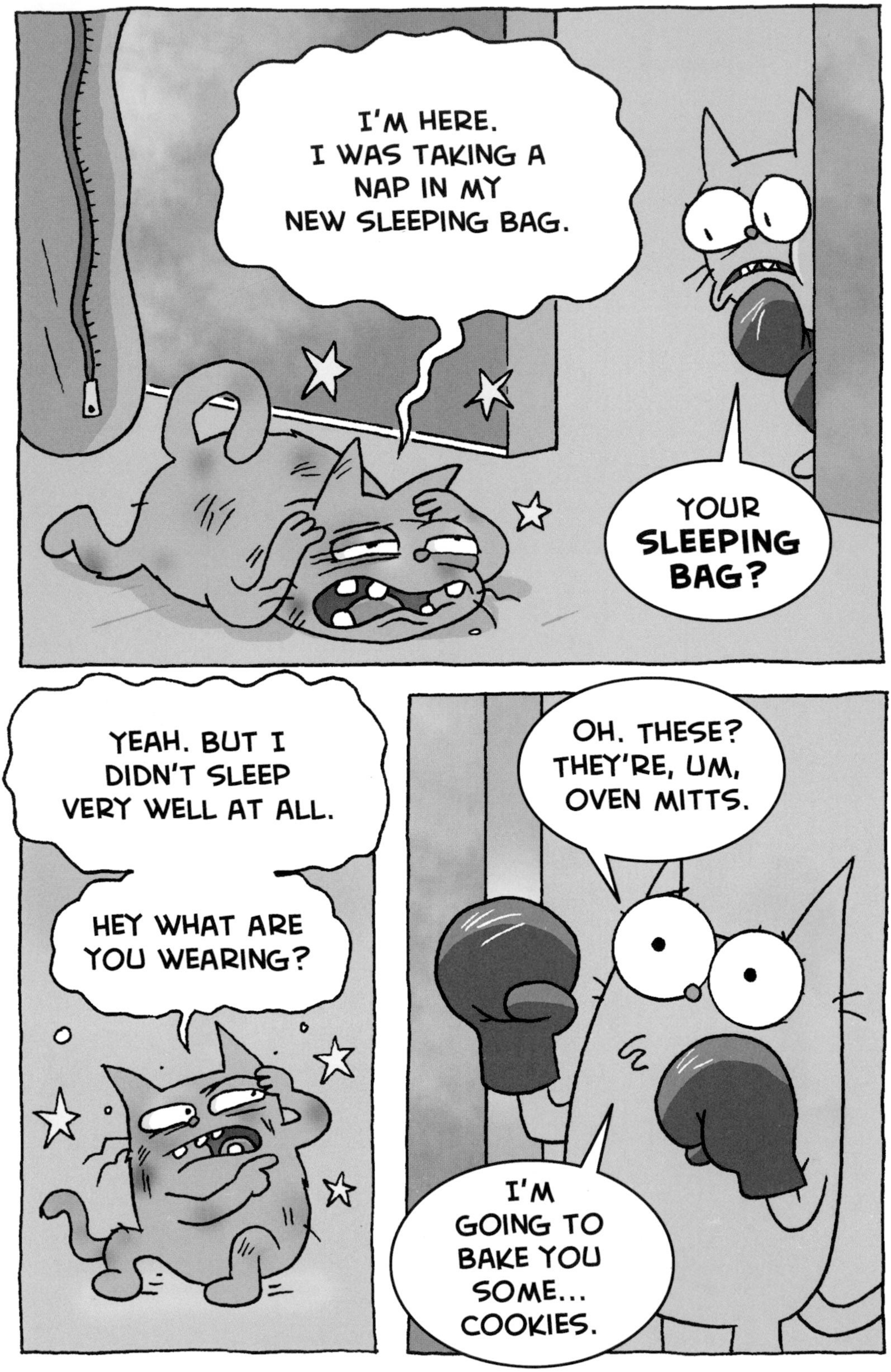
I'M HERE. I WAS TAKING A NAP IN MY NEW SLEEPING BAG.
YOUR **SLEEPING BAG?**
YEAH. BUT I DIDN'T SLEEP VERY WELL AT ALL.
HEY WHAT ARE YOU WEARING?
OH. THESE? THEY'RE, UM, OVEN MITTS.
I'M GOING TO BAKE YOU SOME... COOKIES.

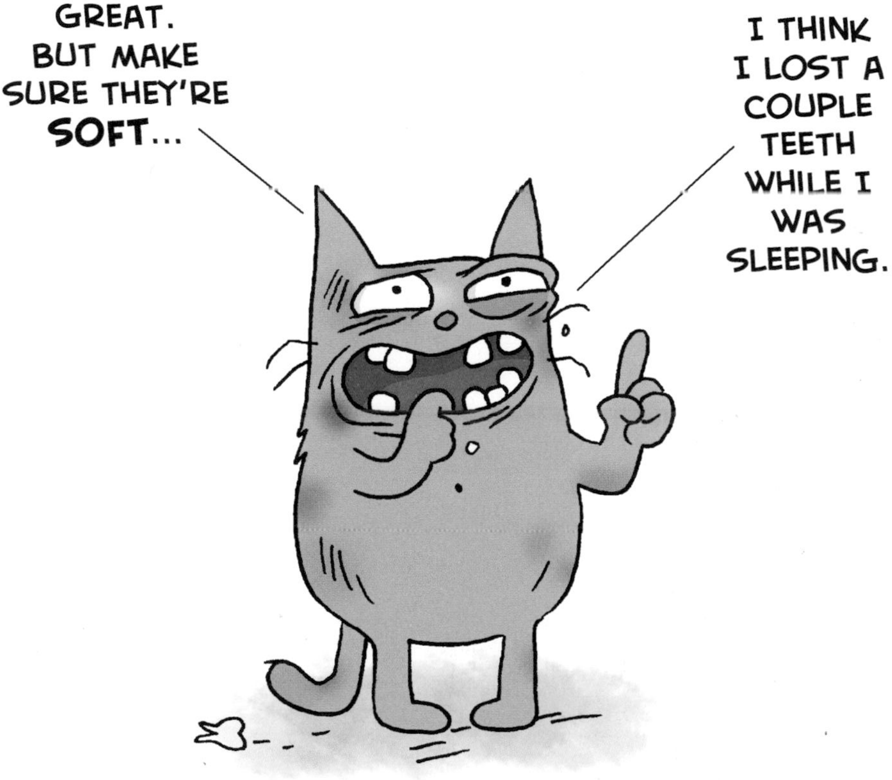
GREAT. BUT MAKE SURE THEY'RE **SOFT**...
I THINK I LOST A COUPLE TEETH WHILE I WAS SLEEPING.

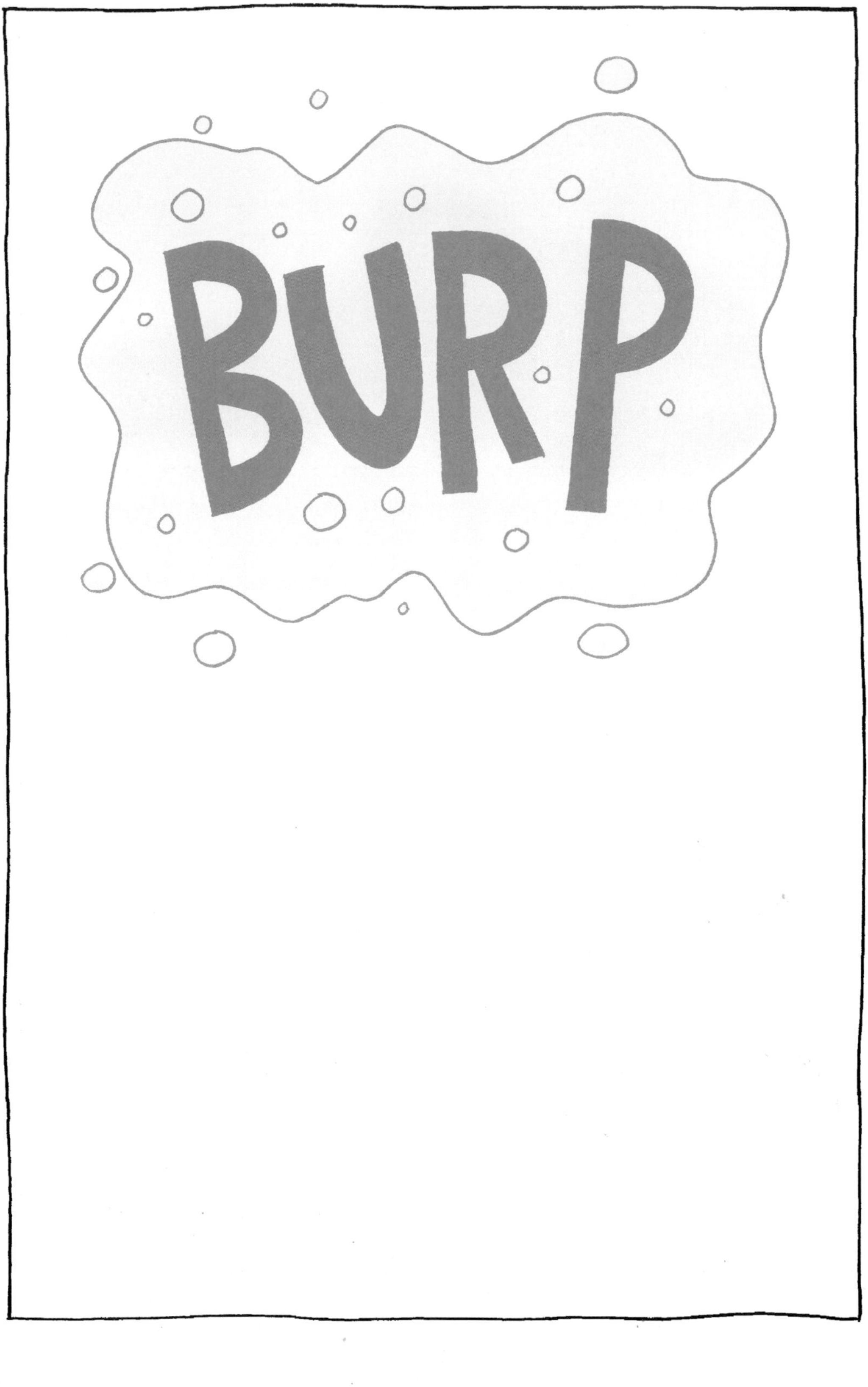
BURP

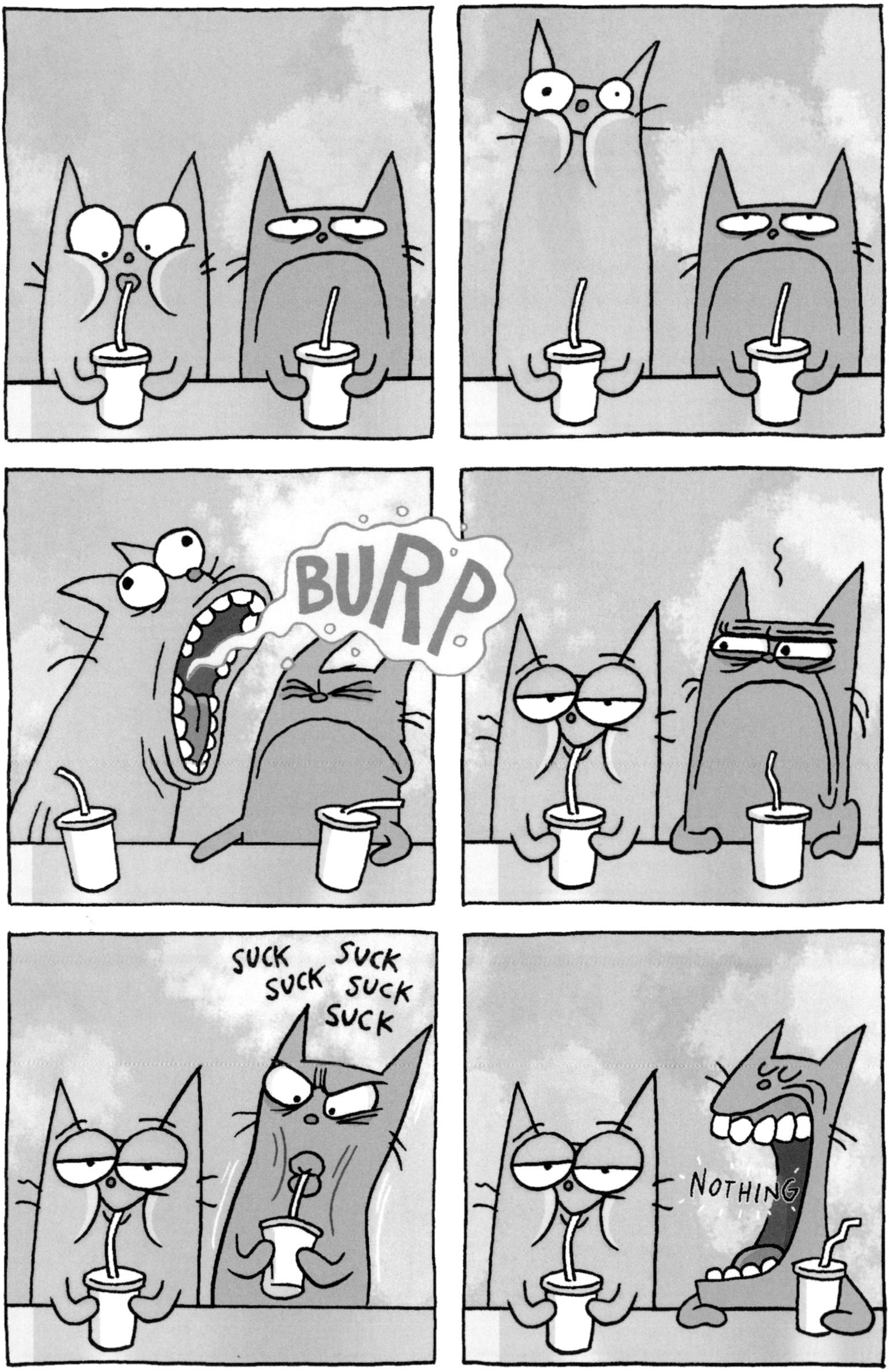
BURP
SUCK SUCK
SUCK SUCK
SUCK SUCK
NOTHING

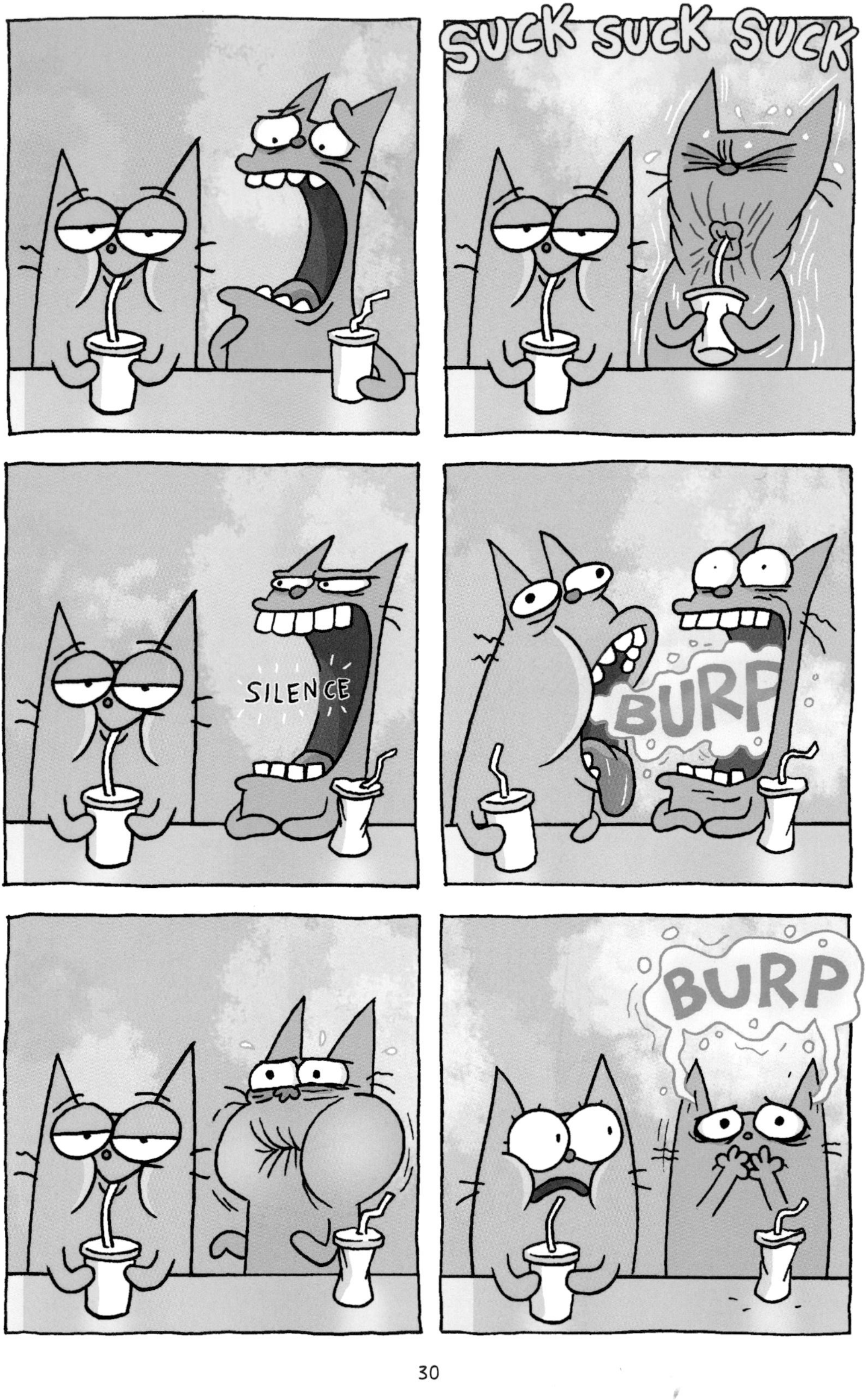
SUCK SUCK SUCK
SILENCE
BURP
BURP

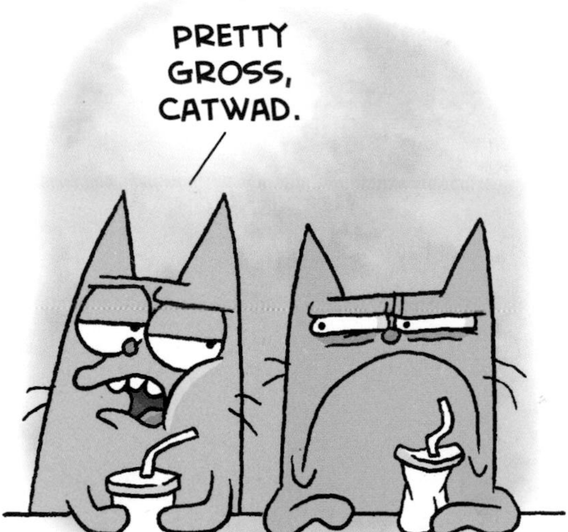
PRETTY
GROSS,
CATWAD.

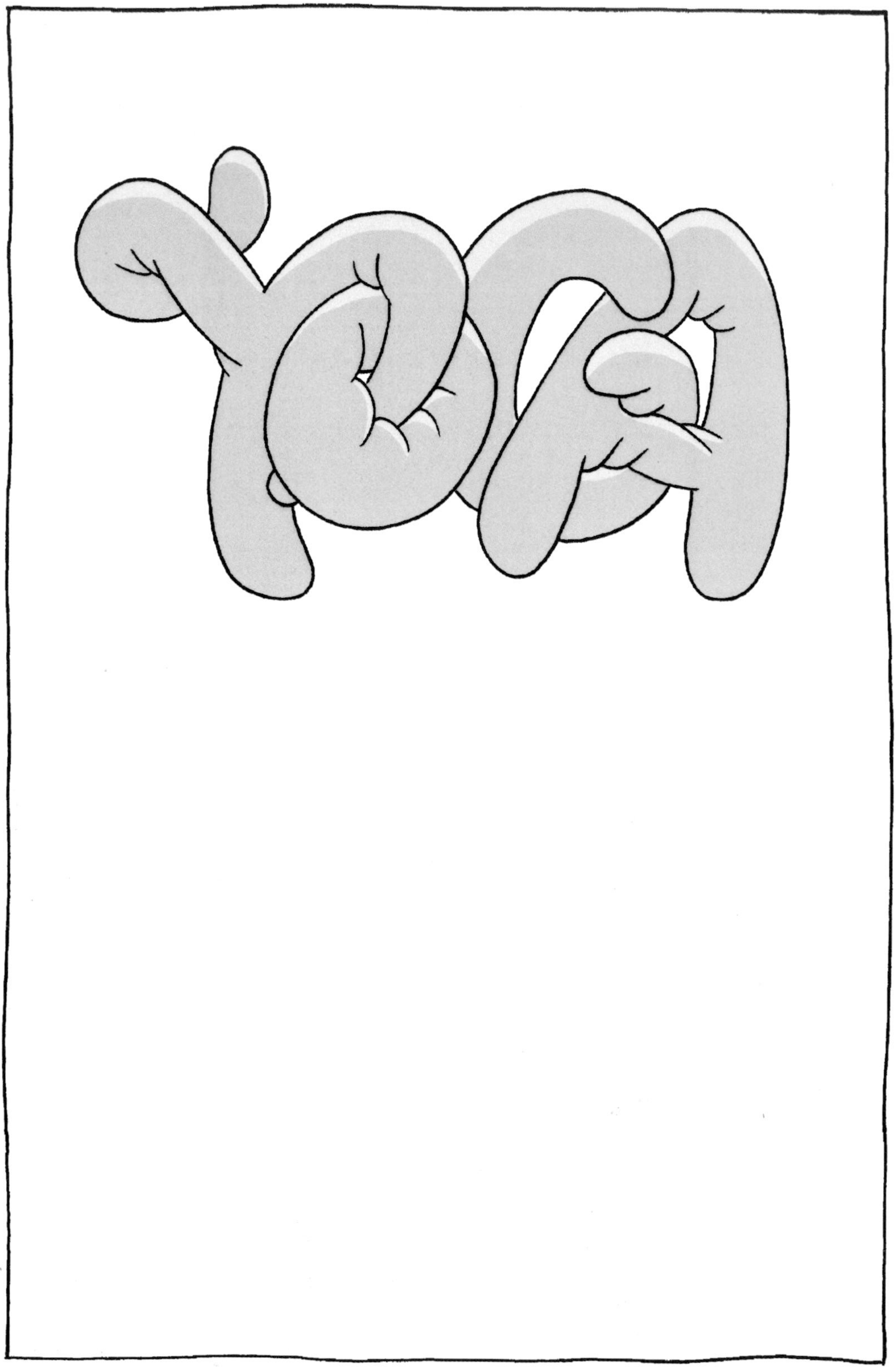
YOGA

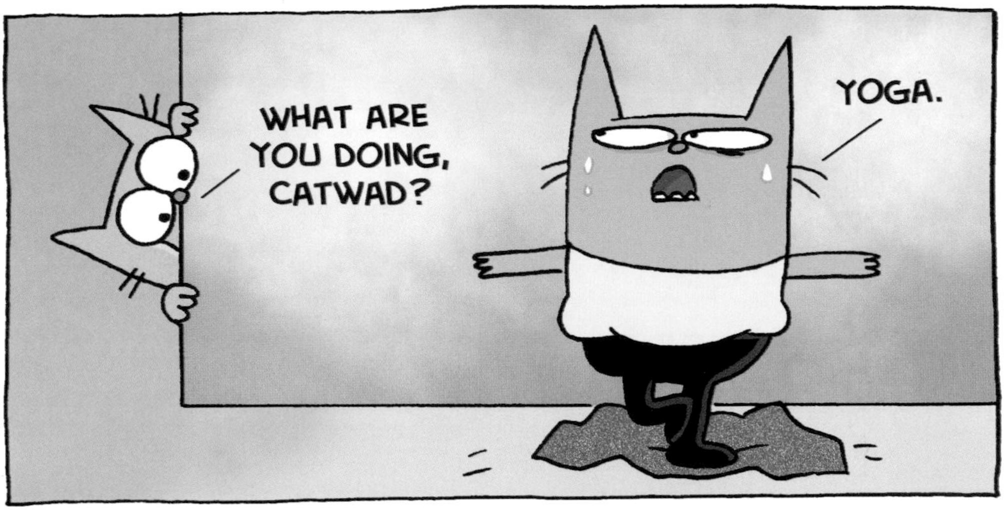
WHAT ARE YOU DOING, CATWAD?
YOGA.

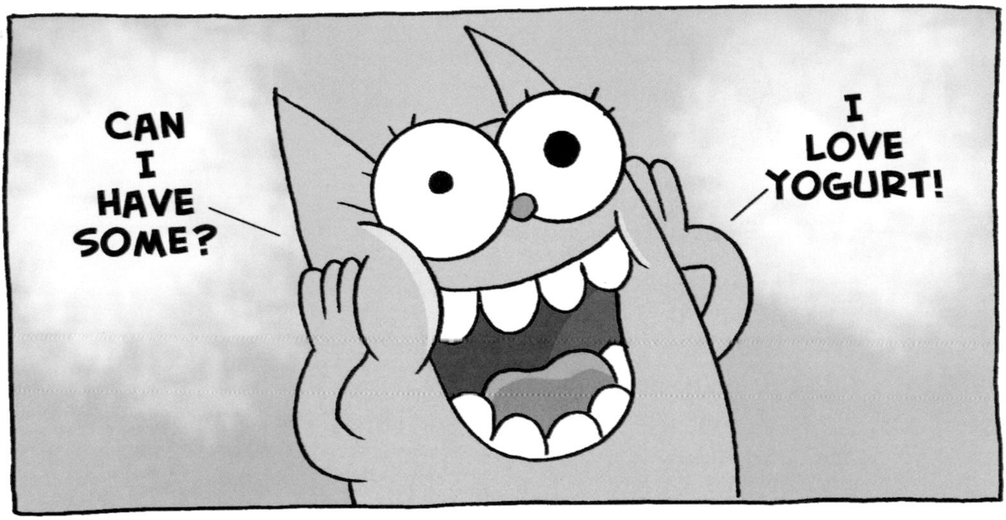
I LOVE YOGURT!
CAN I HAVE SOME?

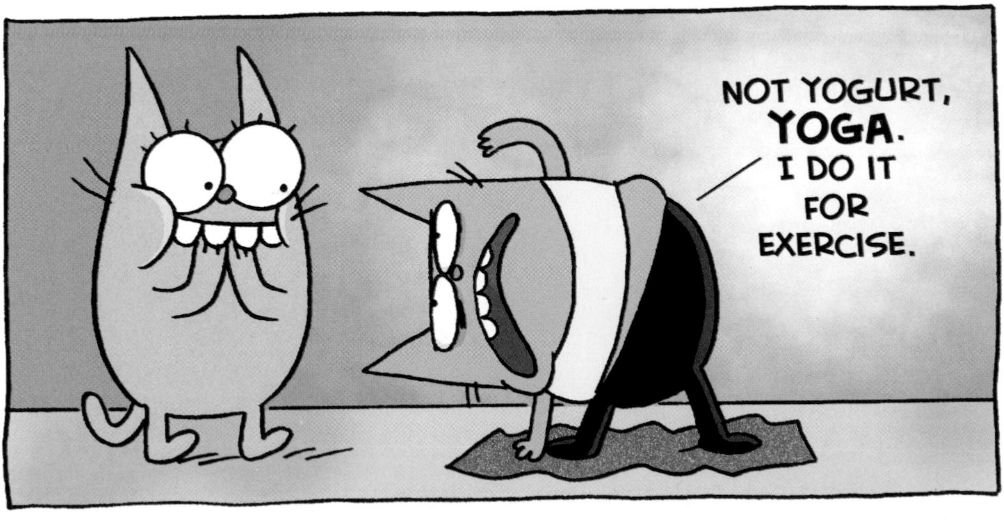
NOT YOGURT, **YOGA**. I DO IT FOR EXERCISE.

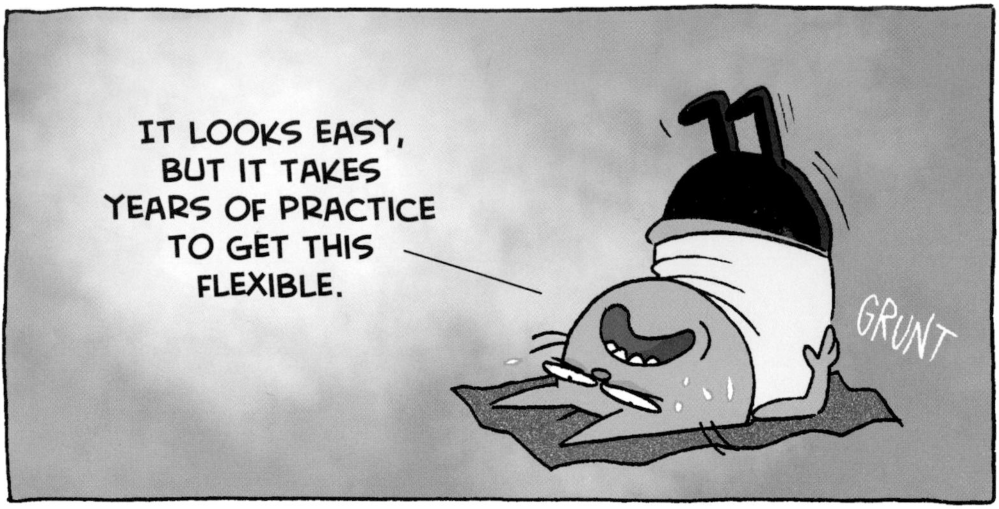
IT LOOKS EASY, BUT IT TAKES YEARS OF PRACTICE TO GET THIS FLEXIBLE.
GRUNT

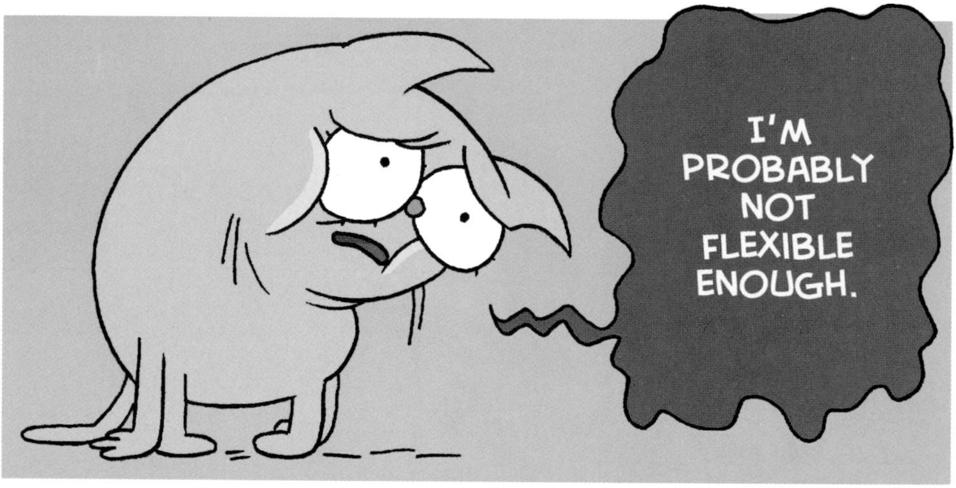
I'M PROBABLY NOT FLEXIBLE ENOUGH.

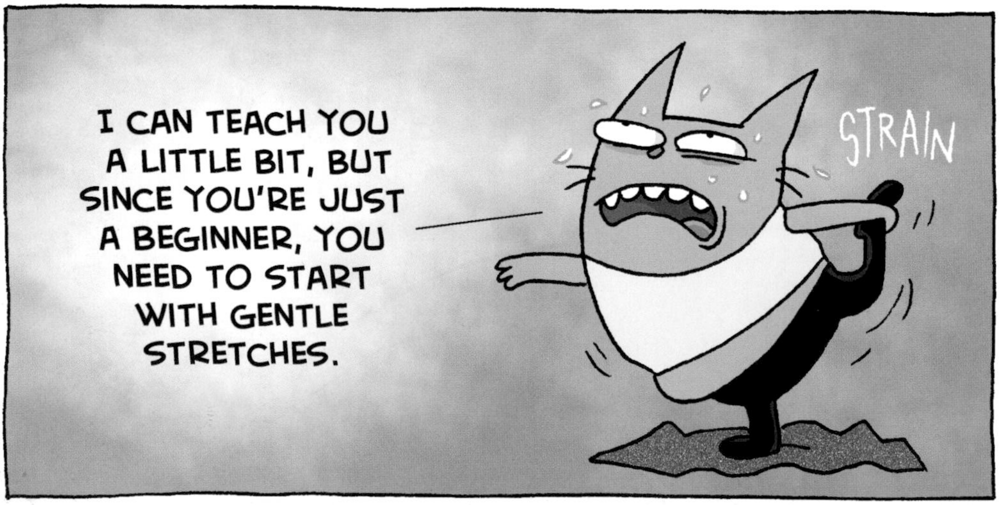
I CAN TEACH YOU A LITTLE BIT, BUT SINCE YOU'RE JUST A BEGINNER, YOU NEED TO START WITH GENTLE STRETCHES.
STRAIN

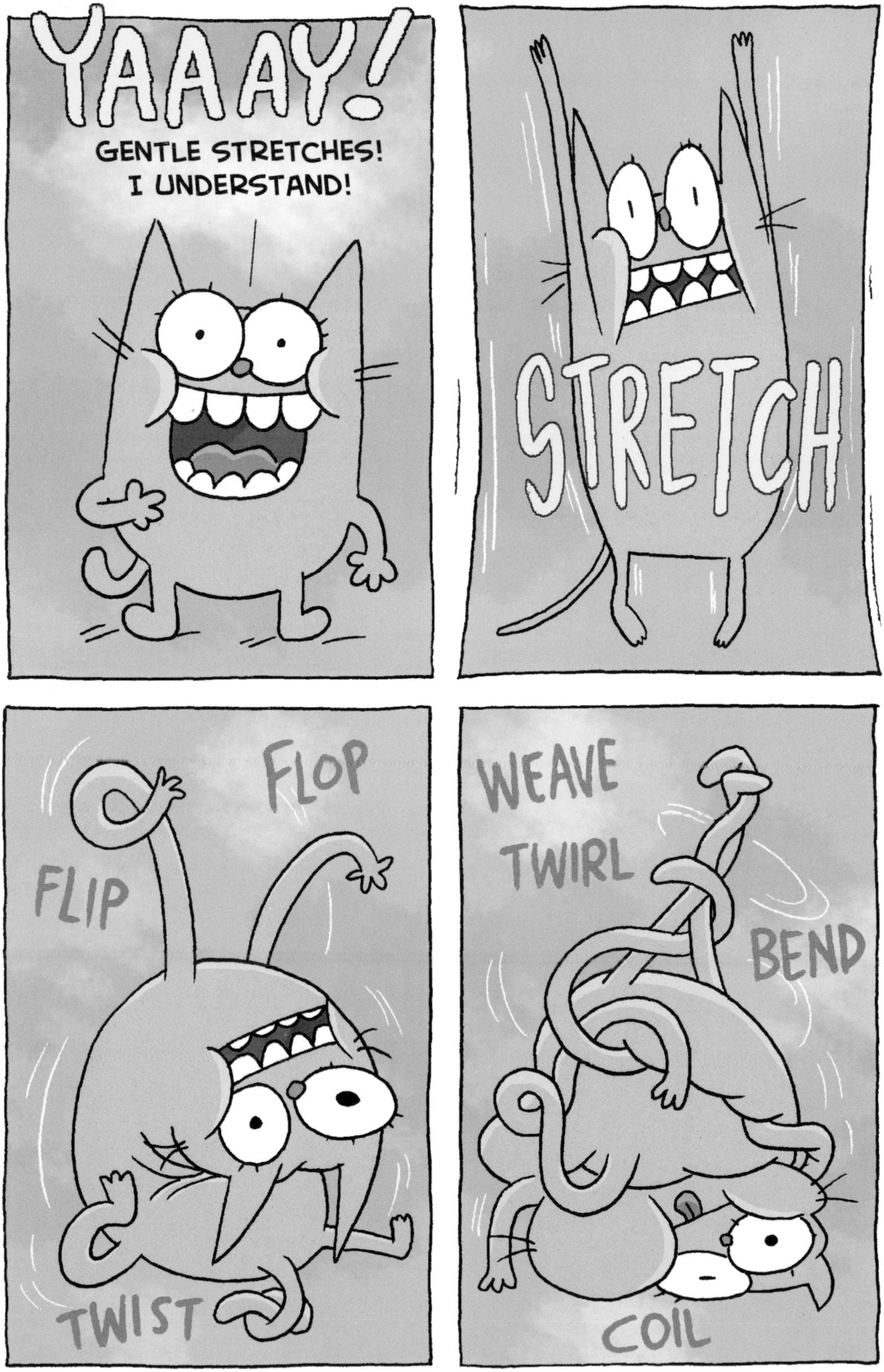
YAAAY!
GENTLE STRETCHES! I UNDERSTAND!
STRETCH
FLOP
FLIP
TWIST
WEAVE
TWIRL
BEND
COIL

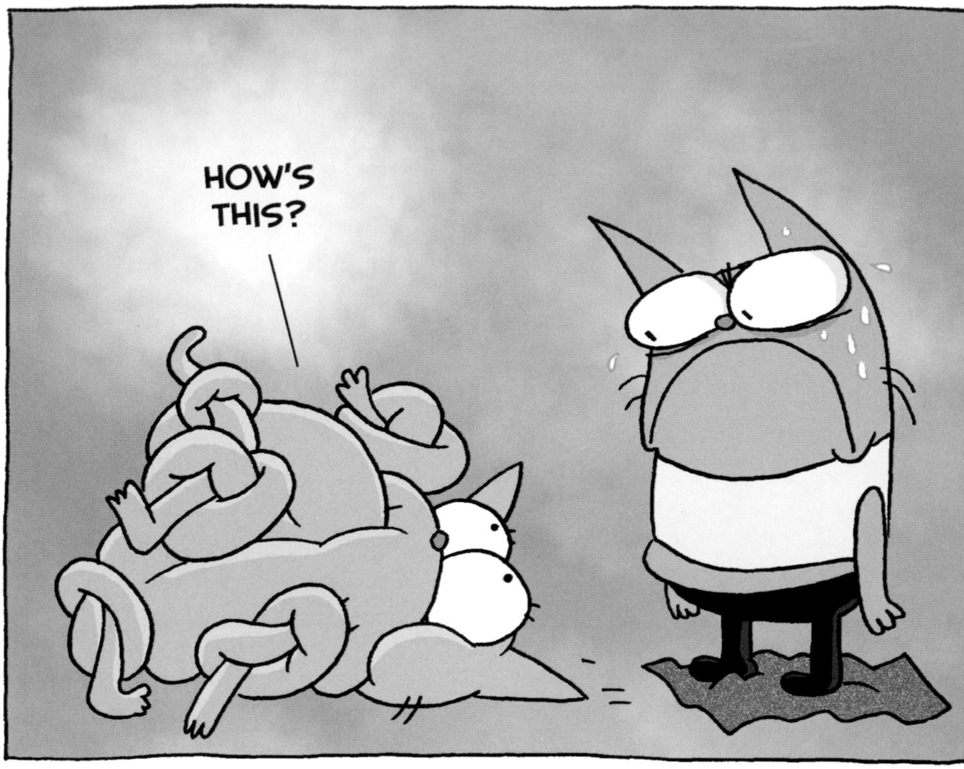
HOW'S THIS?

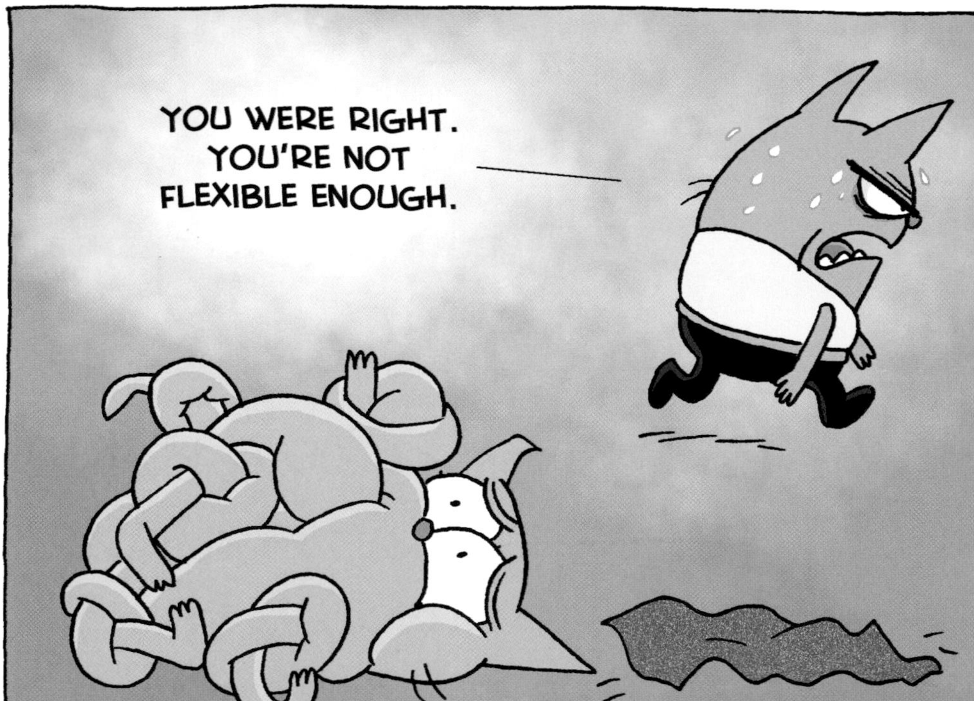
YOU WERE RIGHT. YOU'RE NOT FLEXIBLE ENOUGH.

BUT I WAS
JUST GETTING
WARMED UP.

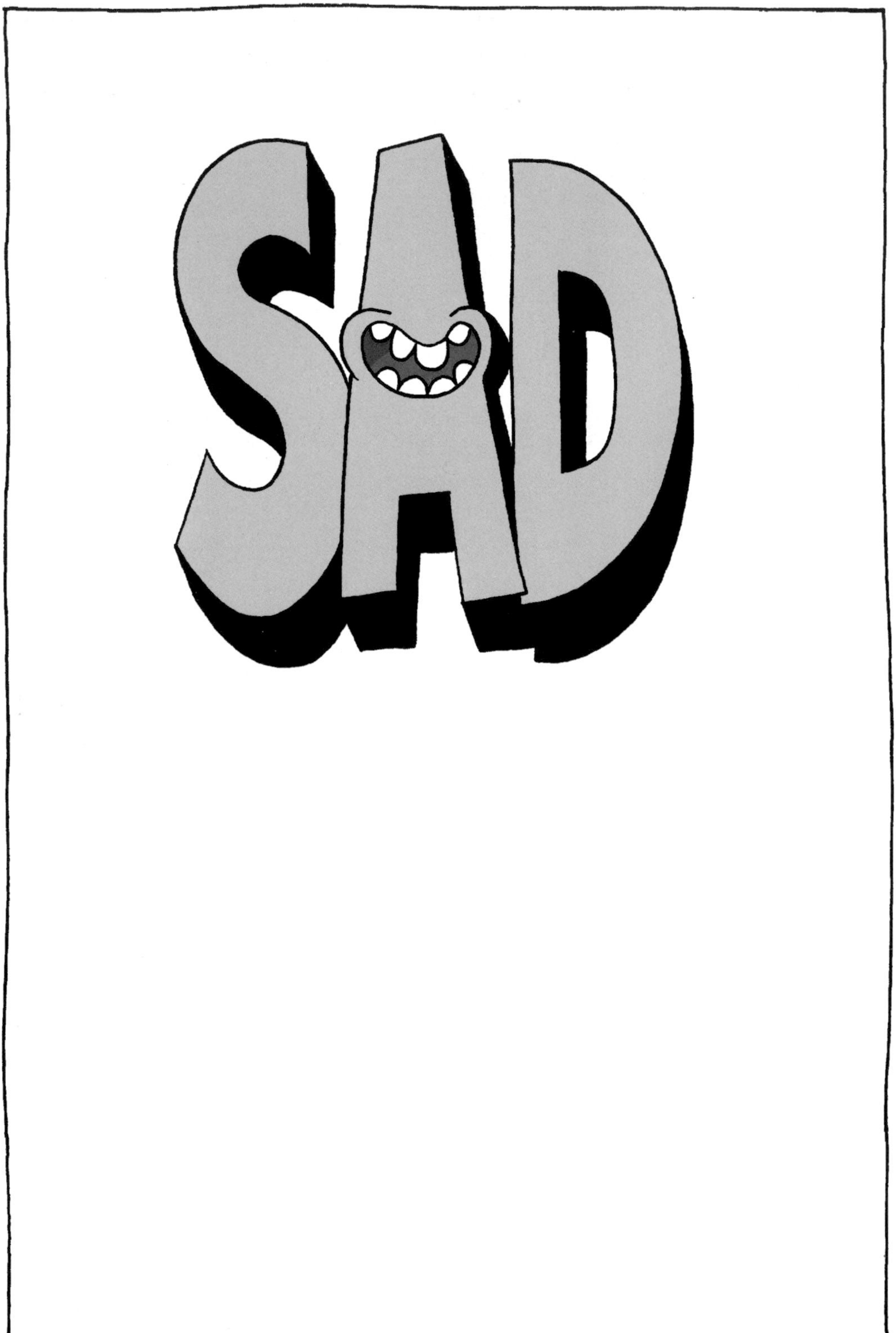
SAD

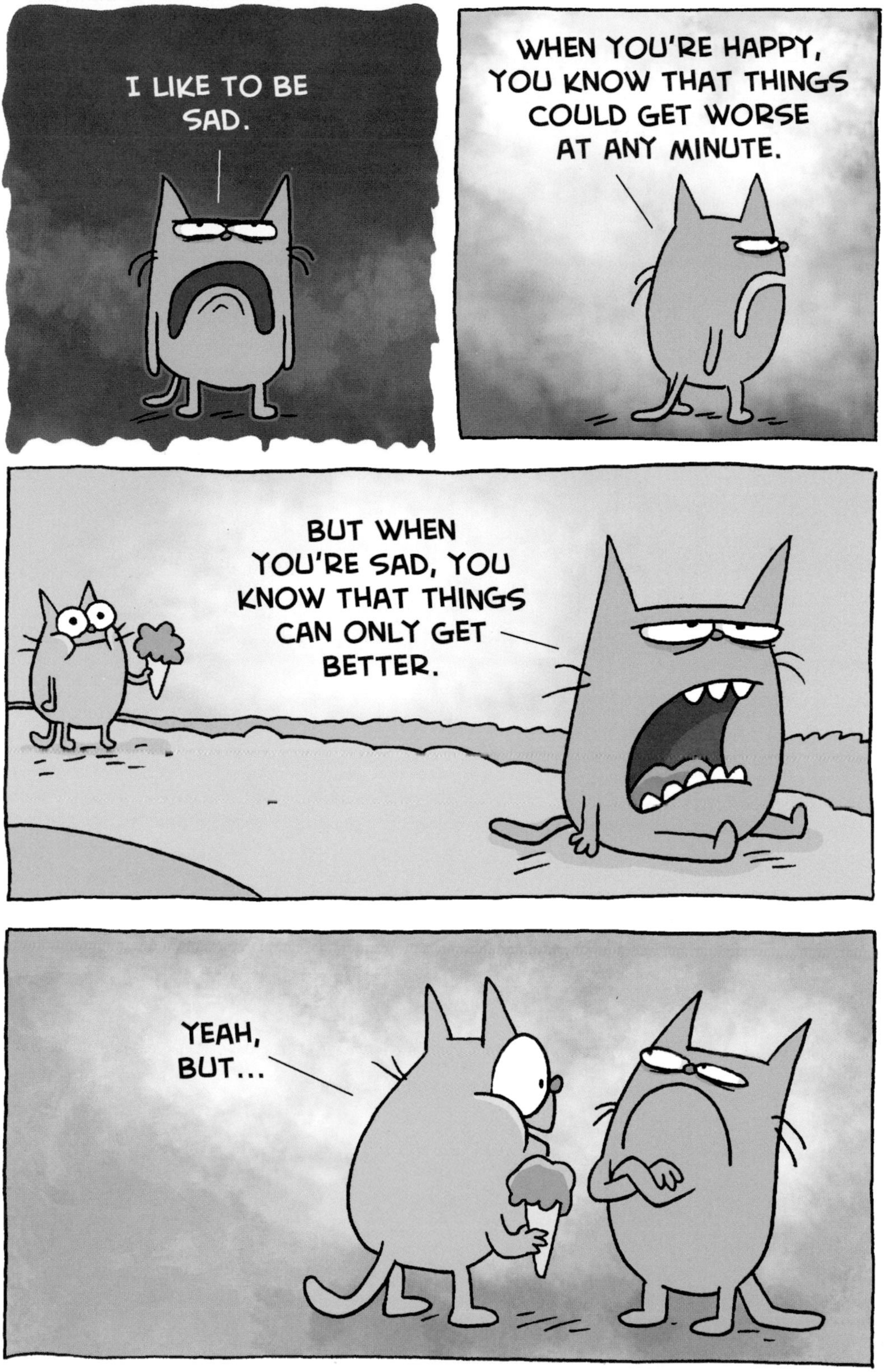
I LIKE TO BE SAD.
WHEN YOU'RE HAPPY, YOU KNOW THAT THINGS COULD GET WORSE AT ANY MINUTE.
BUT WHEN YOU'RE SAD, YOU KNOW THAT THINGS CAN ONLY GET BETTER.
YEAH, BUT...

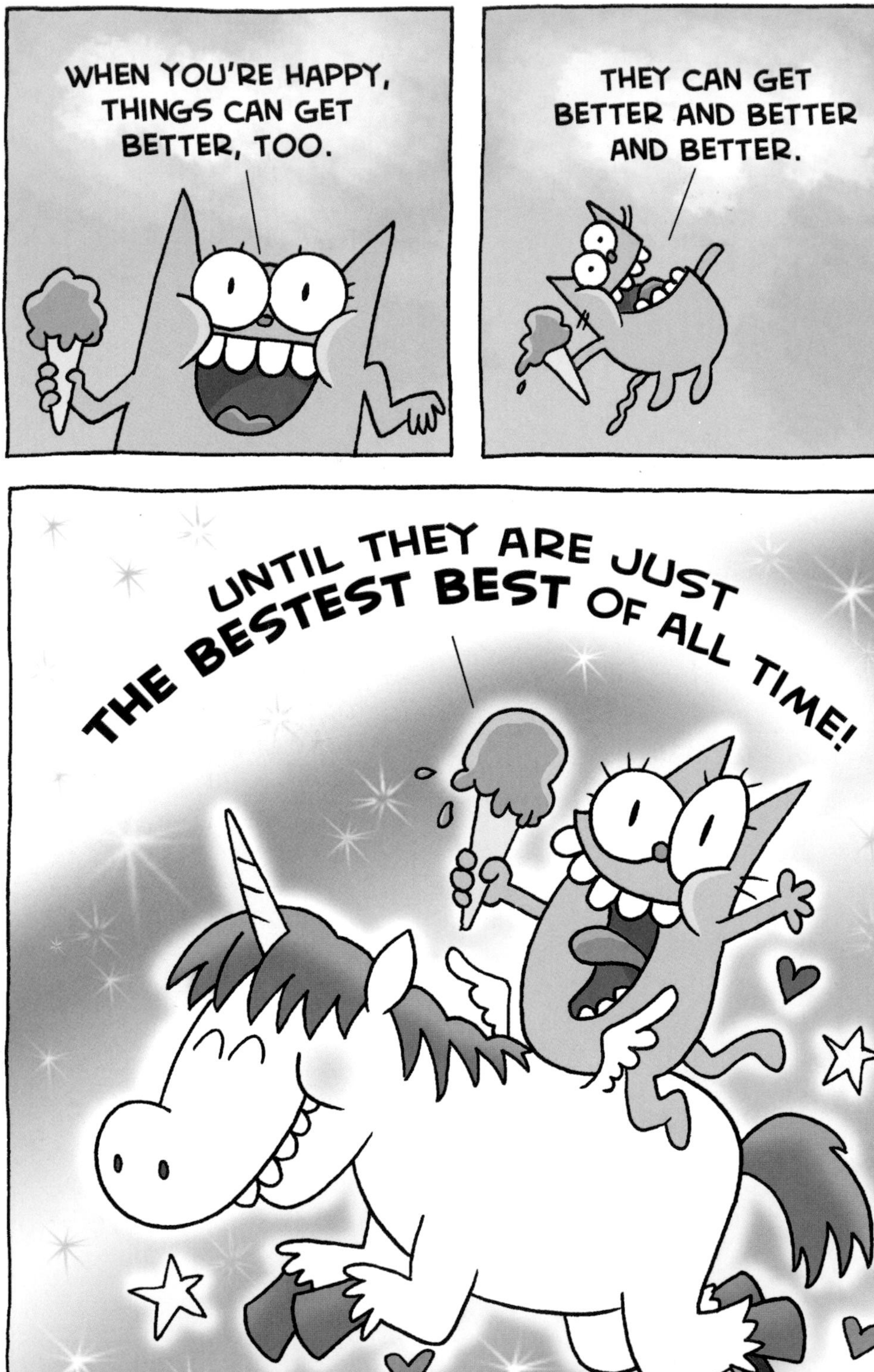
WHEN YOU'RE HAPPY, THINGS CAN GET BETTER, TOO.
THEY CAN GET BETTER AND BETTER AND BETTER.
UNTIL THEY ARE JUST THE BESTEST BEST OF ALL TIME!

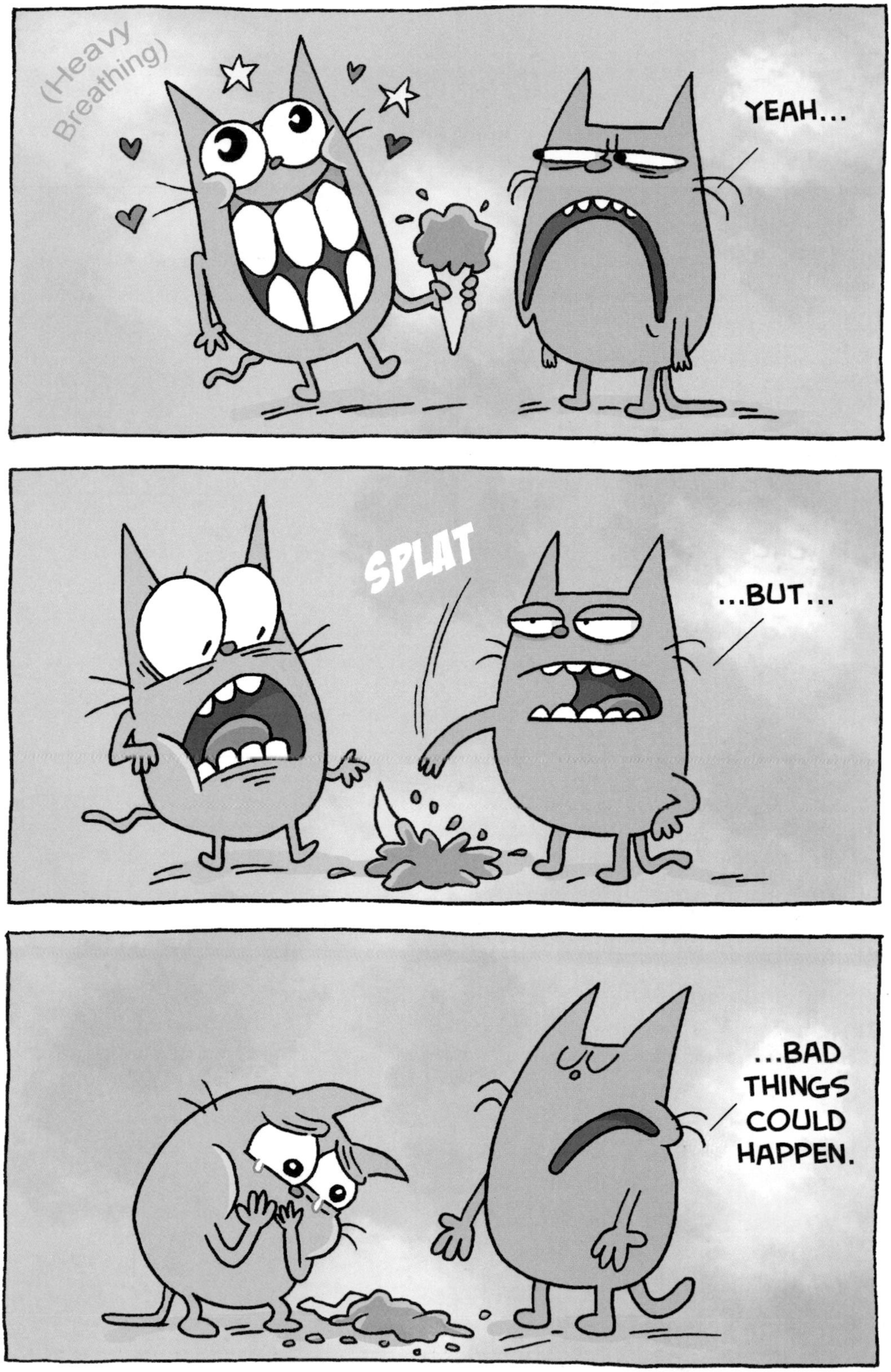
(Heavy Breathing)
YEAH...
SPLAT
...BUT...
...BAD THINGS COULD HAPPEN.

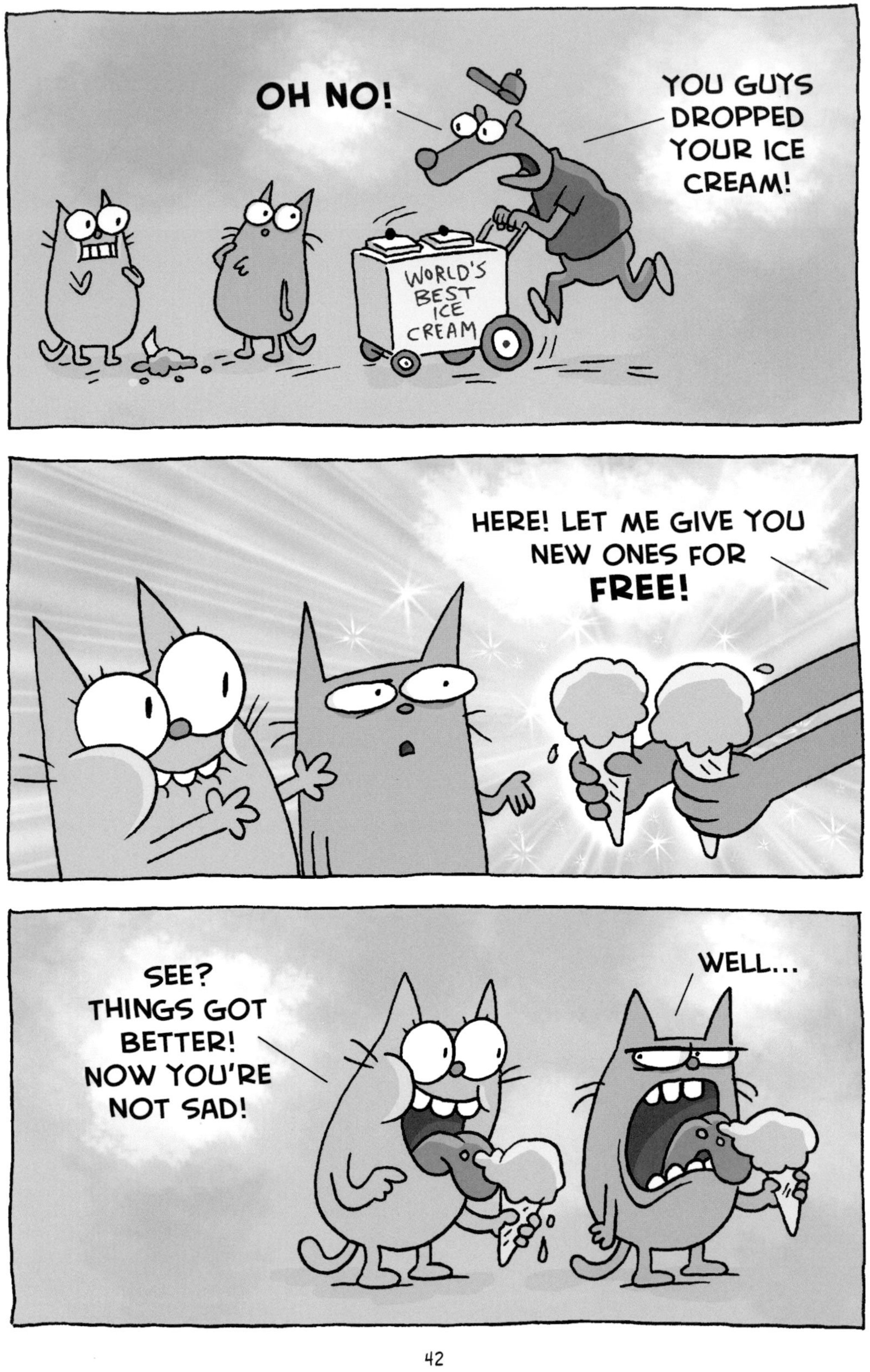
OH NO!
YOU GUYS DROPPED YOUR ICE CREAM!
WORLD'S BEST ICE CREAM
HERE! LET ME GIVE YOU NEW ONES FOR FREE!
SEE? THINGS GOT BETTER! NOW YOU'RE NOT SAD!
WELL...

JUST BECAUSE I'M
NOT SAD DOESN'T
MEAN I'M HAPPY
ABOUT IT.

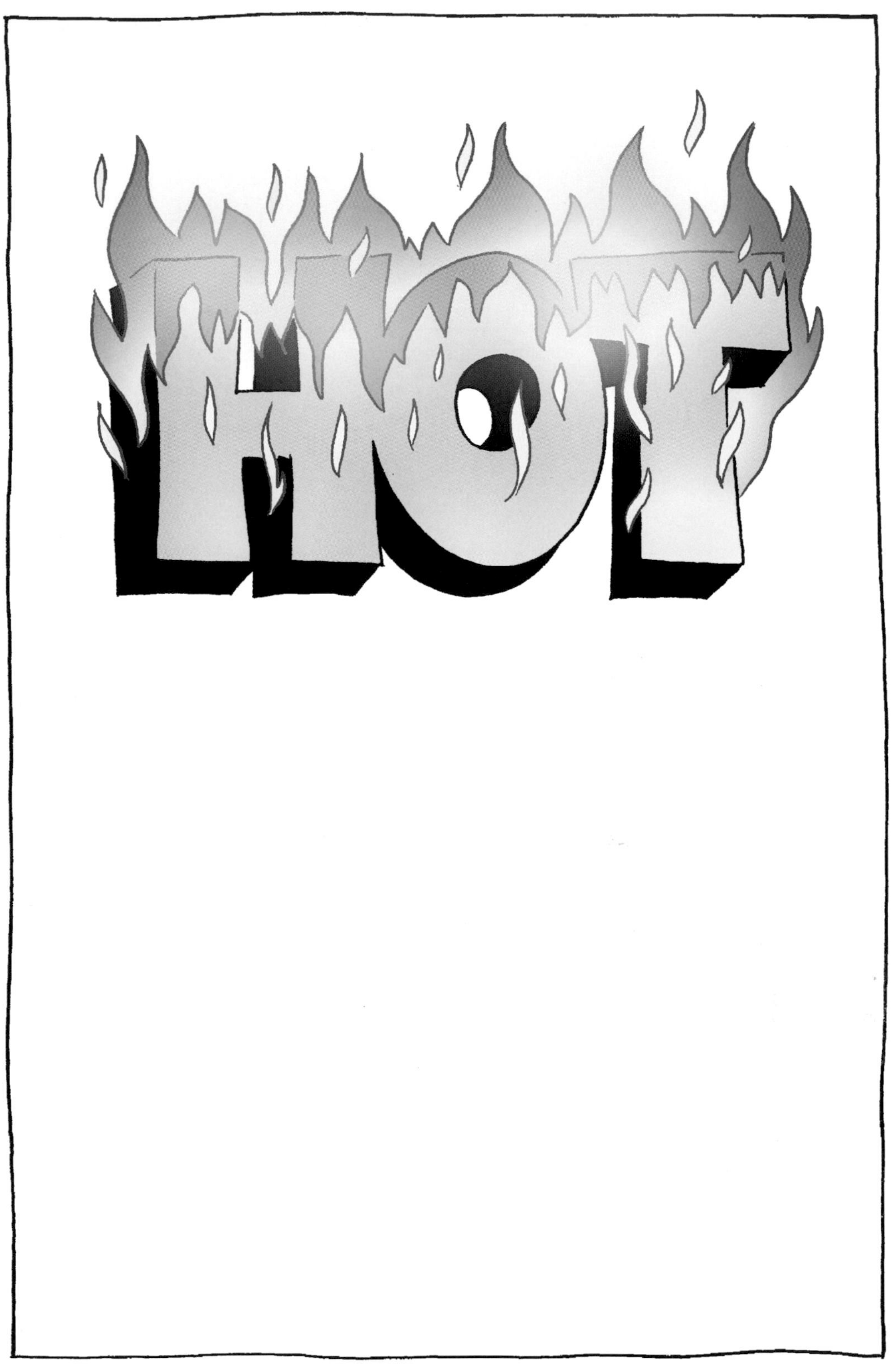
HOT

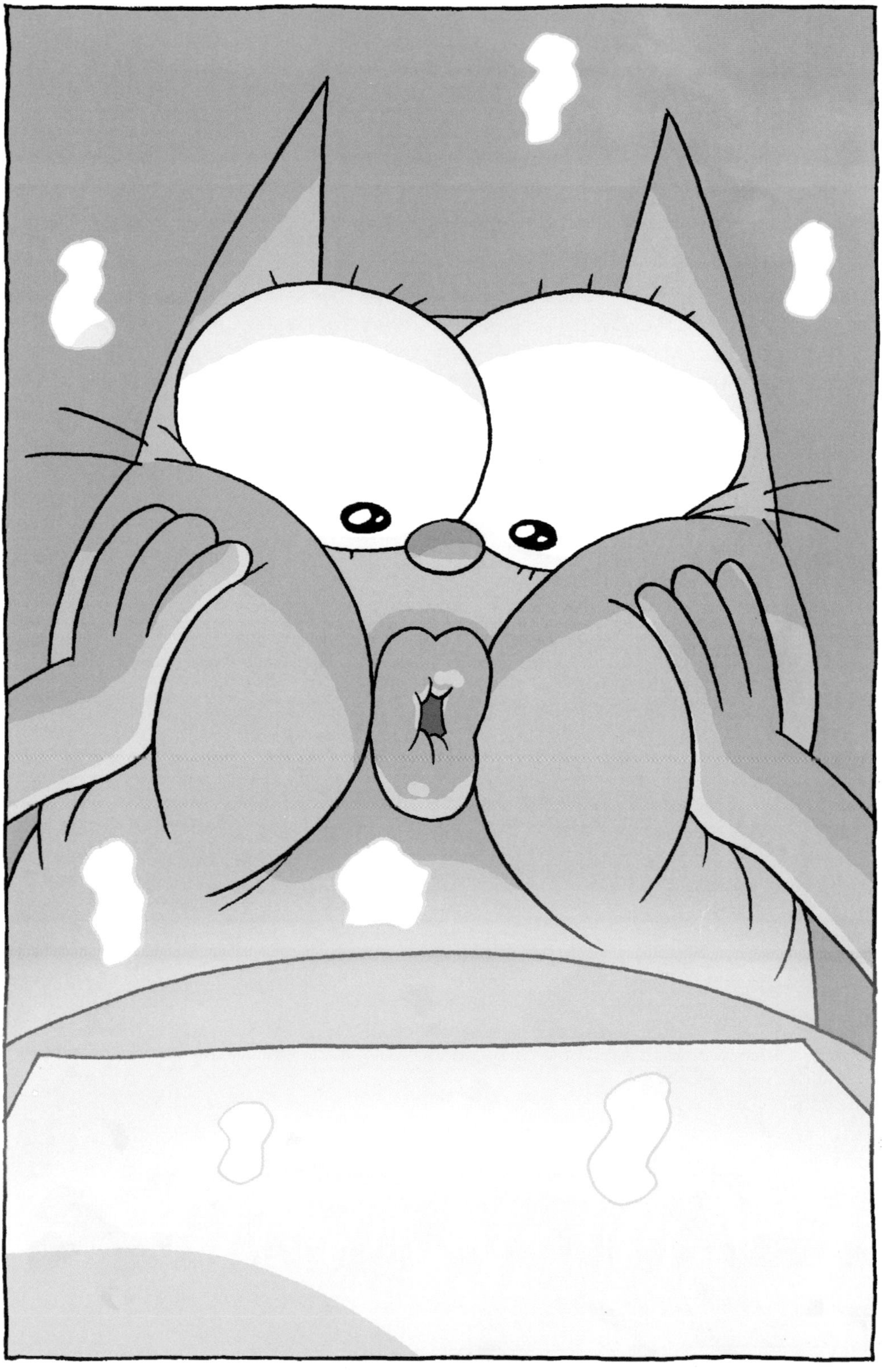

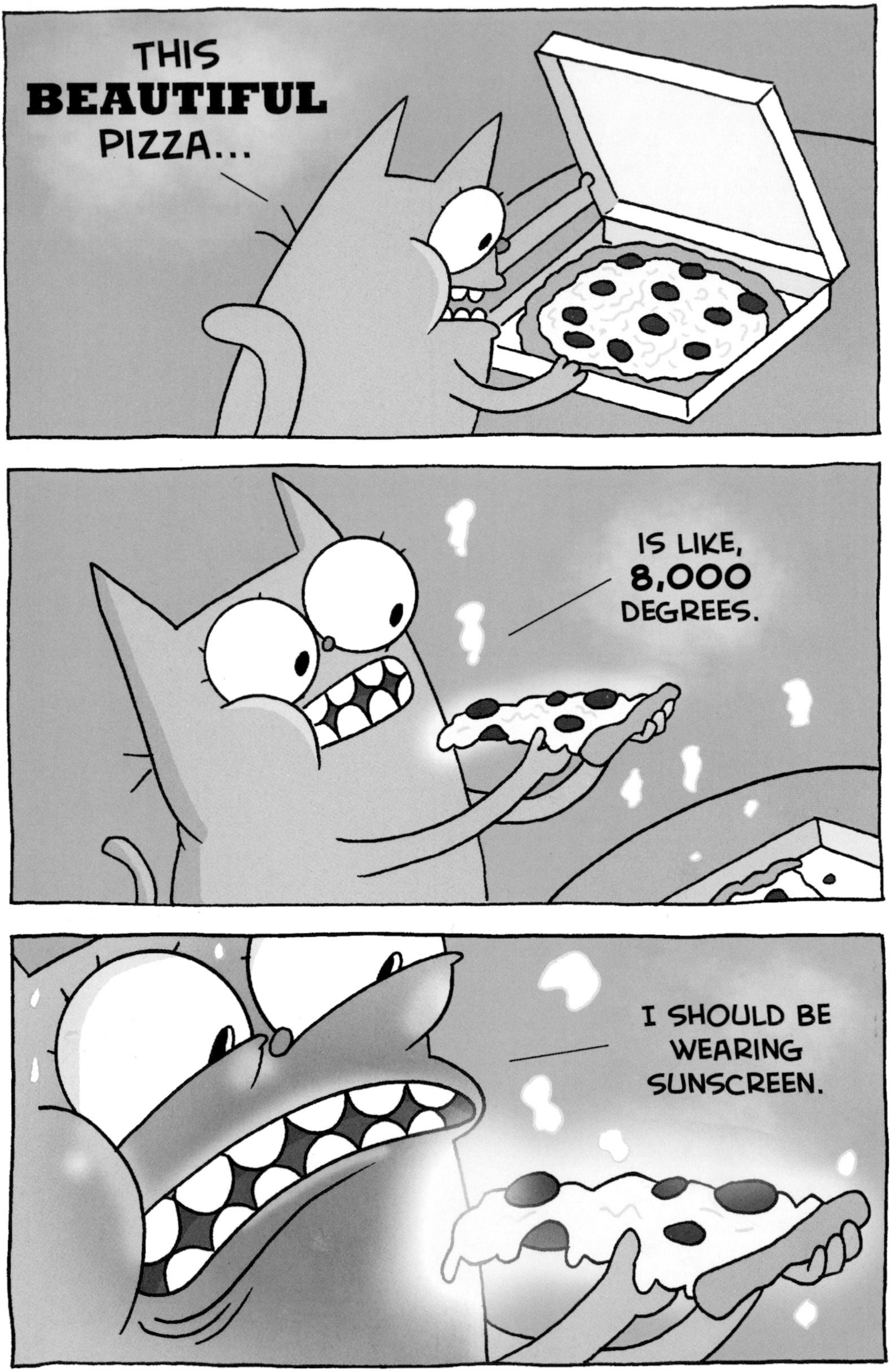
THIS **BEAUTIFUL** PIZZA...
IS LIKE, 8,000 DEGREES.
I SHOULD BE WEARING SUNSCREEN.

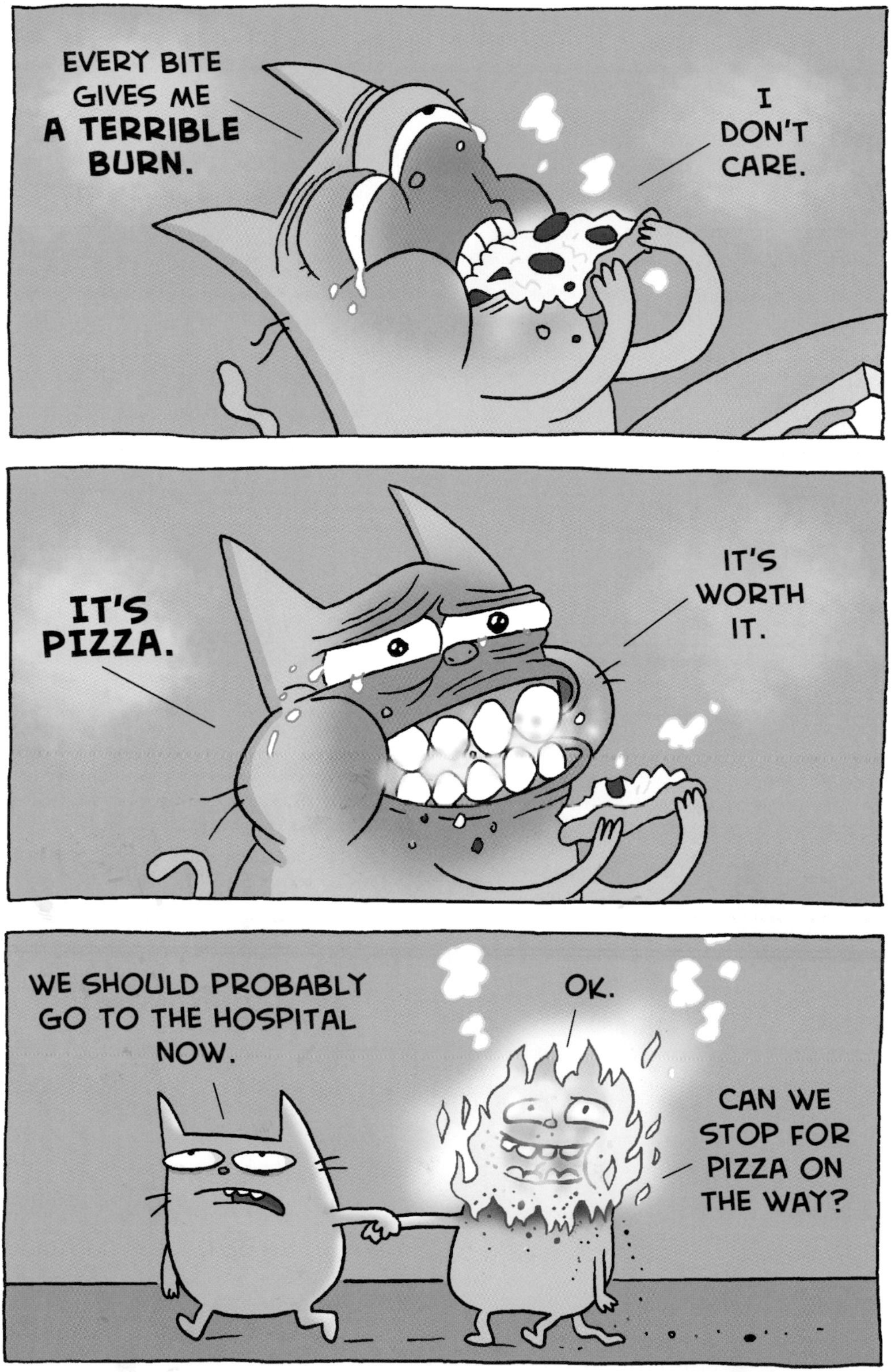
EVERY BITE GIVES ME A TERRIBLE BURN.
I DON'T CARE.
IT'S PIZZA.
IT'S WORTH IT.
WE SHOULD PROBABLY GO TO THE HOSPITAL NOW.
OK.
CAN WE STOP FOR PIZZA ON THE WAY?

PHONE

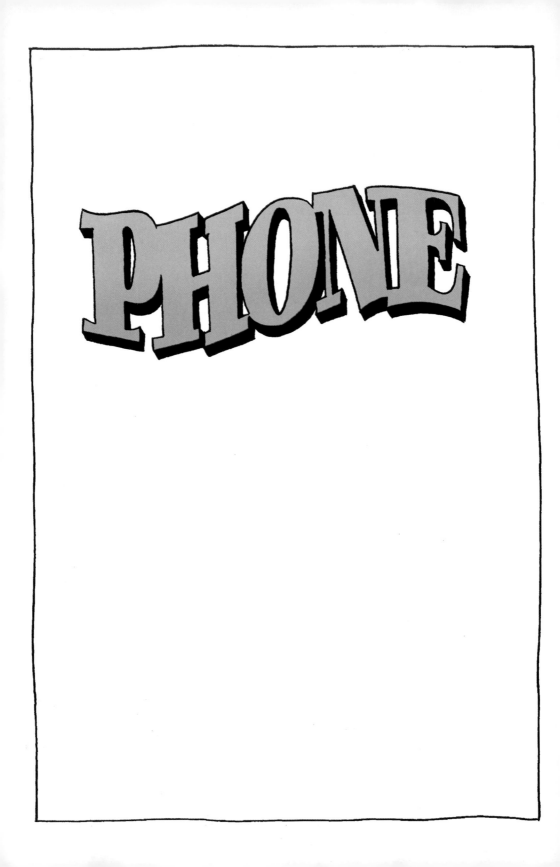

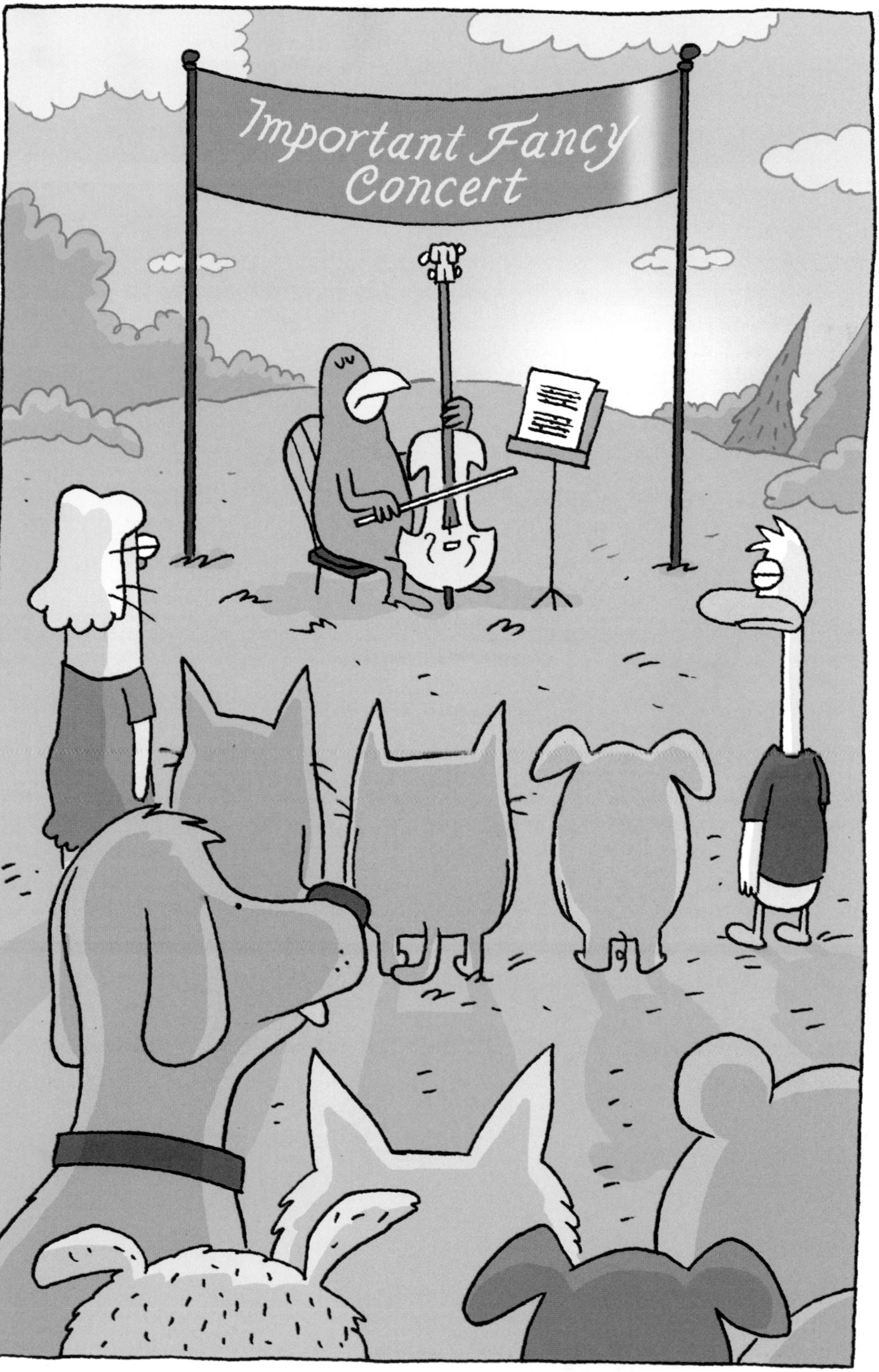
Important Fancy
Concert

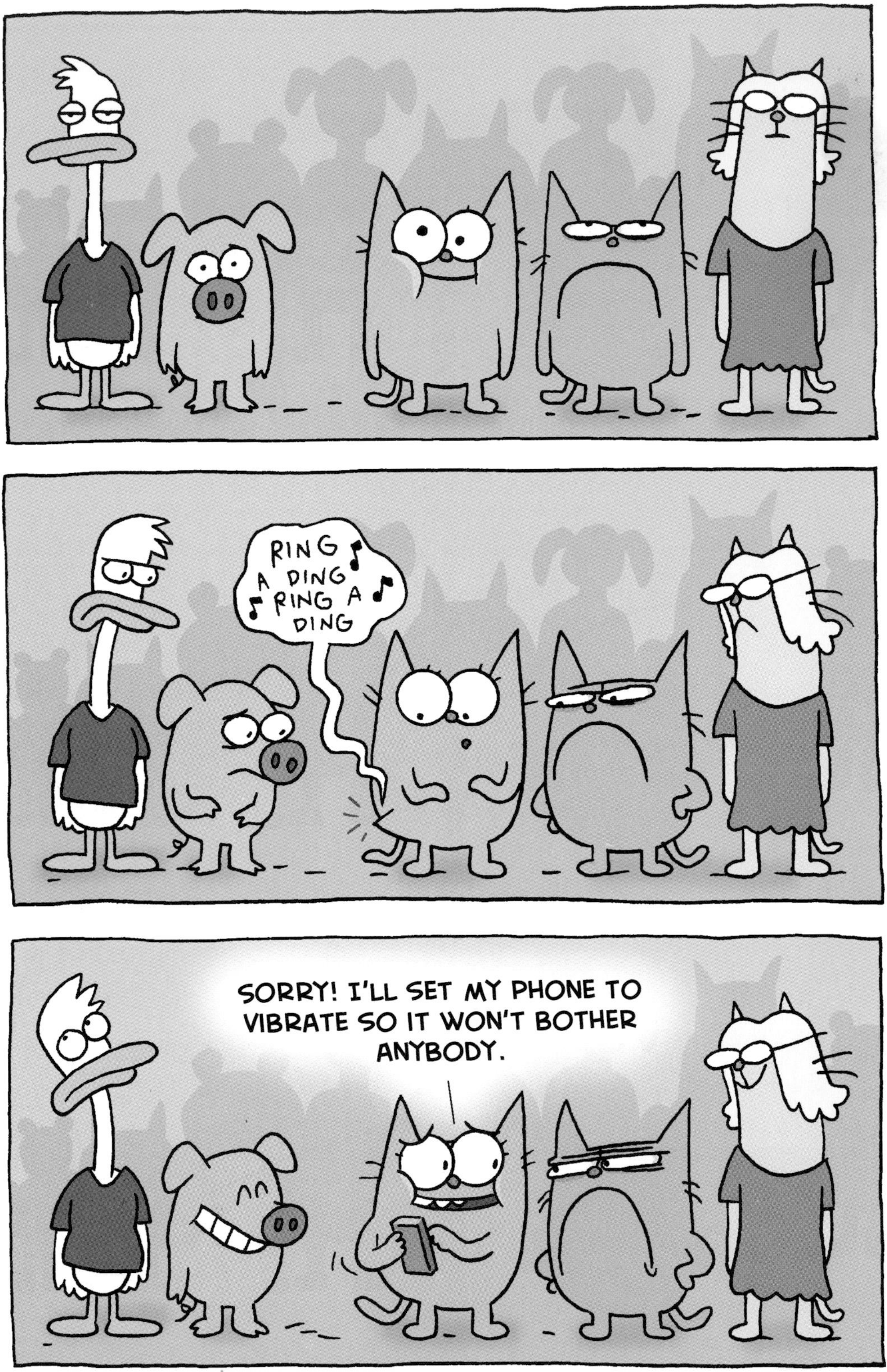
RING A DING RING A DING
SORRY! I'LL SET MY PHONE TO VIBRATE SO IT WON'T BOTHER ANYBODY.

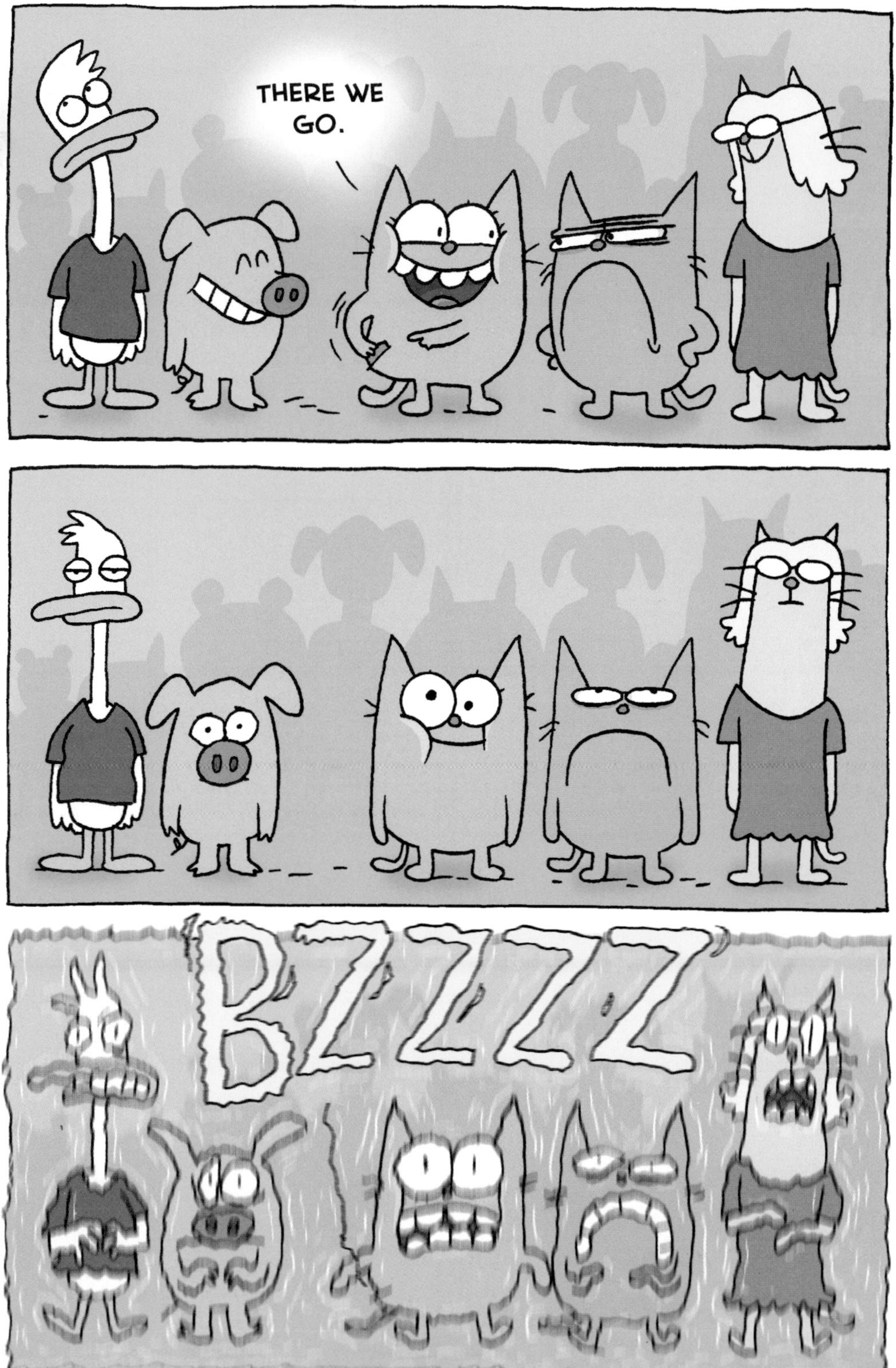
THERE WE GO.
BZZZZ

PLUGGED IN

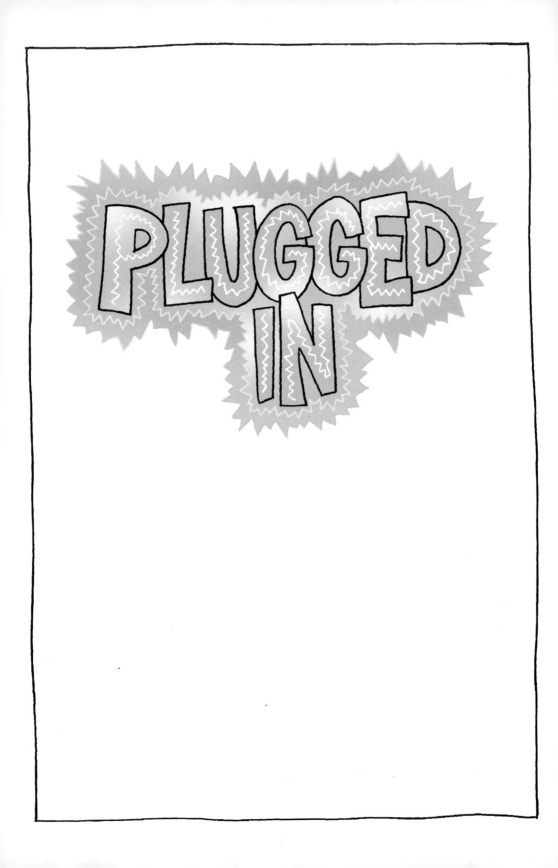

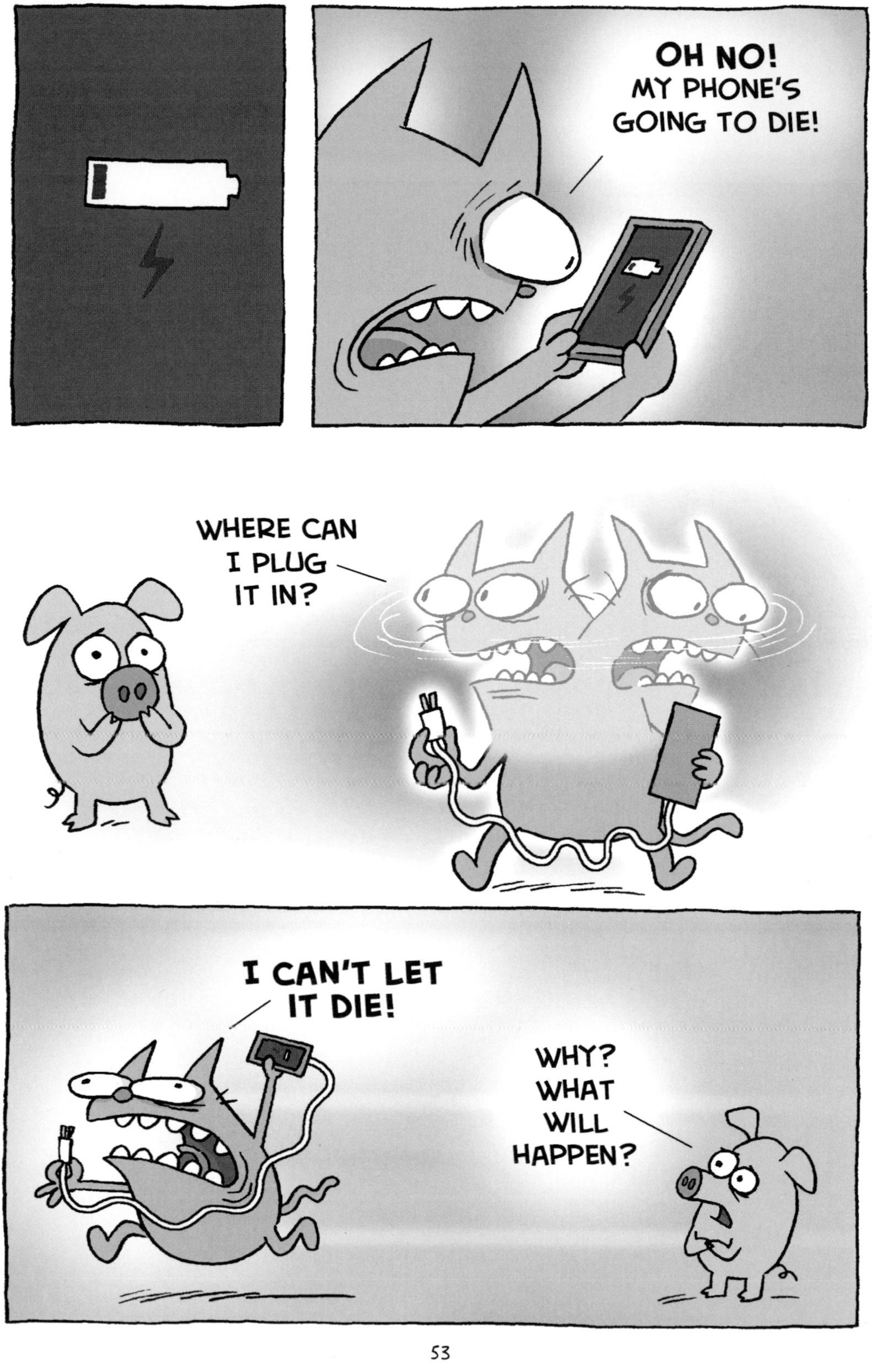
OH NO!
MY PHONE'S
GOING TO DIE!
WHERE CAN
I PLUG
IT IN?
I CAN'T LET
IT DIE!
WHY?
WHAT
WILL
HAPPEN?

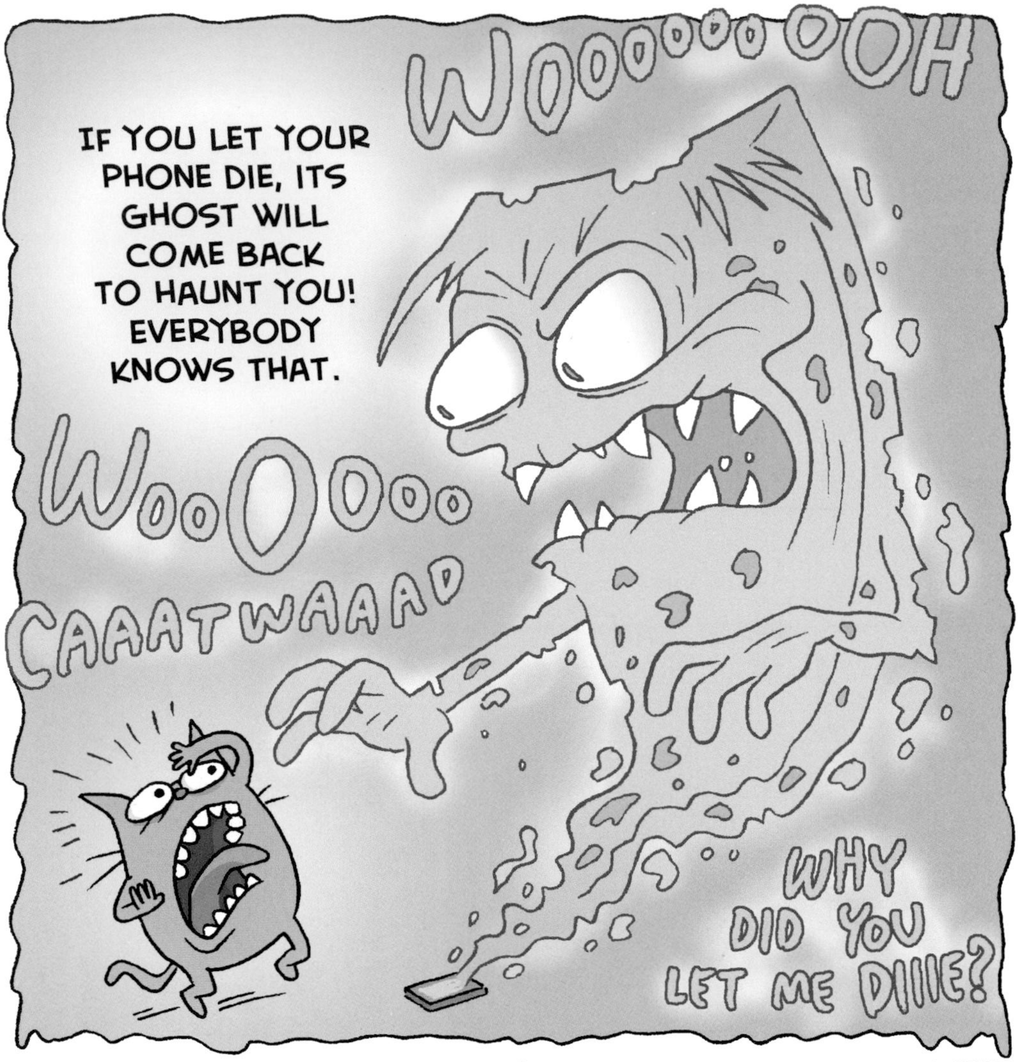
IF YOU LET YOUR PHONE DIE, ITS GHOST WILL COME BACK TO HAUNT YOU! EVERYBODY KNOWS THAT.
WOOOOOOOOH
WooOOoo
CAAATWAAAD
WHY DID YOU LET ME DIIIE?

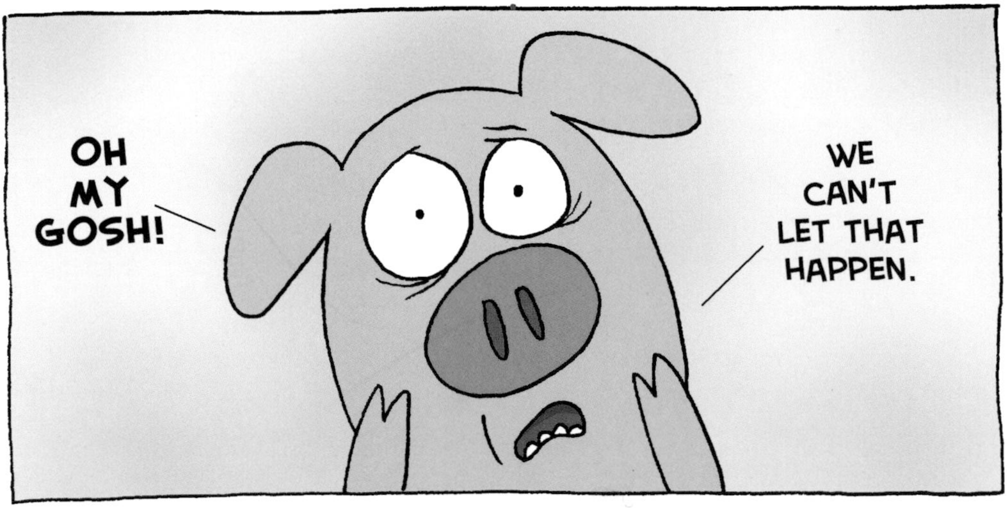
OH MY GOSH!
WE CAN'T LET THAT HAPPEN.

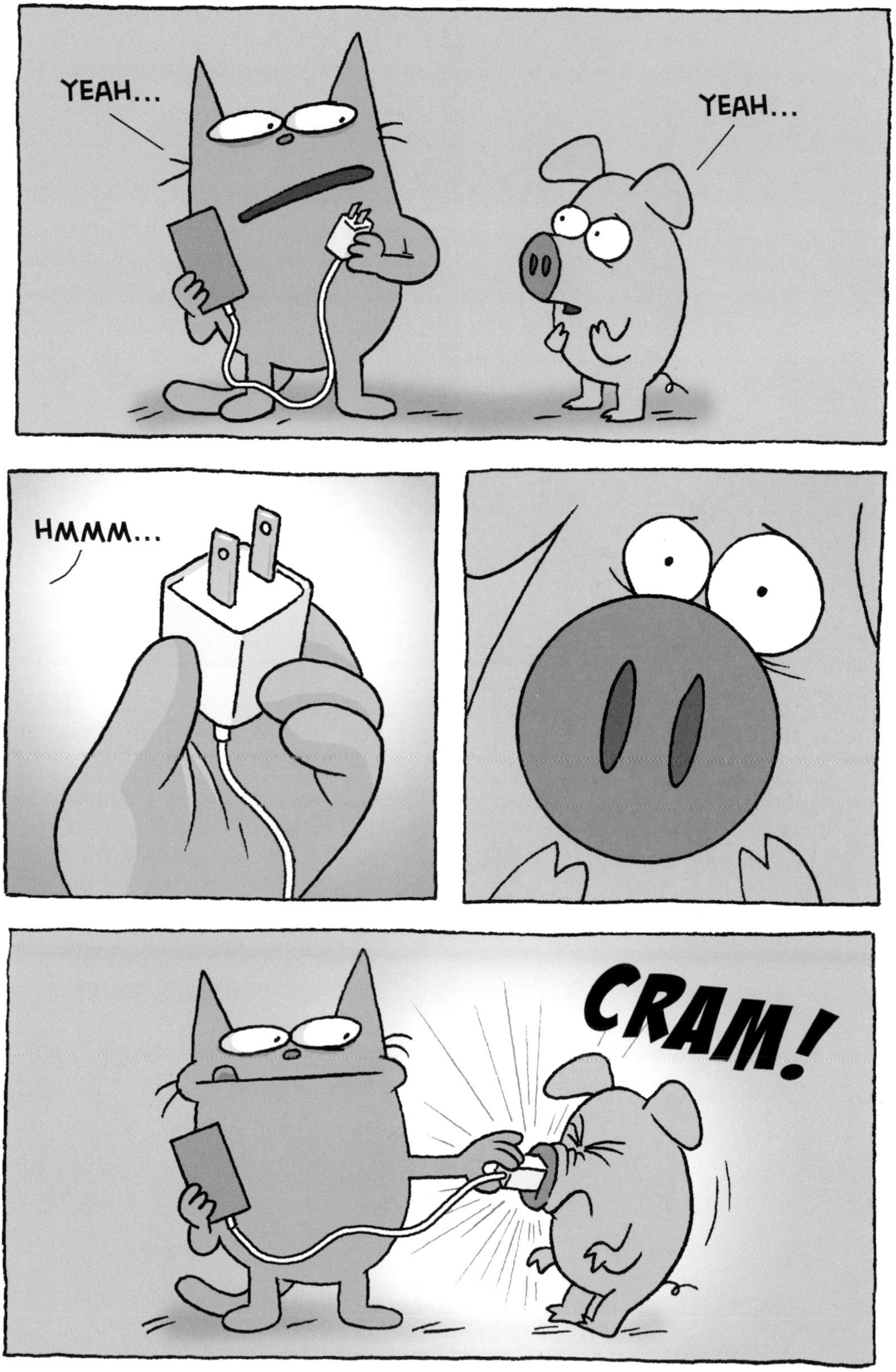
YEAH...
YEAH...
HMMM...
CRAM!

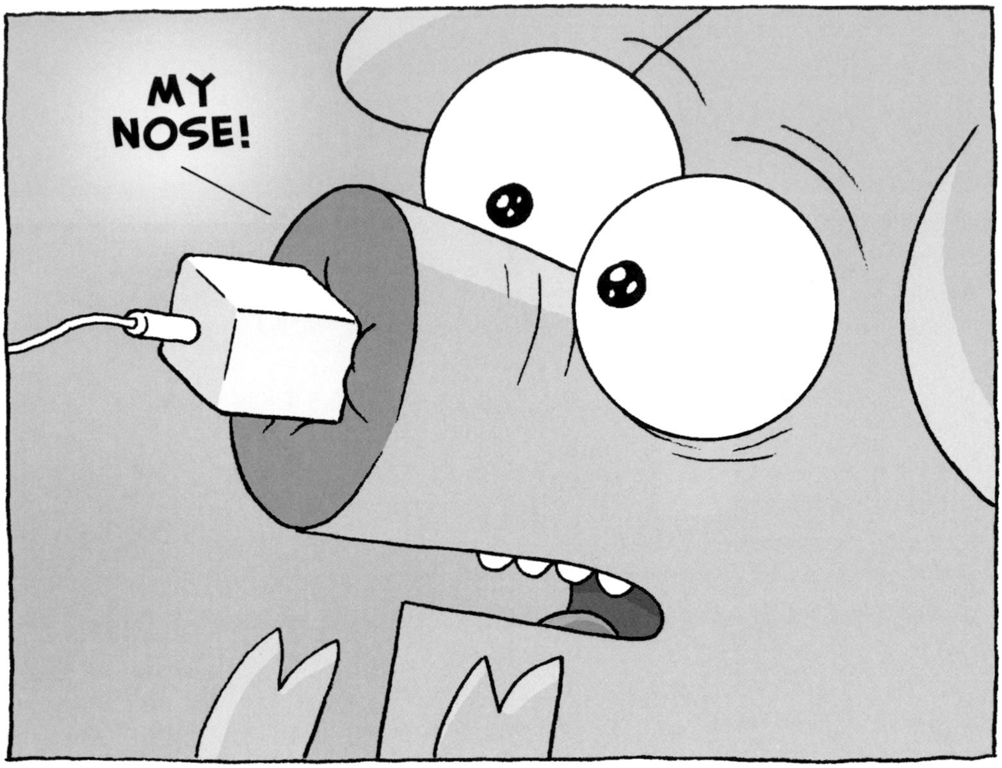
MY NOSE!

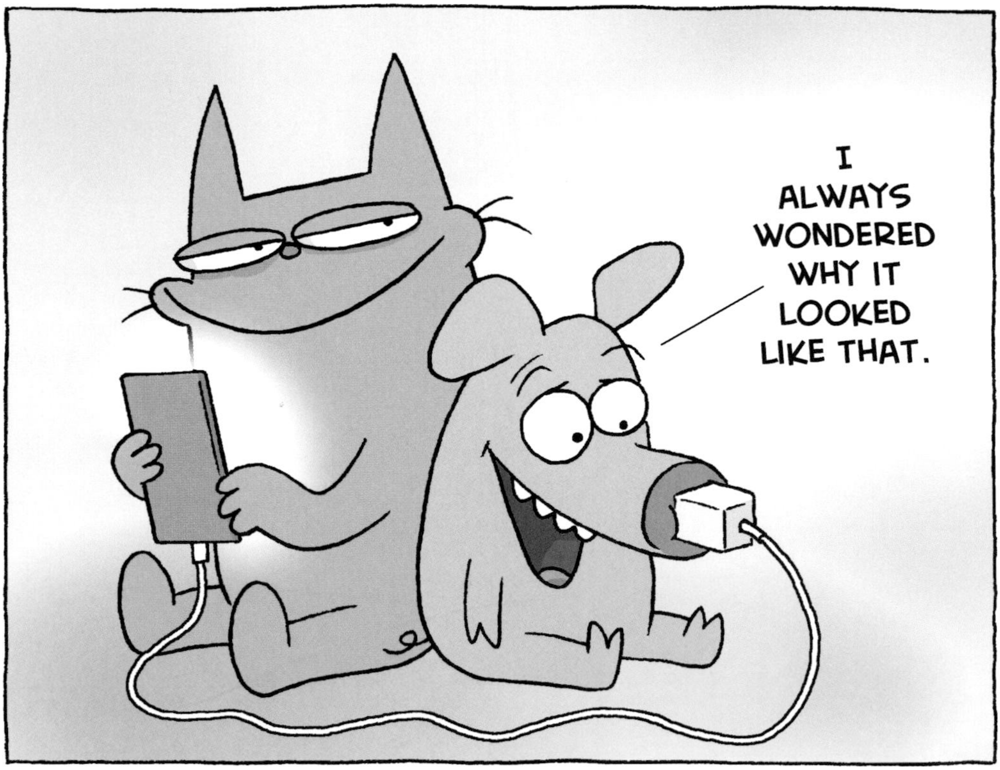
I ALWAYS WONDERED WHY IT LOOKED LIKE THAT.

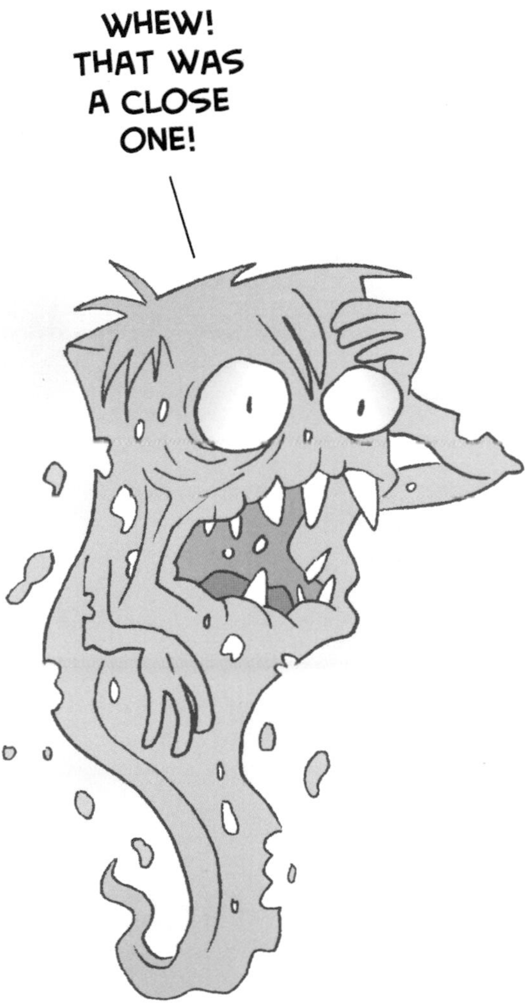
WHEW! THAT WAS A CLOSE ONE!

THE BABY BUNNY

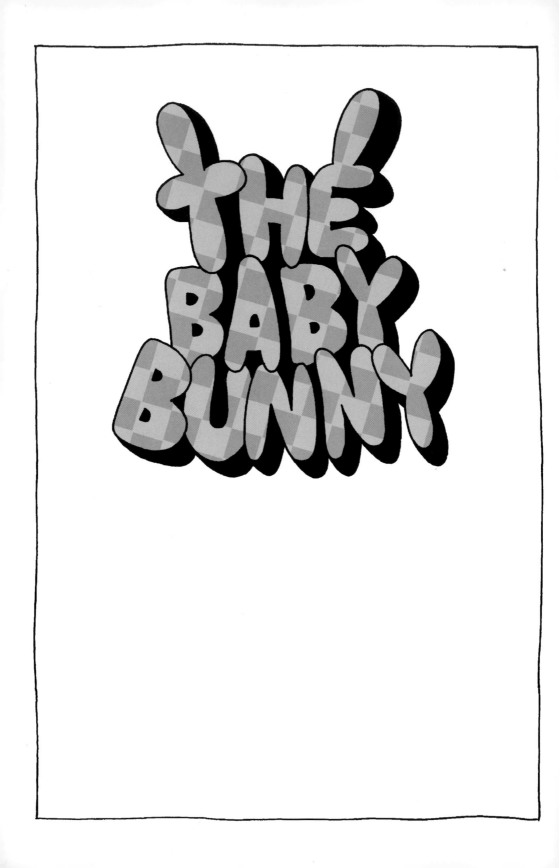

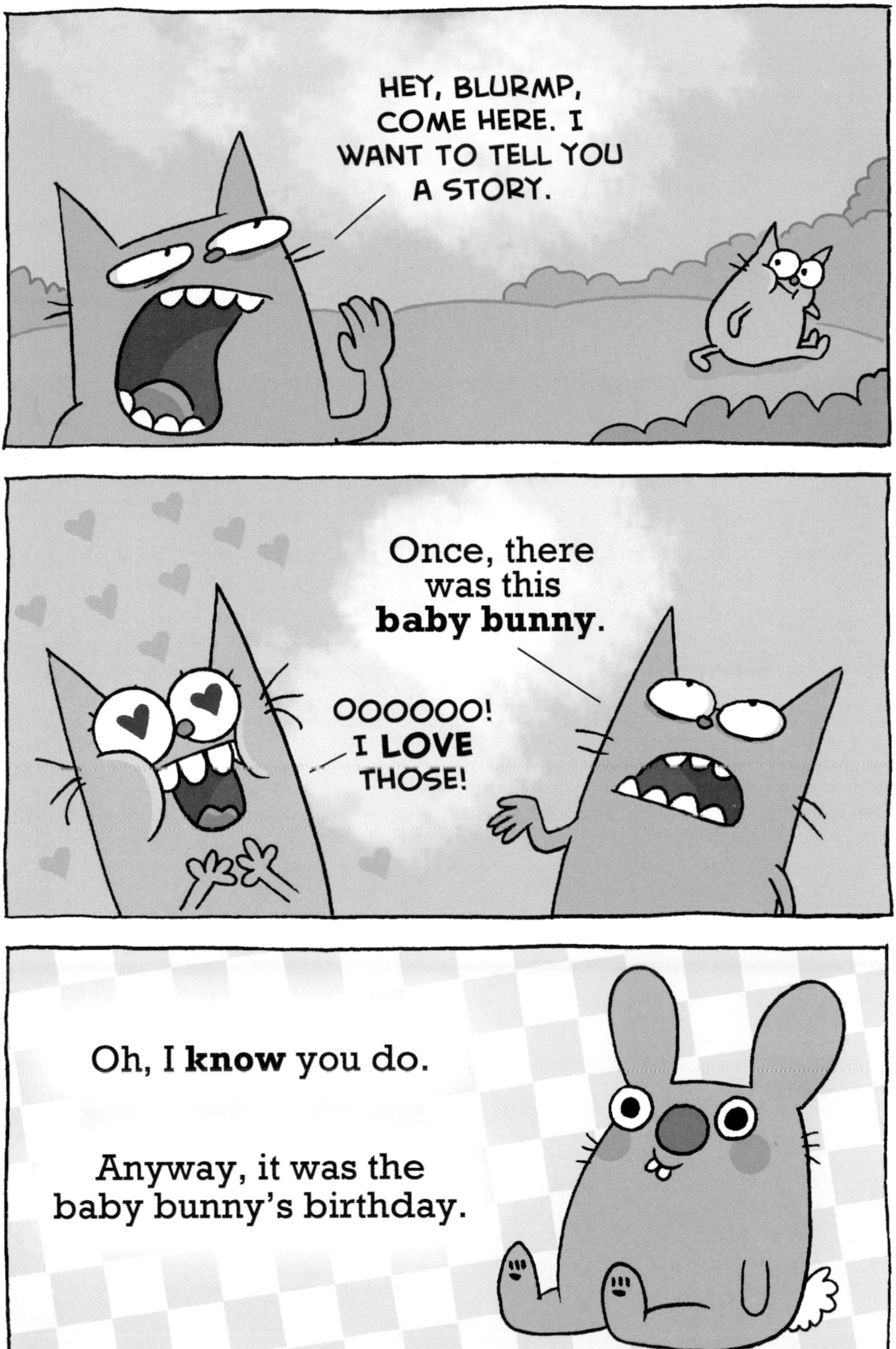
HEY, BLURMP, COME HERE. I WANT TO TELL YOU A STORY.
Once, there was this **baby bunny**.
OOOOOO! I **LOVE** THOSE!
Oh, I **know** you do.
Anyway, it was the baby bunny's birthday.

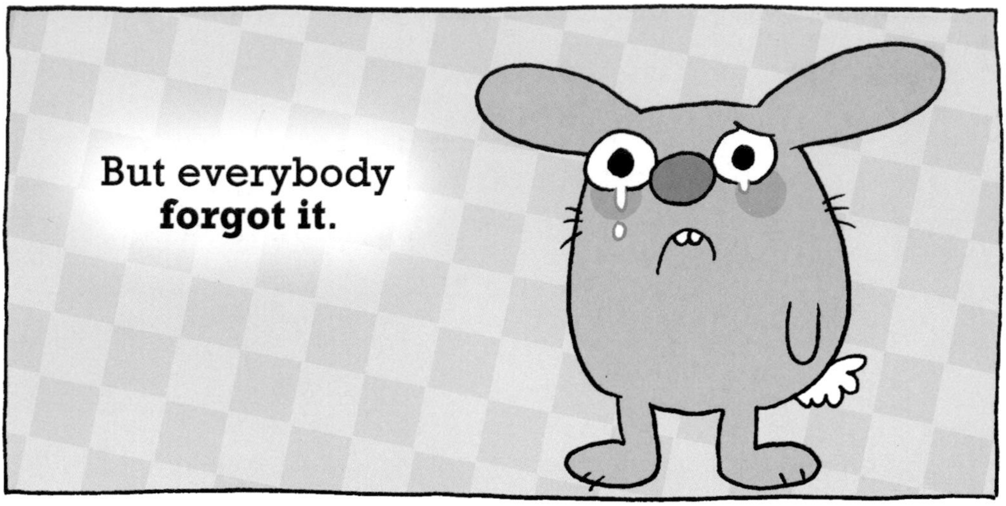
But everybody **forgot it**.

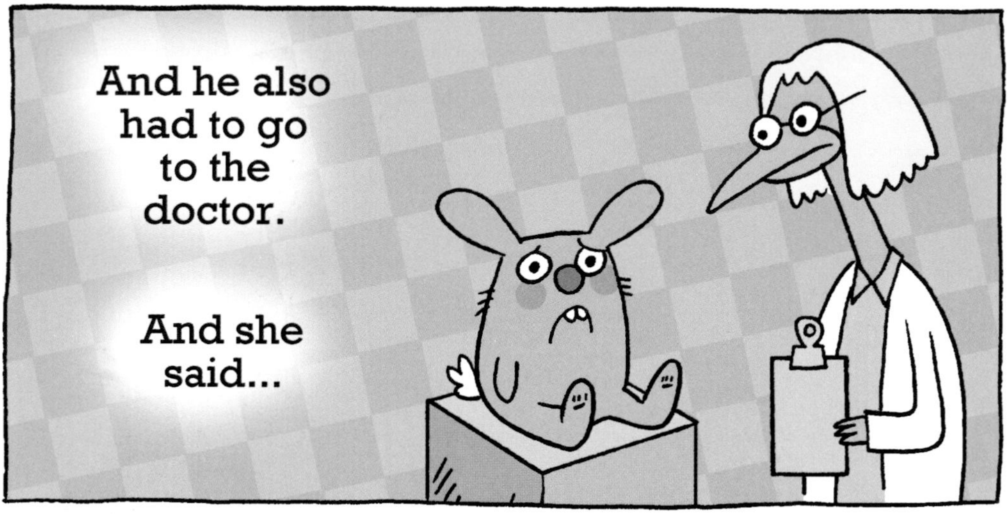
And he also had to go to the doctor.
And she said...

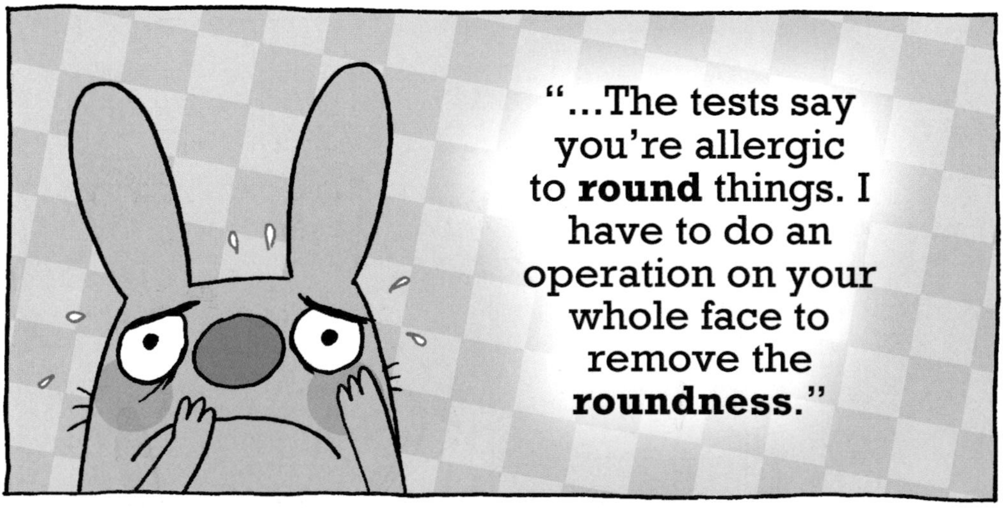
"...The tests say you're allergic to **round** things. I have to do an operation on your whole face to remove the **roundness**."

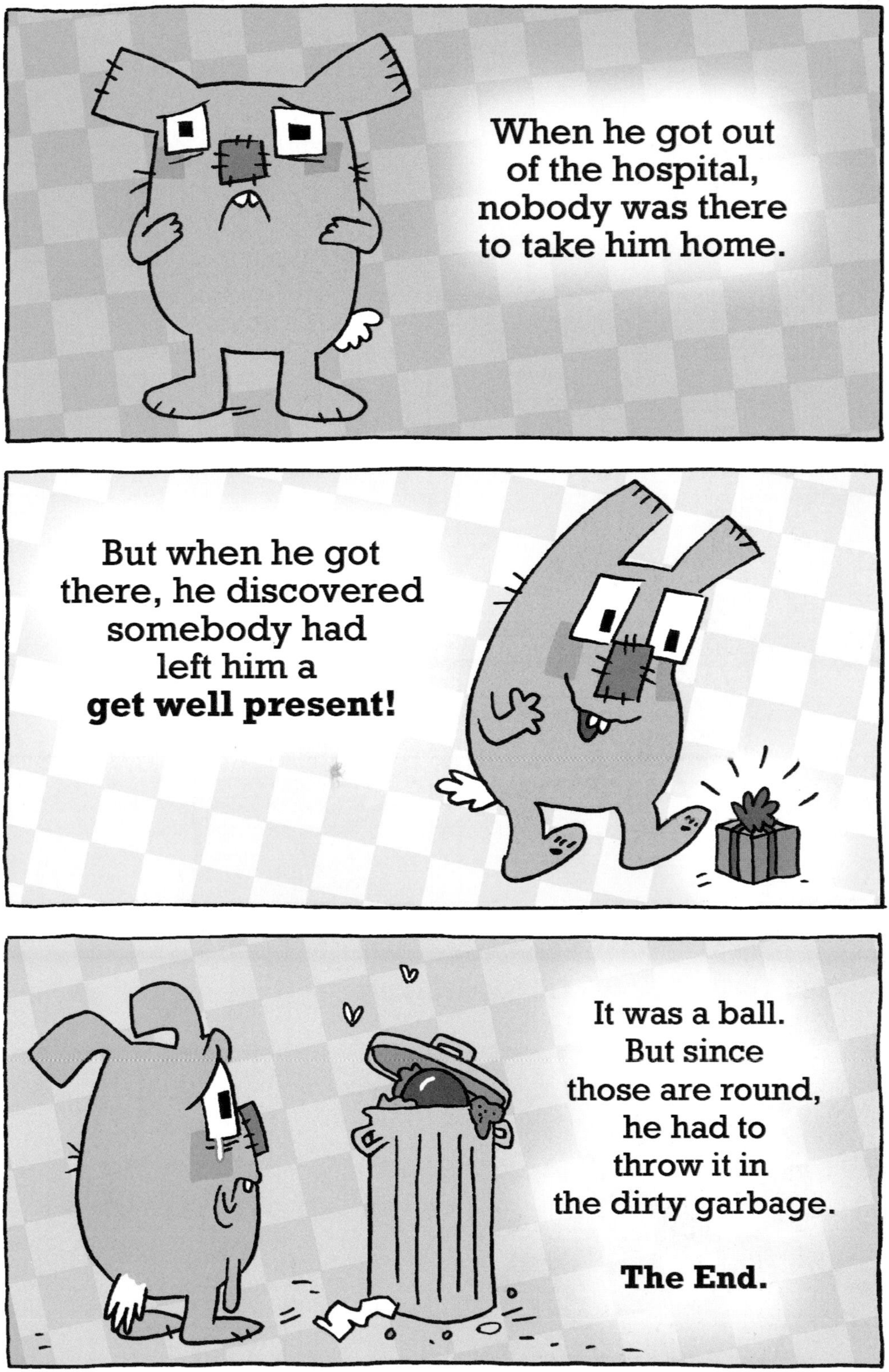
When he got out of the hospital, nobody was there to take him home.
But when he got there, he discovered somebody had left him a **get well present!**
It was a ball. But since those are round, he had to throw it in the dirty garbage.
The End.

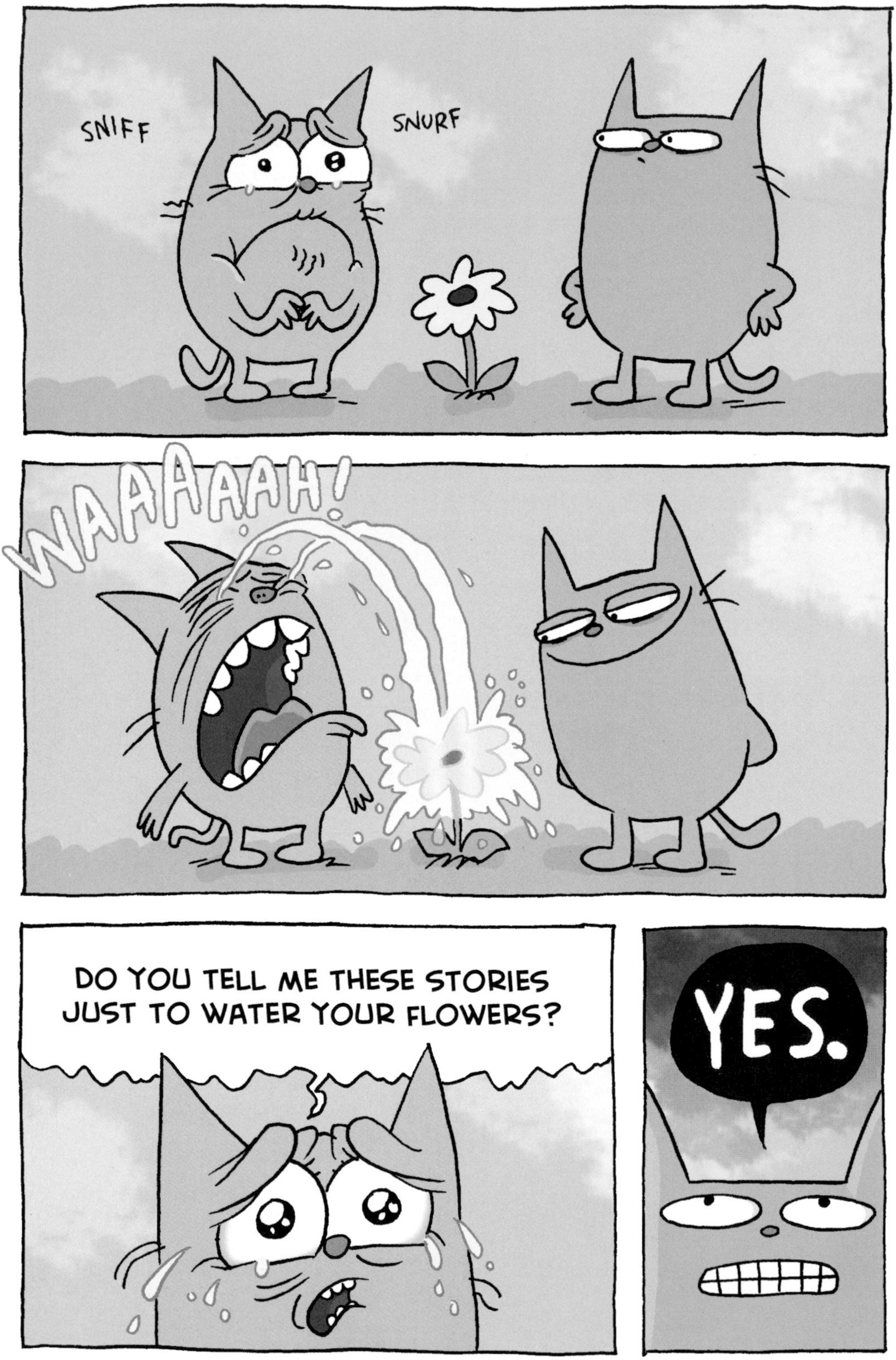
SNIFF
SNURF
WAAAAAAH!
DO YOU TELL ME THESE STORIES JUST TO WATER YOUR FLOWERS?
YES.

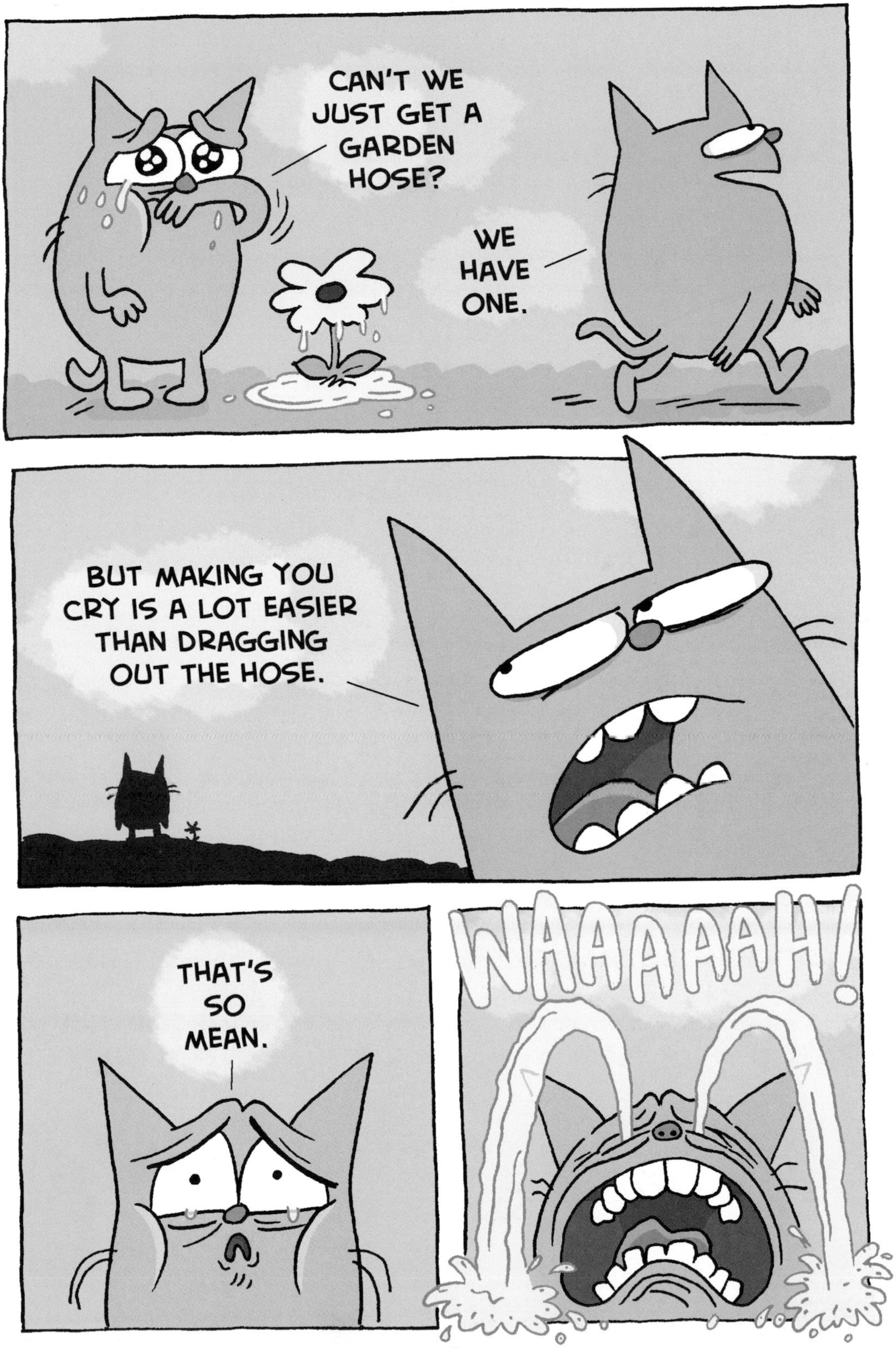
CAN'T WE JUST GET A GARDEN HOSE?
WE HAVE ONE.
BUT MAKING YOU CRY IS A LOT EASIER THAN DRAGGING OUT THE HOSE.
THAT'S SO MEAN.
WAAAAAH!

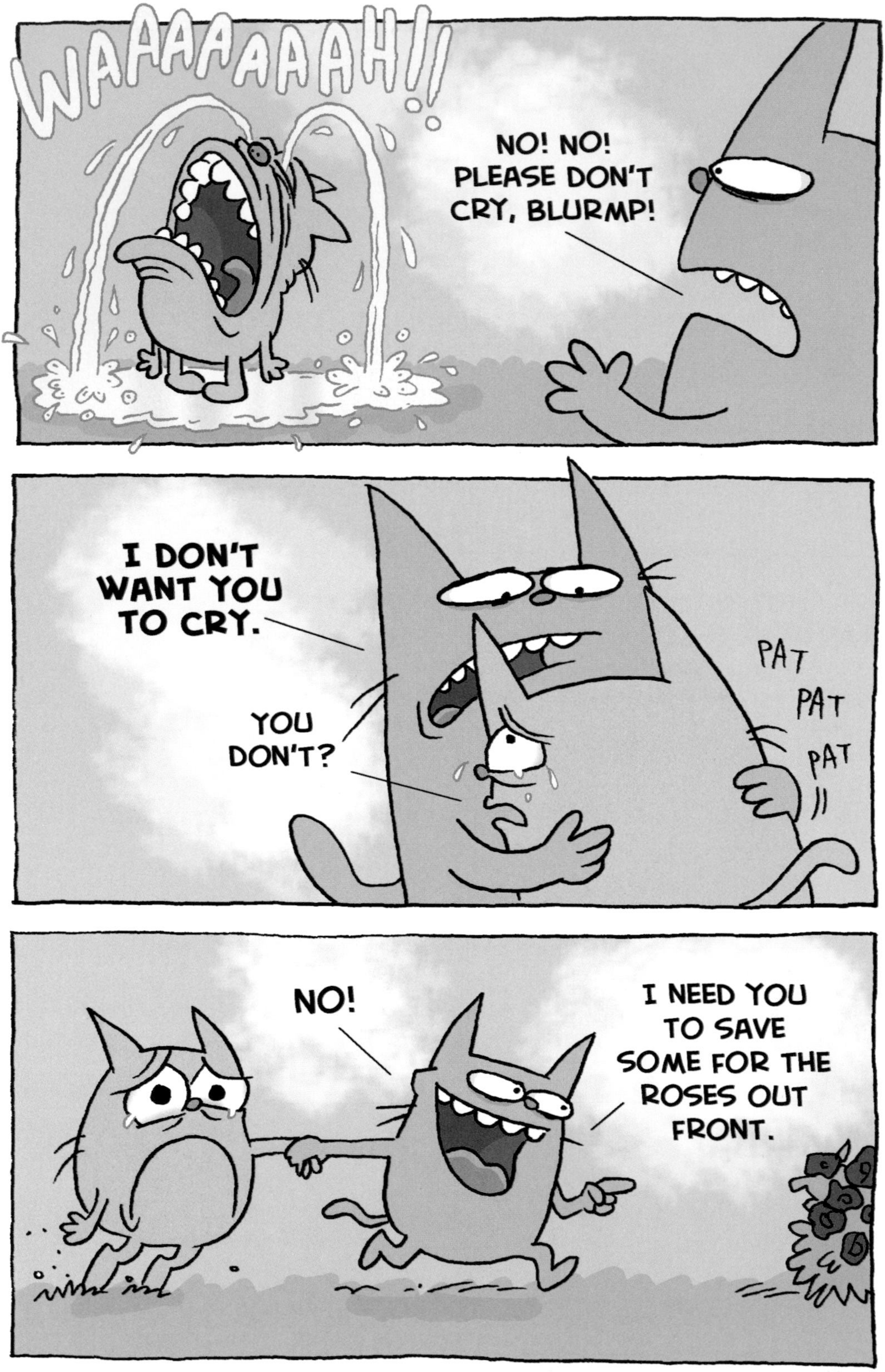
WAAAAAAAH!!
NO! NO! PLEASE DON'T CRY, BLURMP!
I DON'T WANT YOU TO CRY.
YOU DON'T?
PAT PAT PAT
NO!
I NEED YOU TO SAVE SOME FOR THE ROSES OUT FRONT.

Did I ever tell
you the story of the
baby koala who was
stung in the face
by **bees**?

THE JOKE

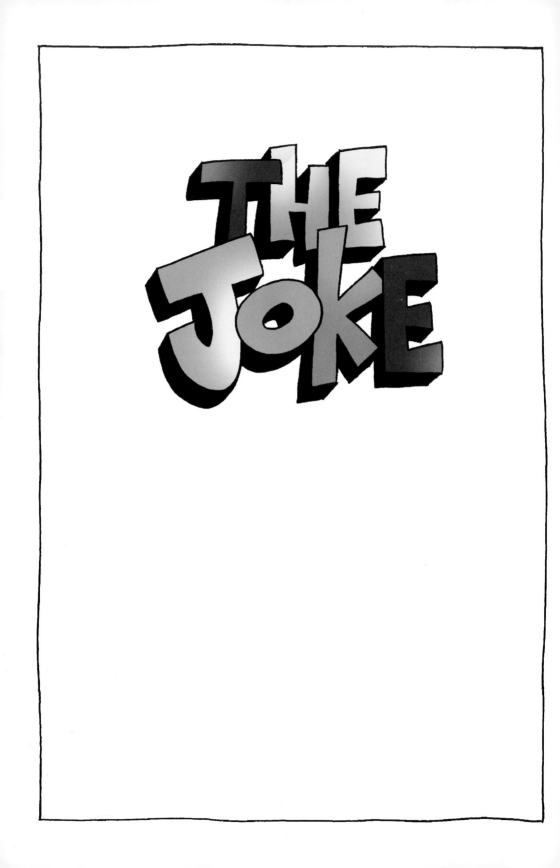

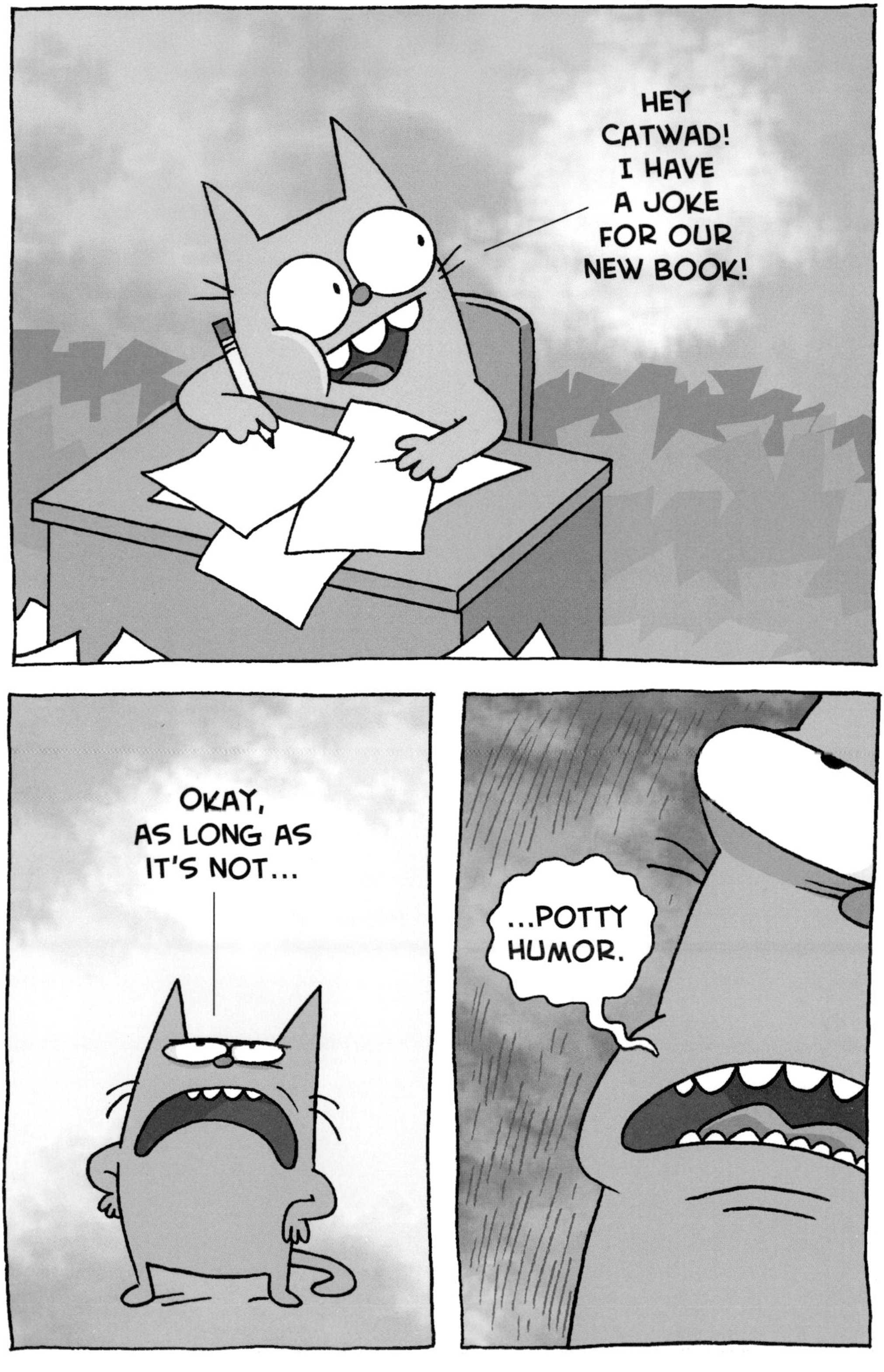
HEY CATWAD! I HAVE A JOKE FOR OUR NEW BOOK!
OKAY, AS LONG AS IT'S NOT...
...POTTY HUMOR.

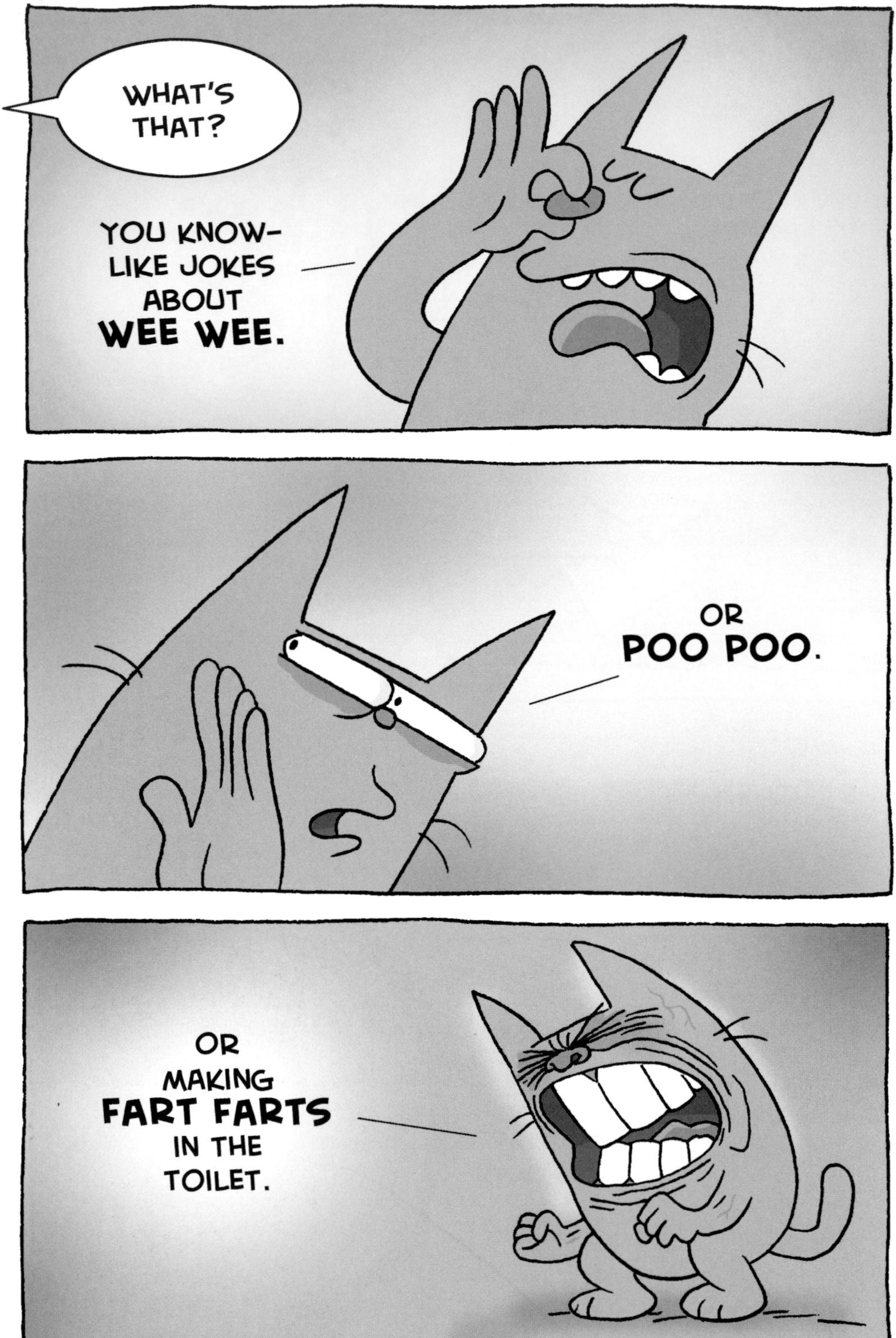

WHAT'S THAT?
YOU KNOW- LIKE JOKES ABOUT **WEE WEE.**
OR **POO POO**.
OR MAKING **FART FARTS** IN THE TOILET.

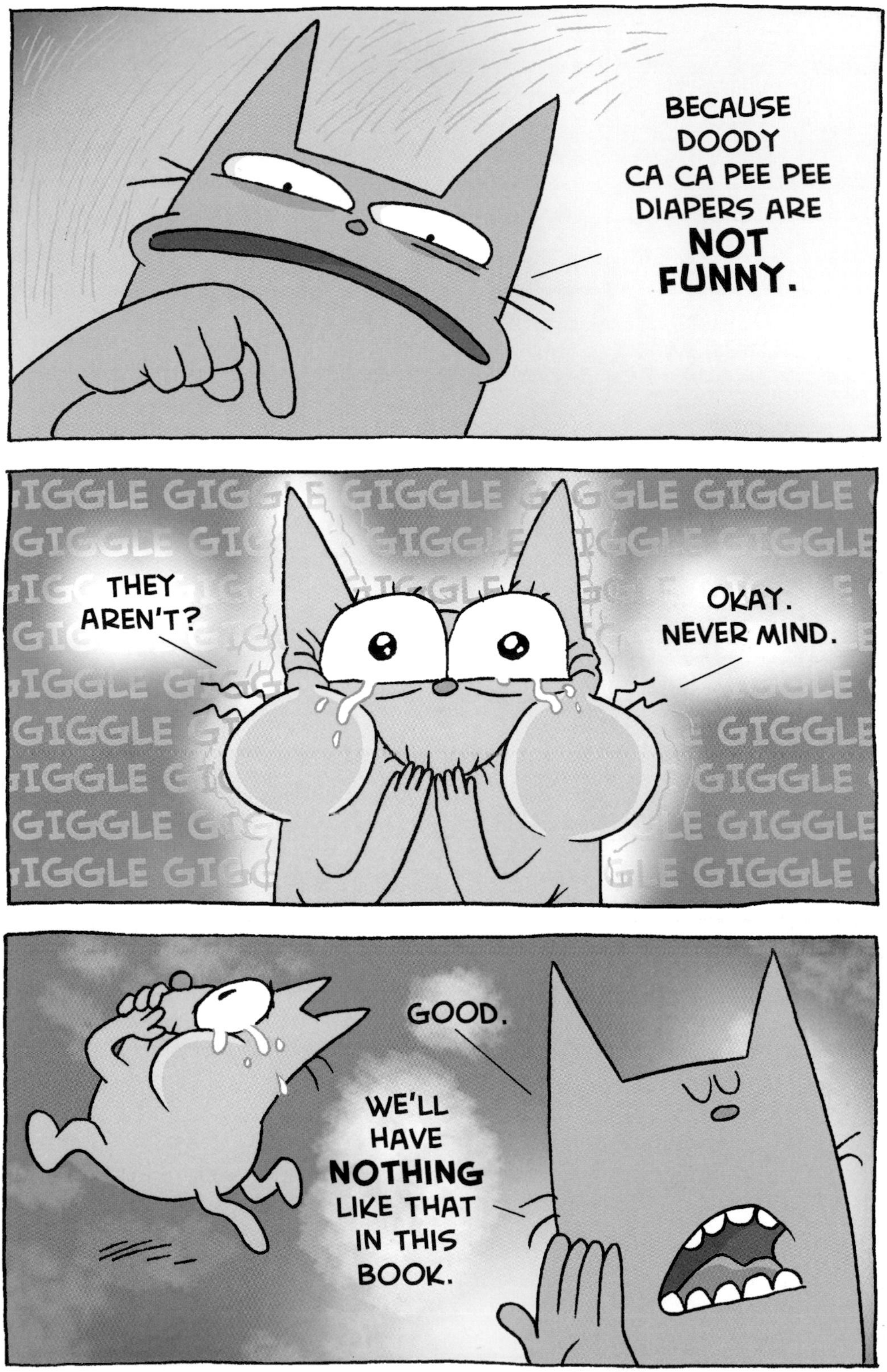
BECAUSE DOODY CA CA PEE PEE DIAPERS ARE NOT FUNNY.
THEY AREN'T?
OKAY. NEVER MIND.
GIGGLE GIGGLE GIGGLE
GOOD.
WE'LL HAVE NOTHING LIKE THAT IN THIS BOOK.

UNDERSEA ADVENTURE

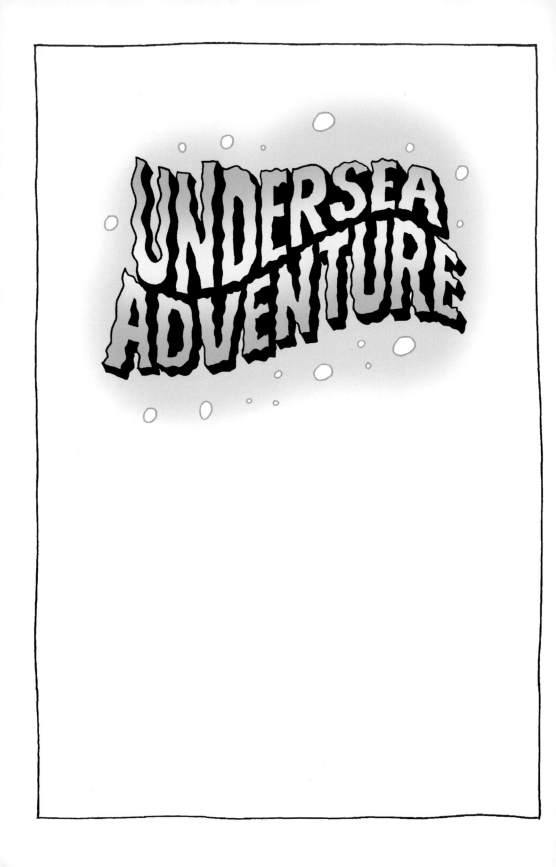

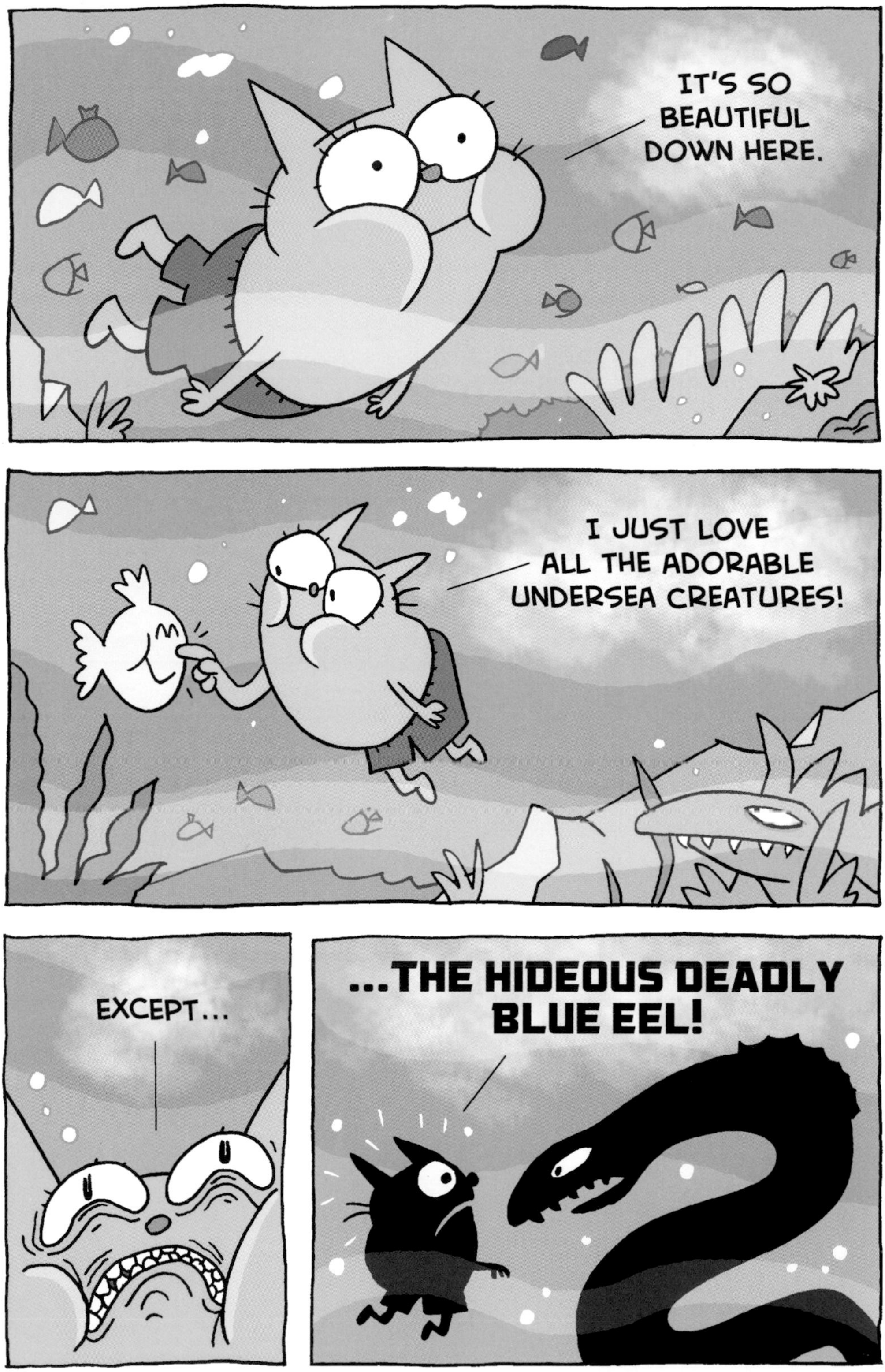
IT'S SO BEAUTIFUL DOWN HERE.
I JUST LOVE ALL THE ADORABLE UNDERSEA CREATURES!
EXCEPT...
...THE HIDEOUS DEADLY BLUE EEL!

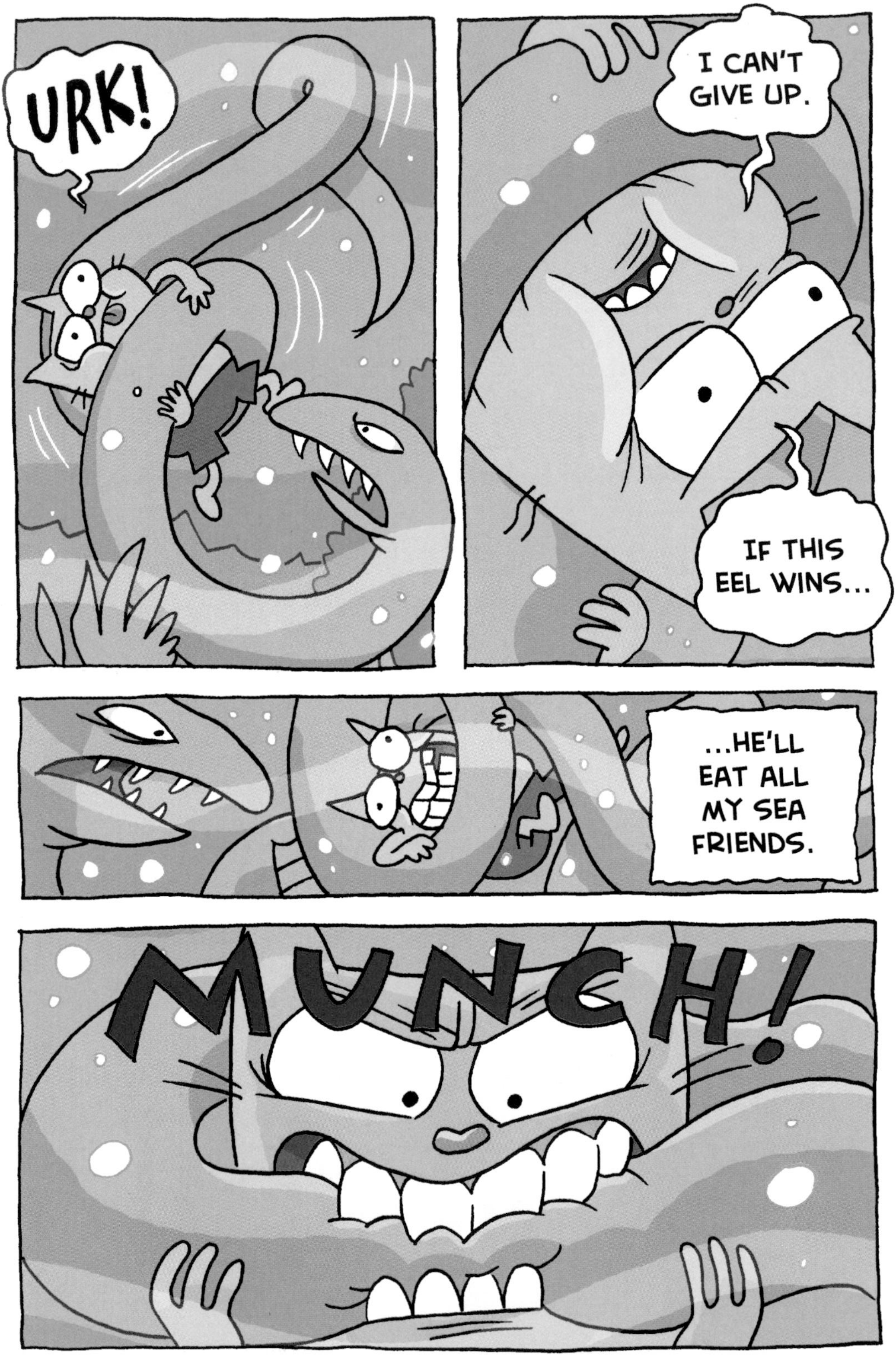
URK!
I CAN'T GIVE UP.
IF THIS EEL WINS...
...HE'LL EAT ALL MY SEA FRIENDS.
MUNCH!

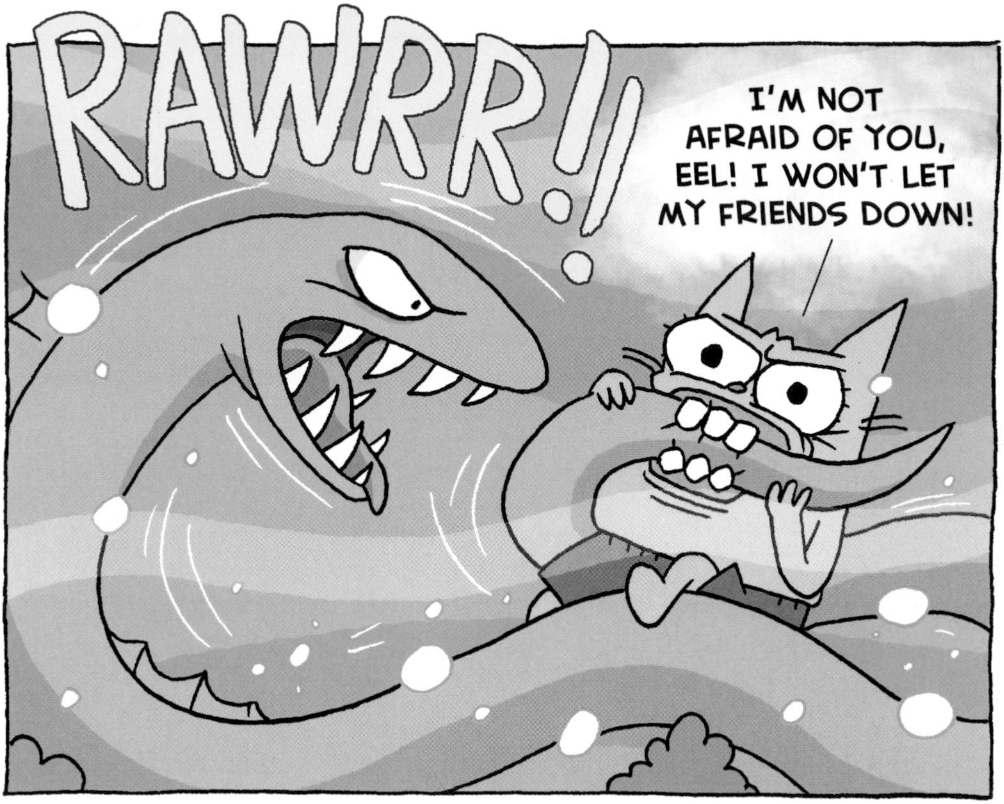
RAWRR!!
I'M NOT AFRAID OF YOU, EEL! I WON'T LET MY FRIENDS DOWN!

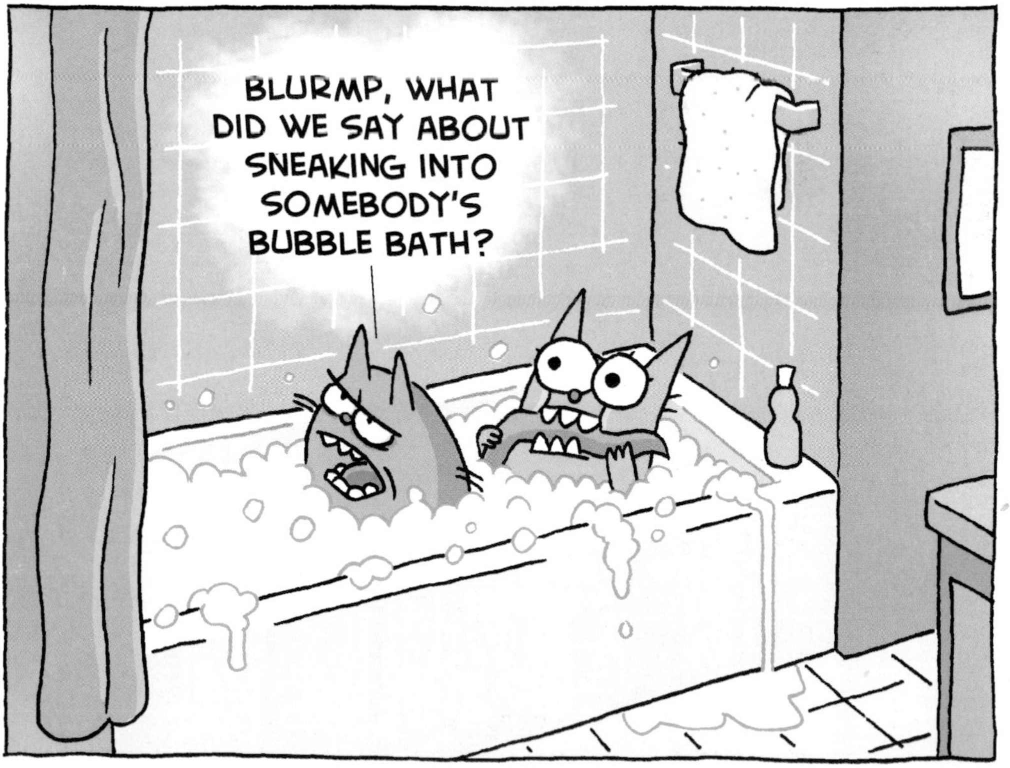
BLURMP, WHAT DID WE SAY ABOUT SNEAKING INTO SOMEBODY'S BUBBLE BATH?

PAJAMAS

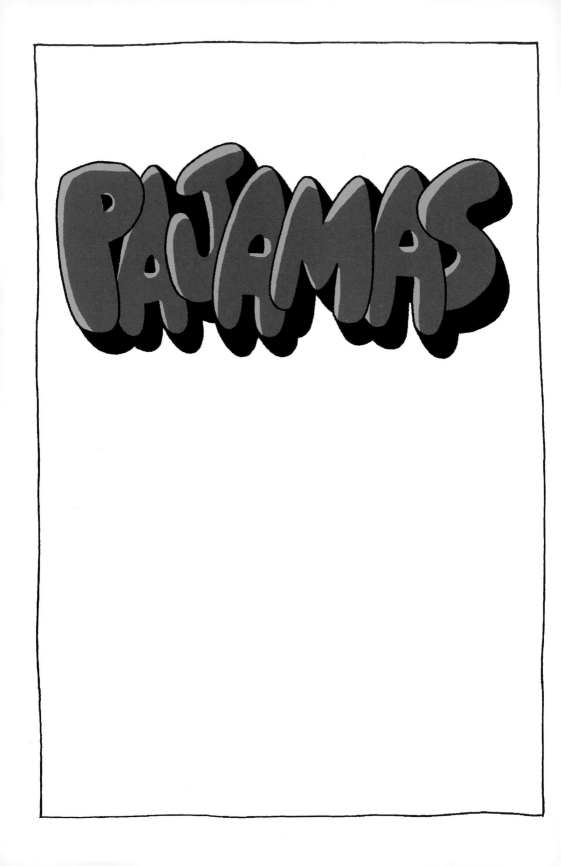

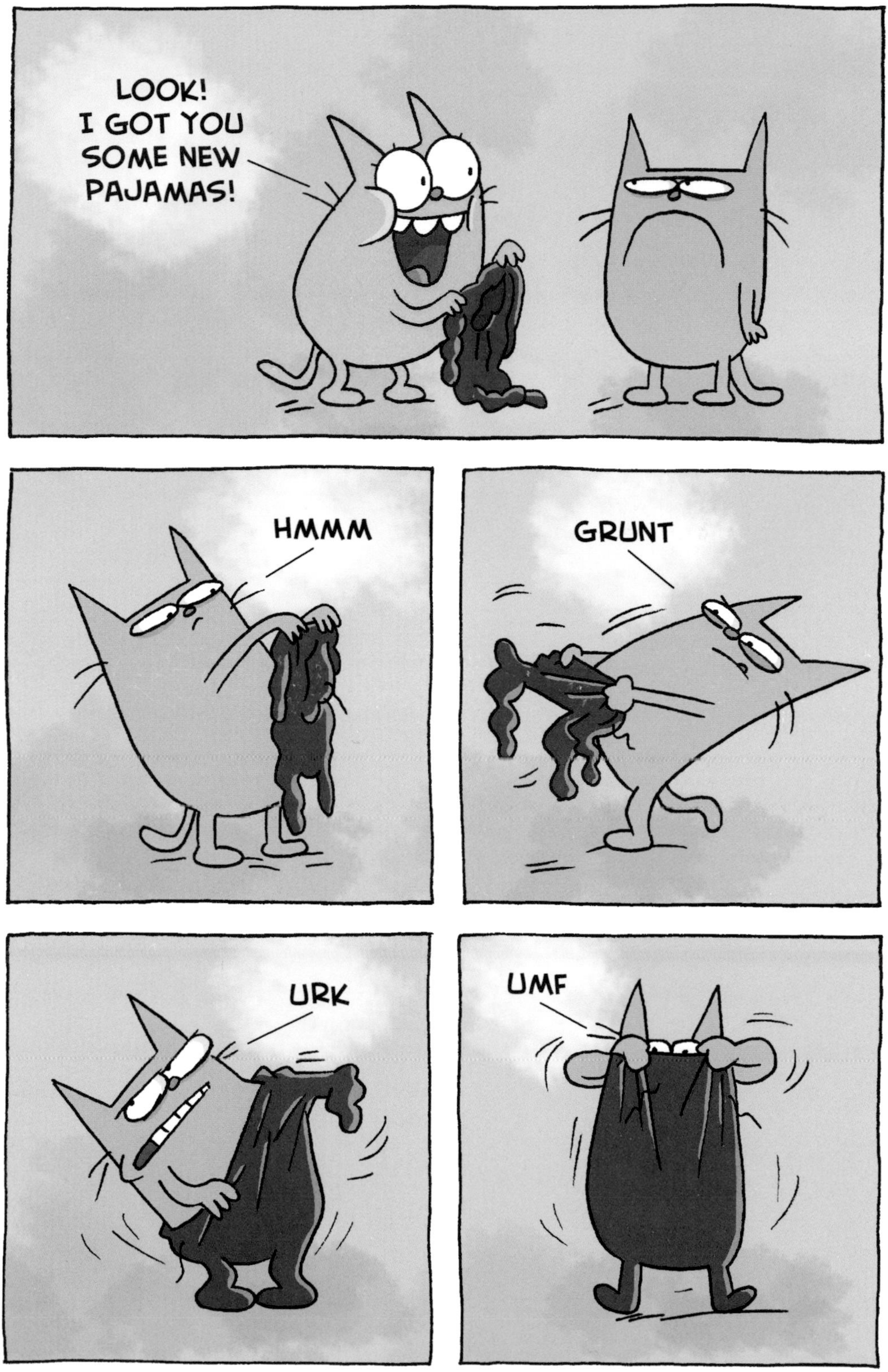
LOOK! I GOT YOU SOME NEW PAJAMAS!
HMMM
GRUNT
URK
UMF

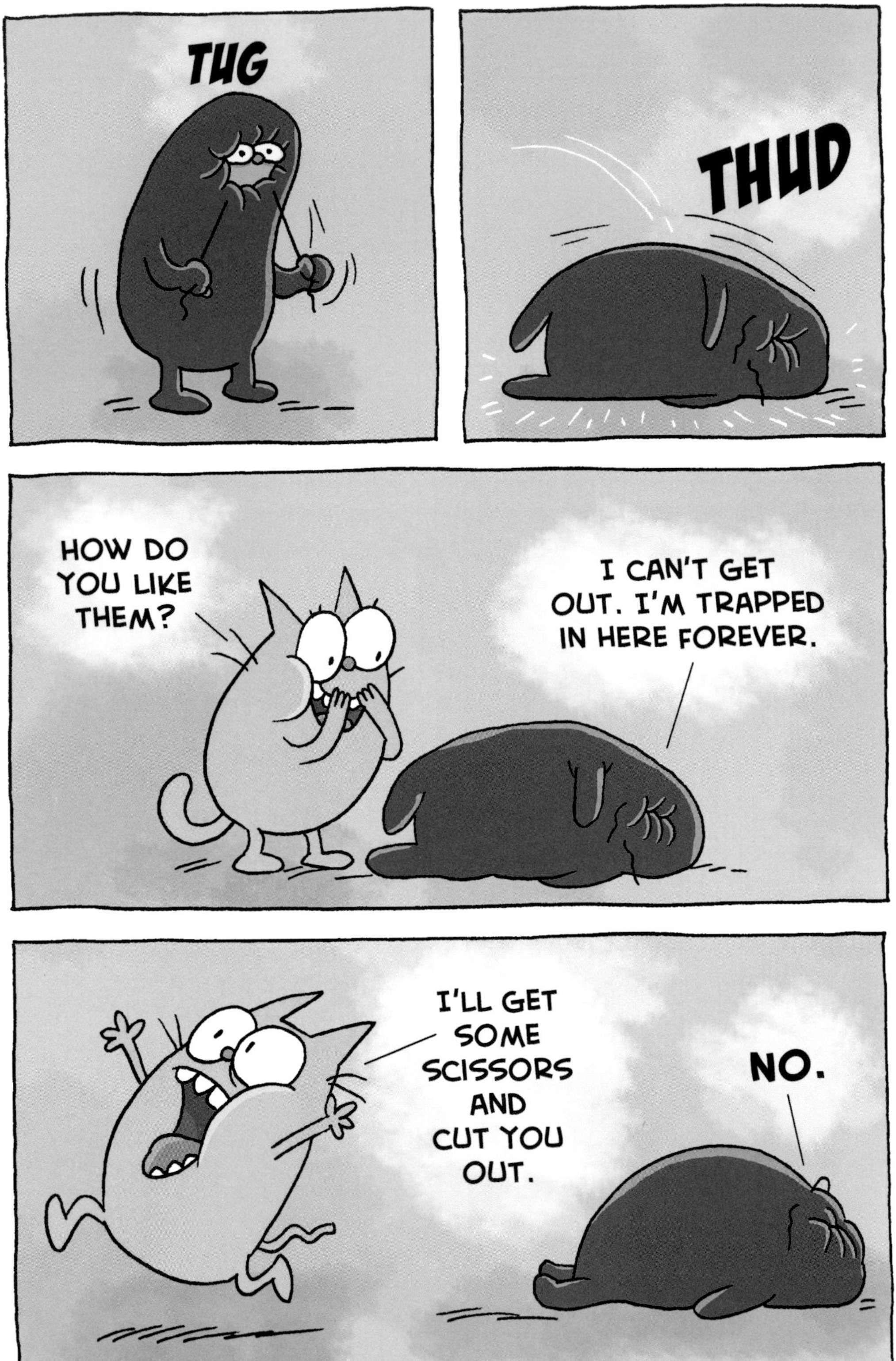
TUG
THUD
HOW DO YOU LIKE THEM?
I CAN'T GET OUT. I'M TRAPPED IN HERE FOREVER.
I'LL GET SOME SCISSORS AND CUT YOU OUT.
NO.

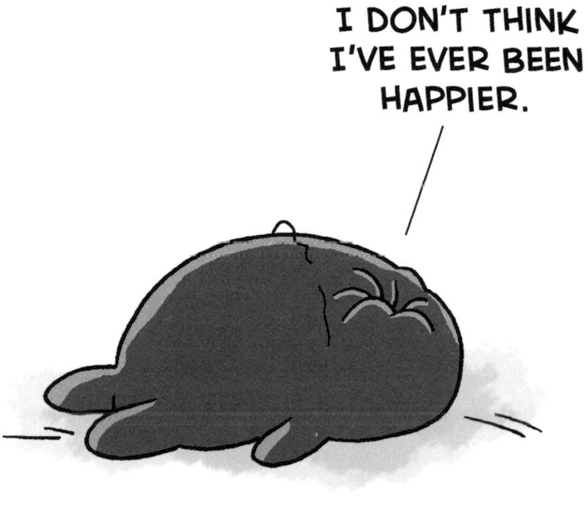
I DON'T THINK I'VE EVER BEEN HAPPIER.

JOURNAL

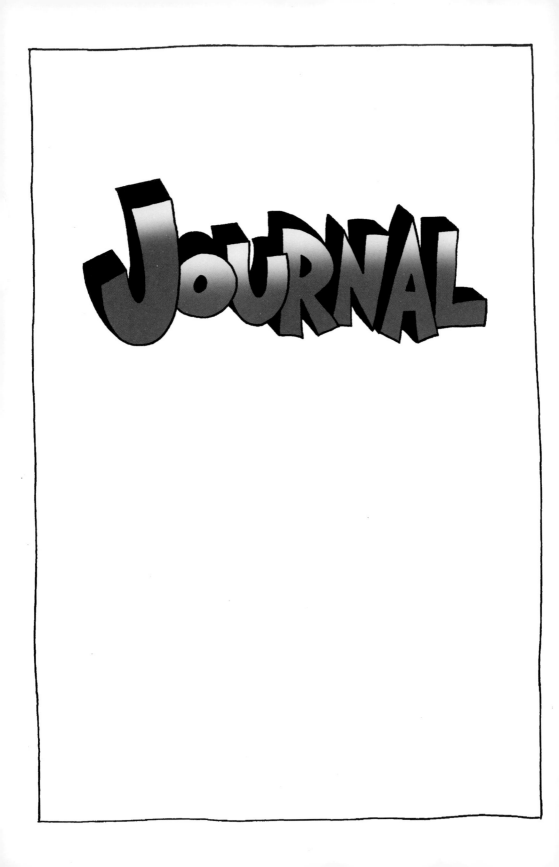

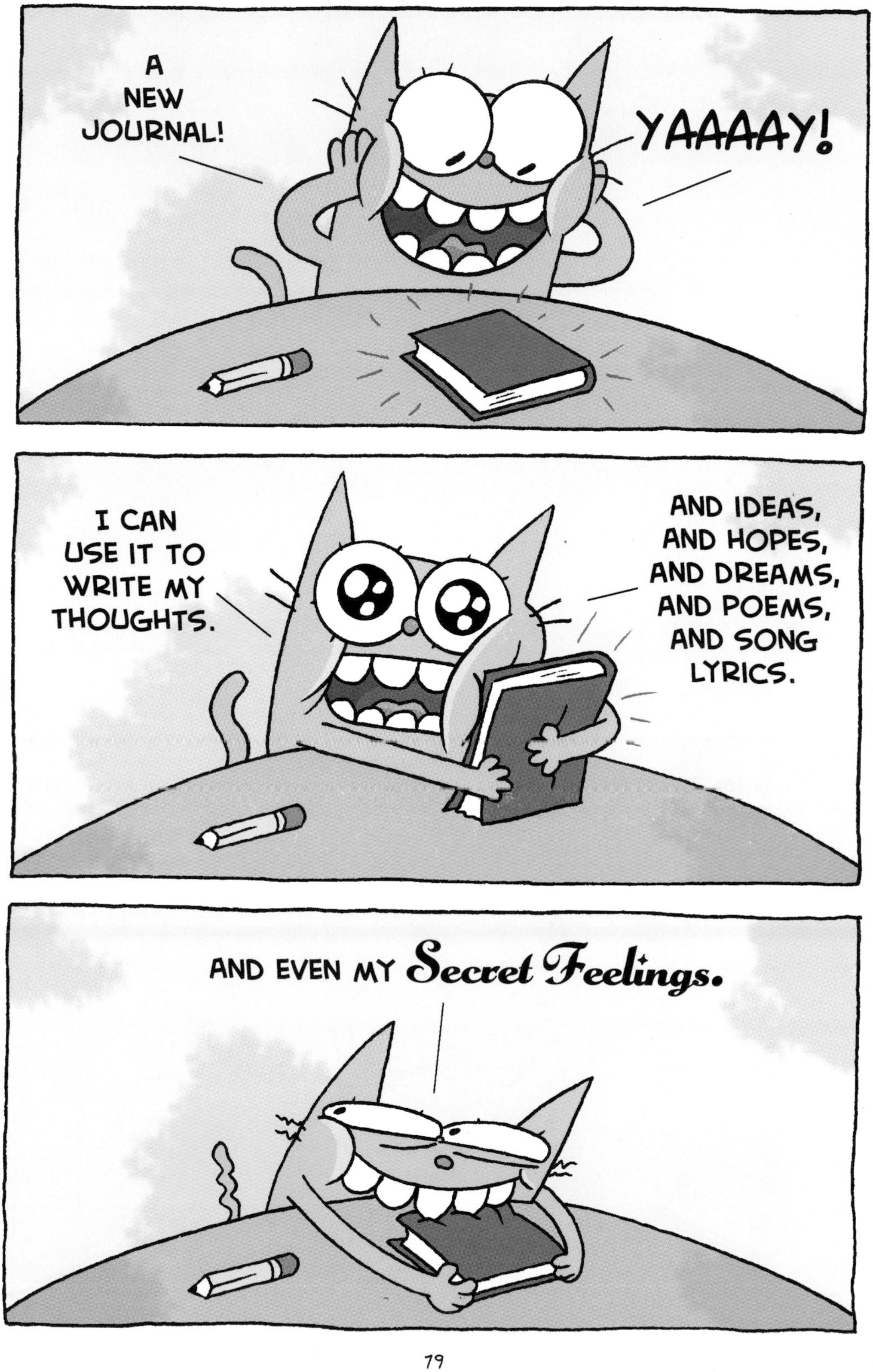
A NEW JOURNAL!
YAAAAY!
I CAN USE IT TO WRITE MY THOUGHTS.
AND IDEAS, AND HOPES, AND DREAMS, AND POEMS, AND SONG LYRICS.
AND EVEN MY Secret Feelings.

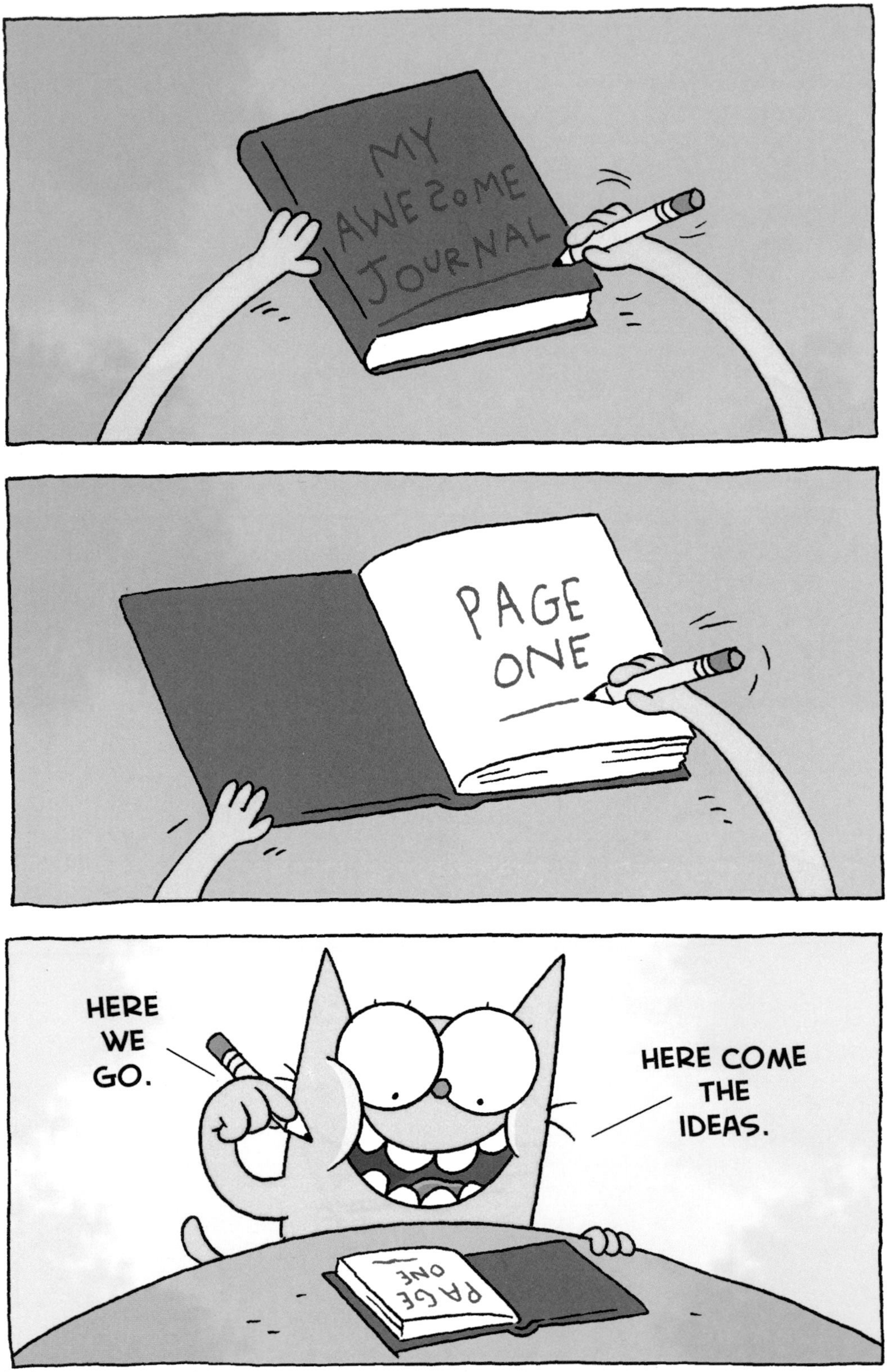
MY AWESOME JOURNAL
PAGE ONE
HERE WE GO.
HERE COME THE IDEAS.

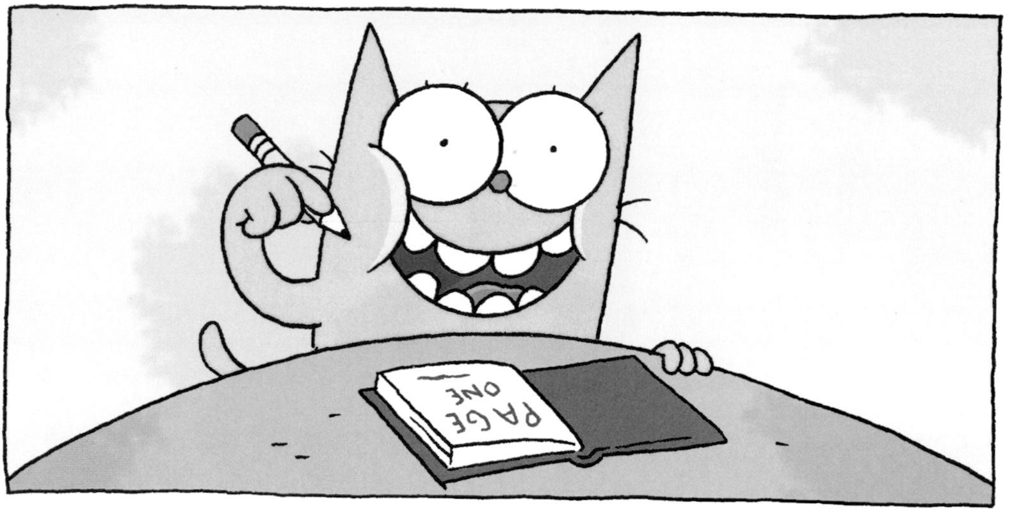
PAGE ONE

NINETY-SIX YEARS LATER

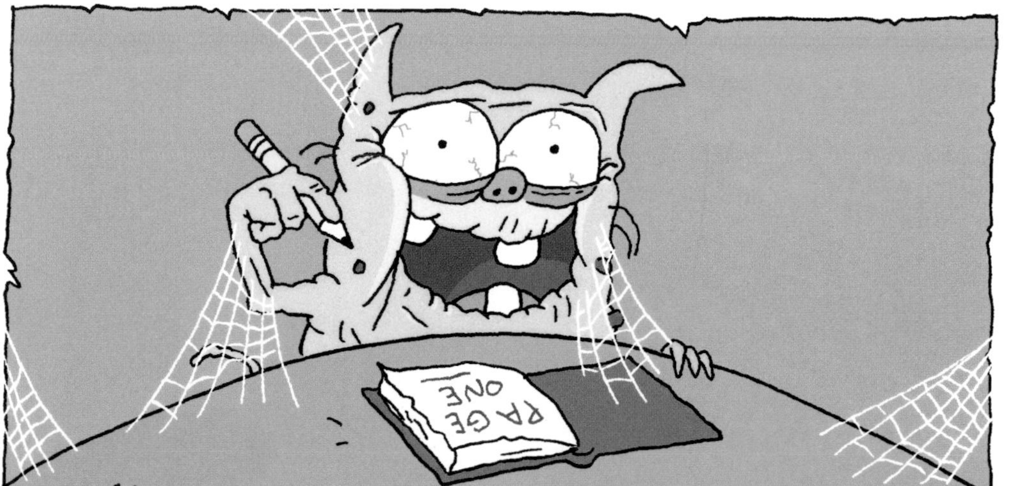
PAGE ONE

THE ULTIMATE HERO

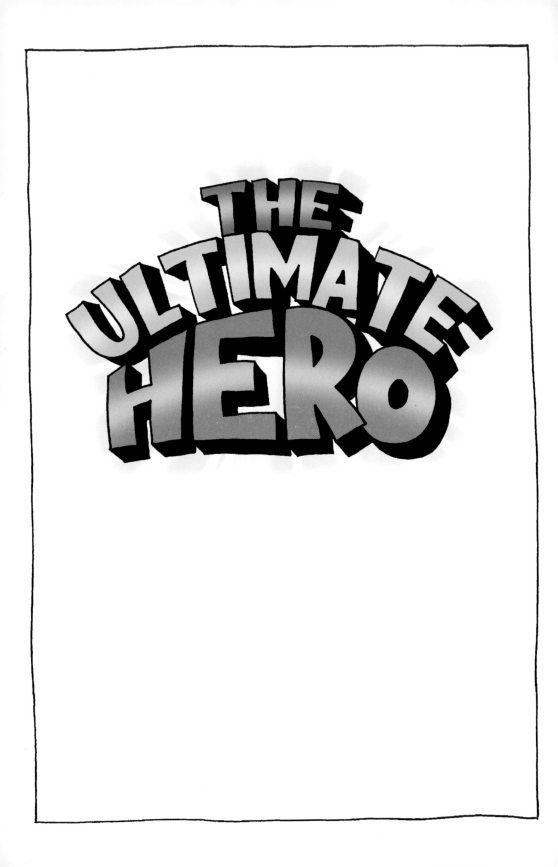

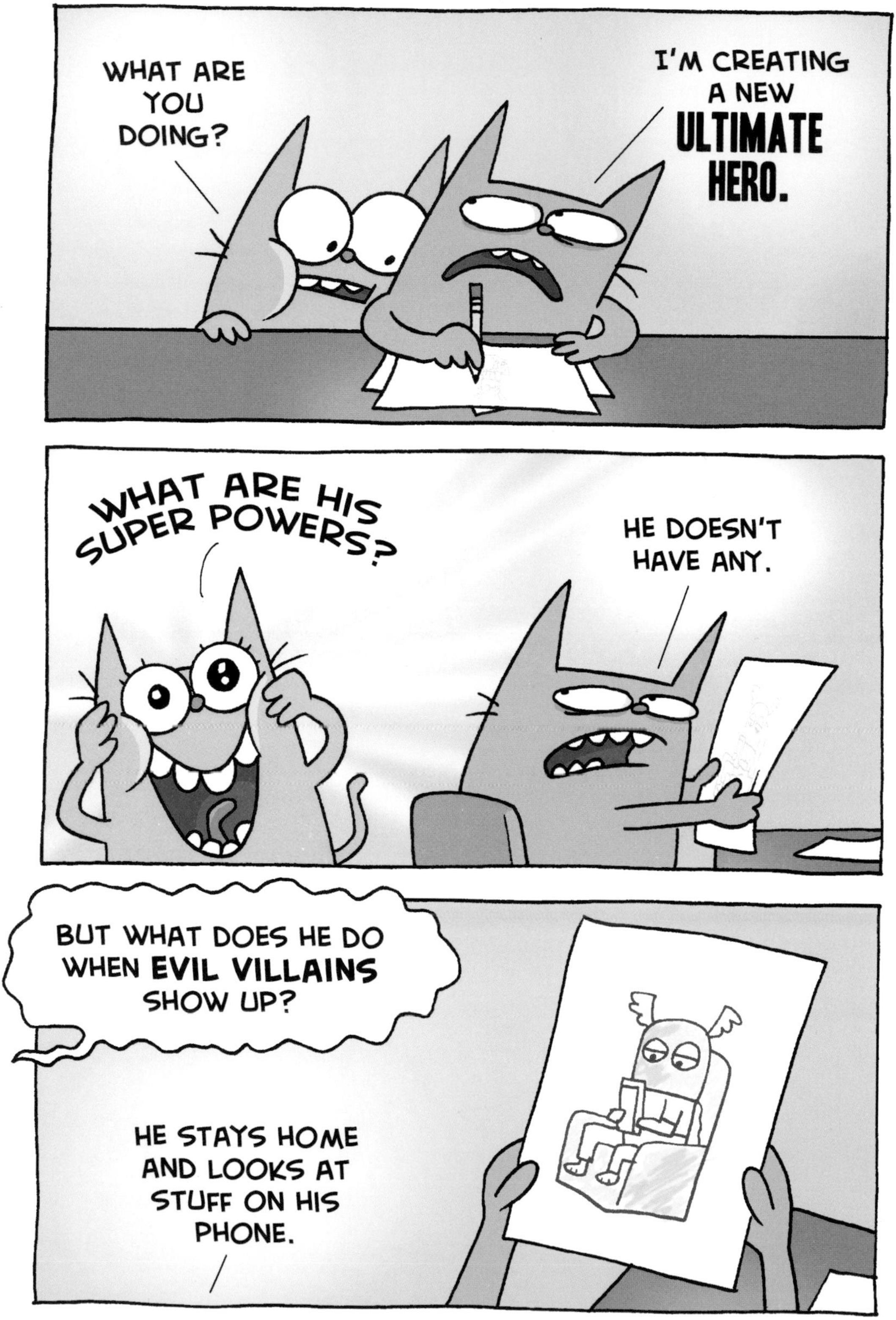
WHAT ARE YOU DOING?
I'M CREATING A NEW ULTIMATE HERO.
WHAT ARE HIS SUPER POWERS?
HE DOESN'T HAVE ANY.
BUT WHAT DOES HE DO WHEN EVIL VILLAINS SHOW UP?
HE STAYS HOME AND LOOKS AT STUFF ON HIS PHONE.

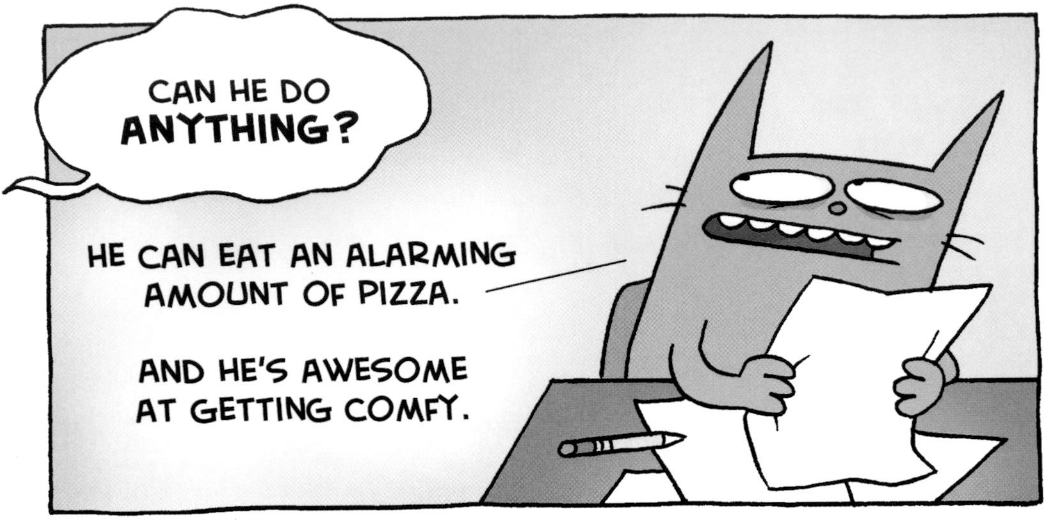
CAN HE DO **ANYTHING?**
HE CAN EAT AN ALARMING AMOUNT OF PIZZA.
AND HE'S AWESOME AT GETTING COMFY.

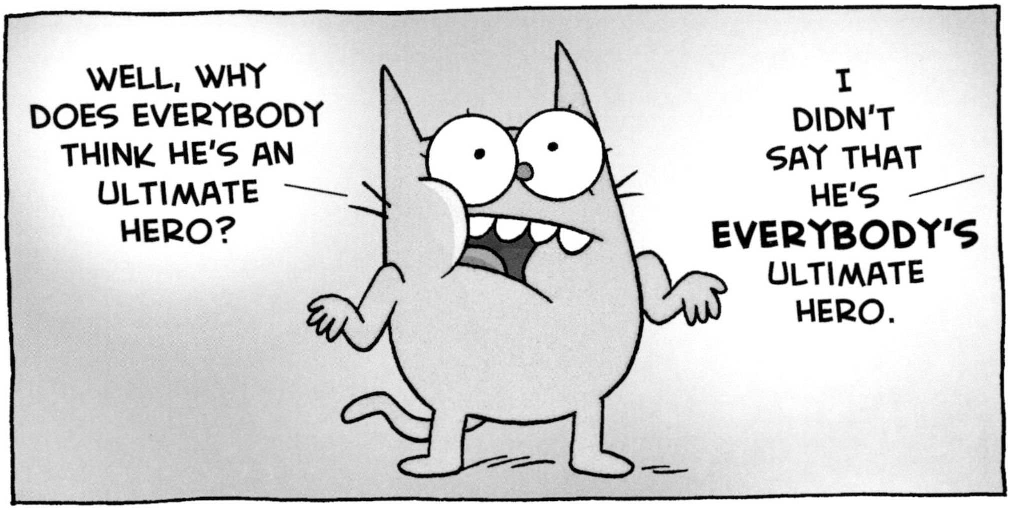
WELL, WHY DOES EVERYBODY THINK HE'S AN ULTIMATE HERO?
I DIDN'T SAY THAT HE'S **EVERYBODY'S** ULTIMATE HERO.

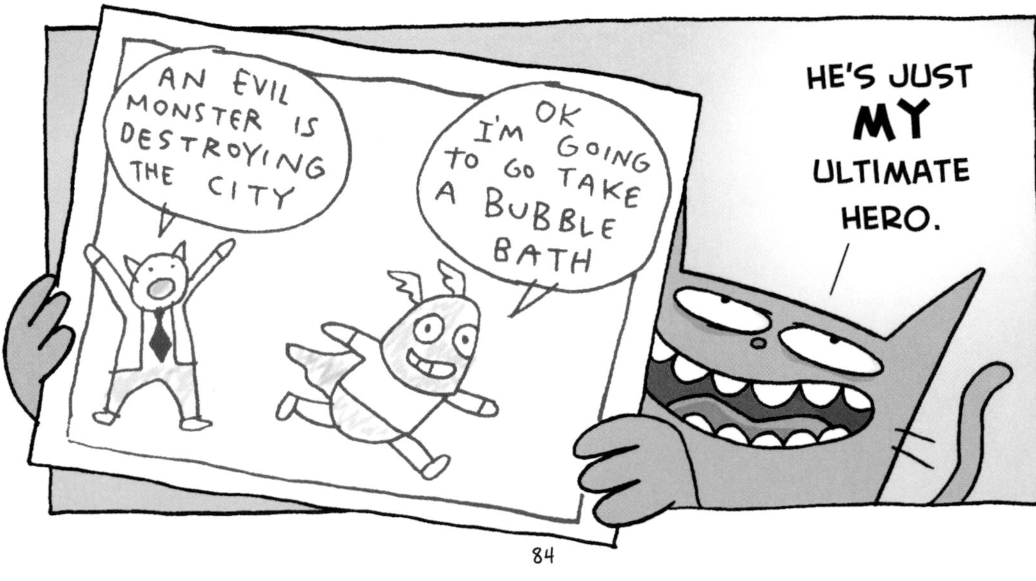
AN EVIL MONSTER IS DESTROYING THE CITY
OK I'M GOING TO GO TAKE A BUBBLE BATH
HE'S JUST **MY** ULTIMATE HERO.

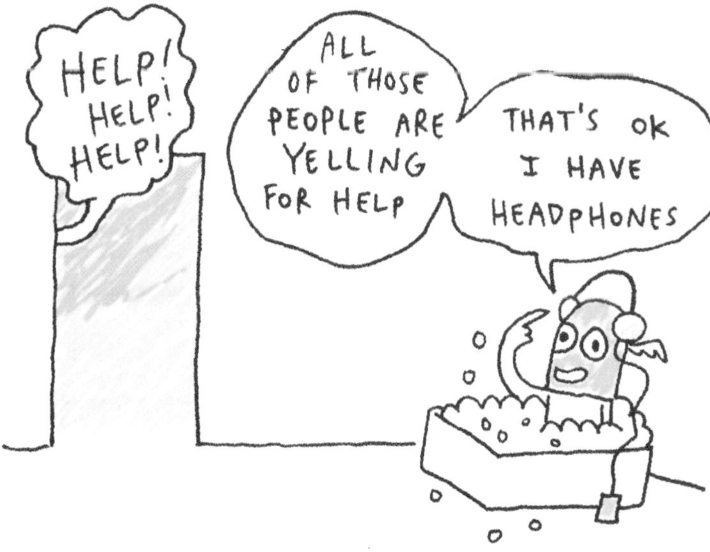
HELP! HELP! HELP!
ALL OF THOSE PEOPLE ARE YELLING FOR HELP
THAT'S OK I HAVE HEADPHONES

The Playlist

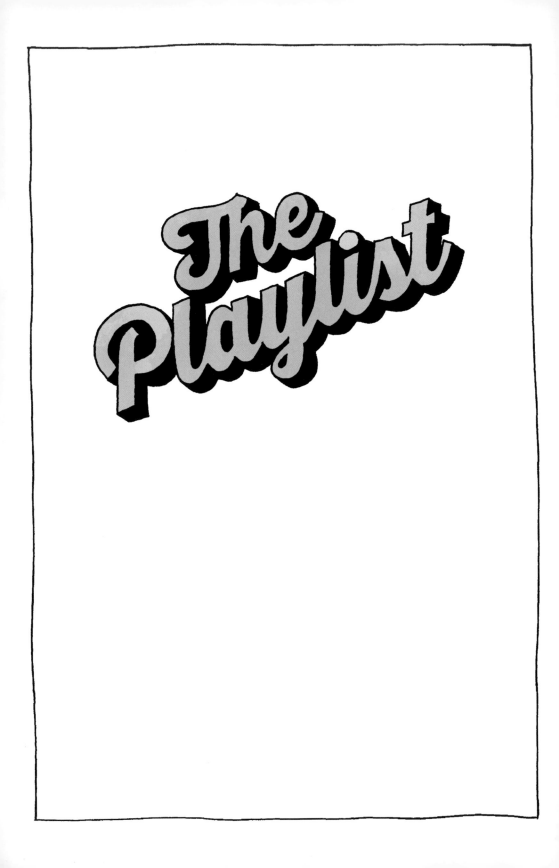

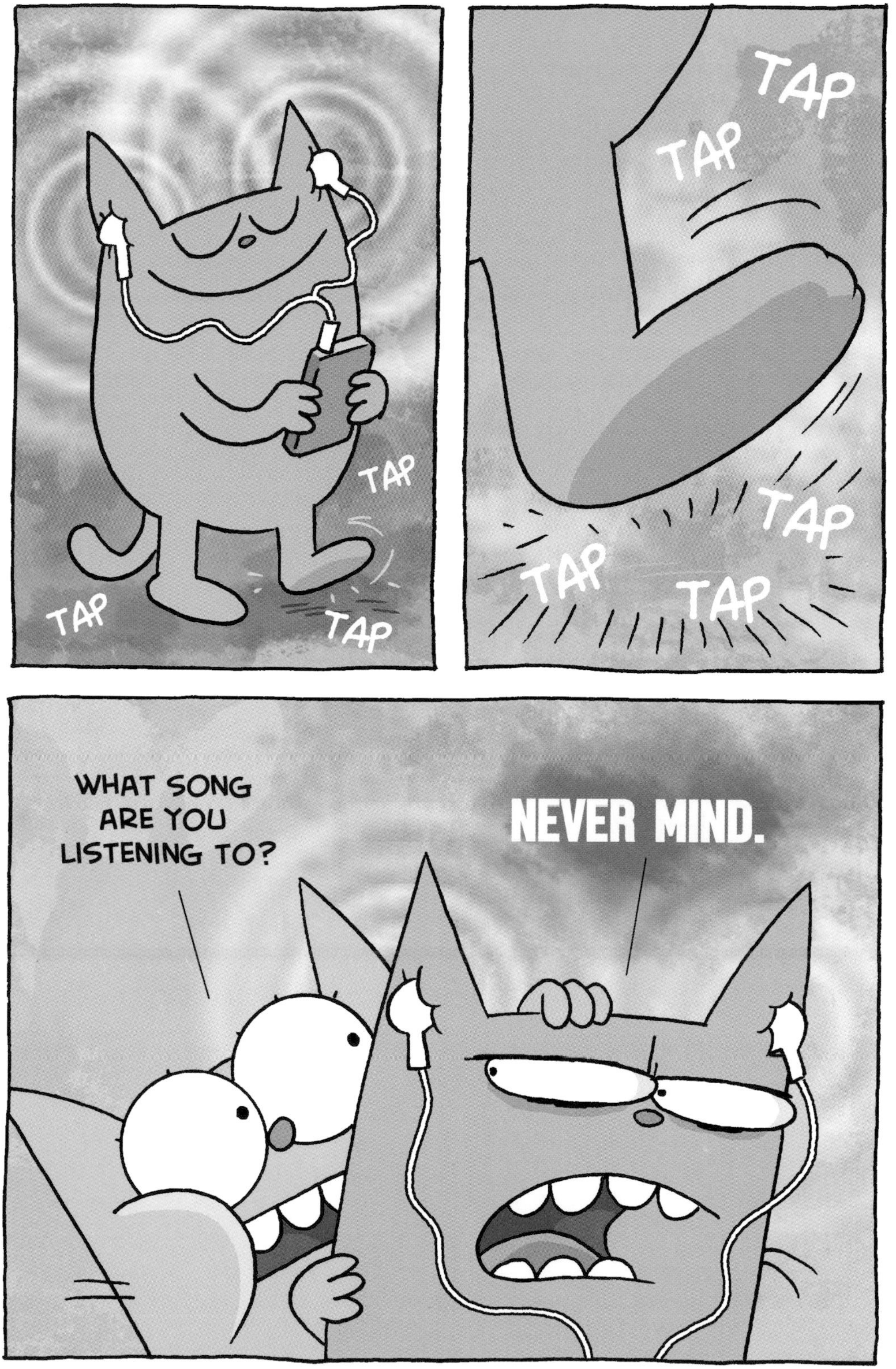
TAP
TAP
TAP
TAP
TAP
TAP
TAP
TAP
TAP
WHAT SONG ARE YOU LISTENING TO?
NEVER MIND.

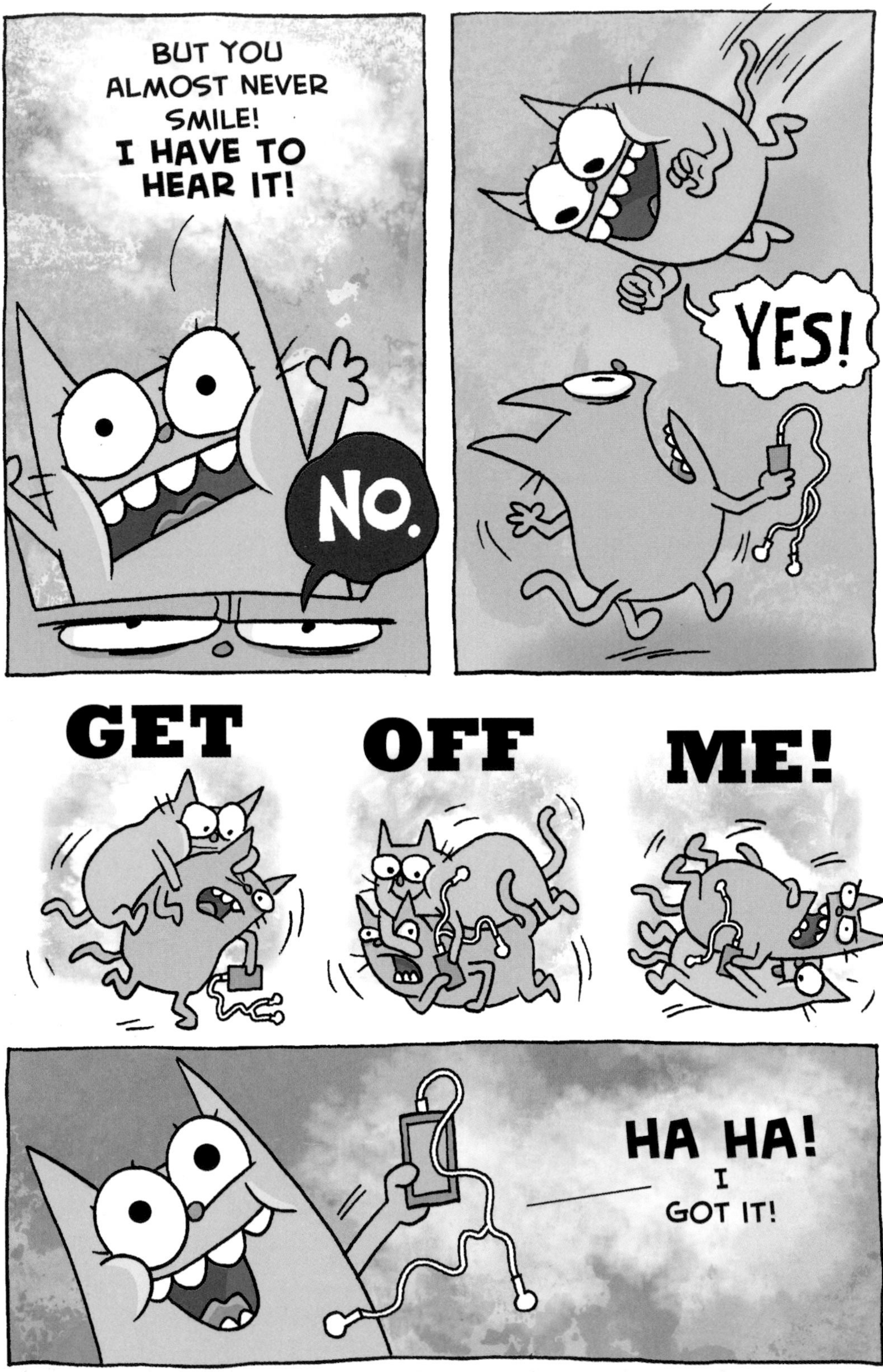
BUT YOU ALMOST NEVER SMILE! I HAVE TO HEAR IT!
NO.
YES!
GET
OFF
ME!
HA HA! I GOT IT!

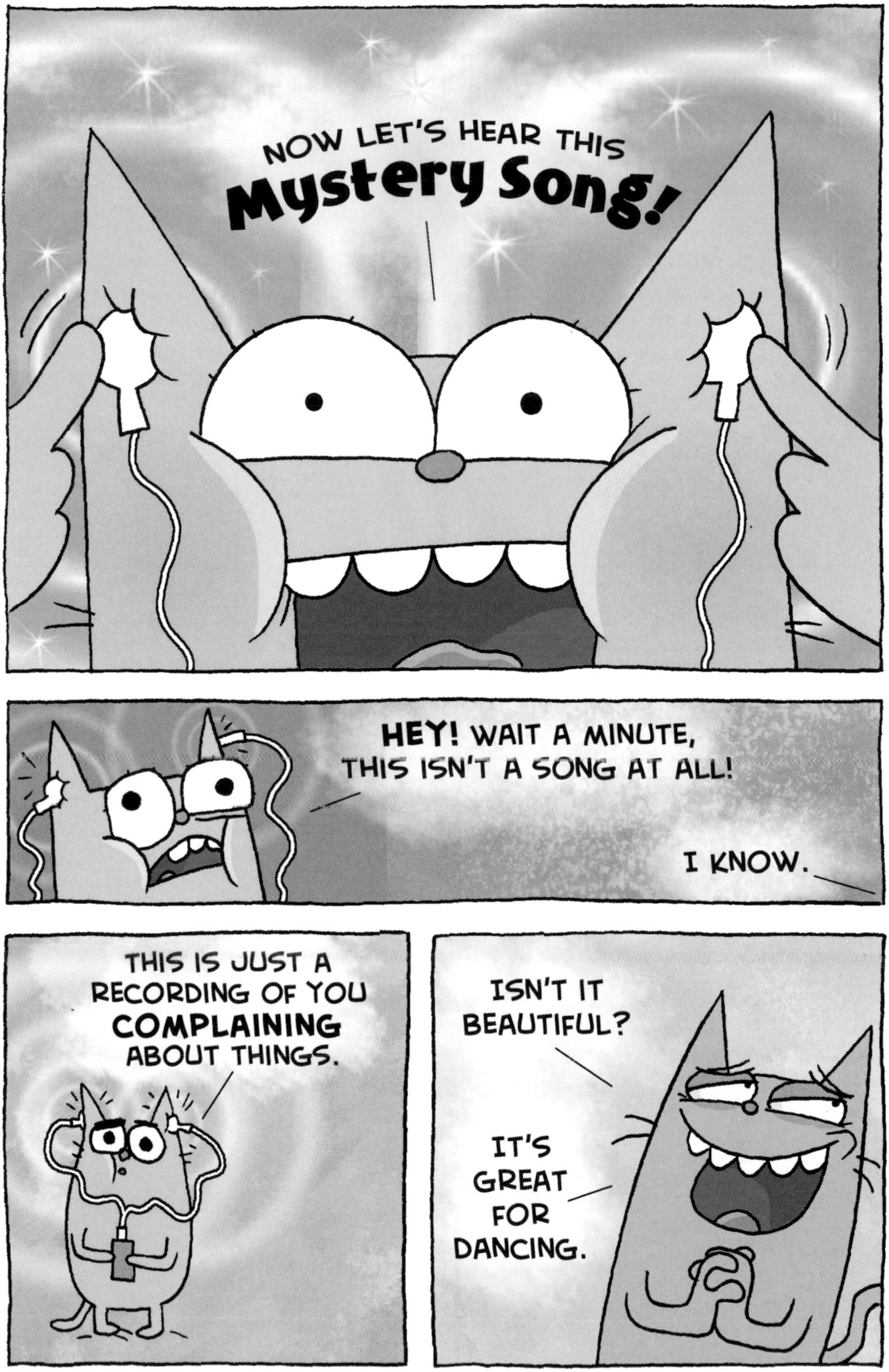
NOW LET'S HEAR THIS
Mystery Song!
HEY! WAIT A MINUTE, THIS ISN'T A SONG AT ALL!
I KNOW.
THIS IS JUST A RECORDING OF YOU COMPLAINING ABOUT THINGS.
ISN'T IT BEAUTIFUL?
IT'S GREAT FOR DANCING.

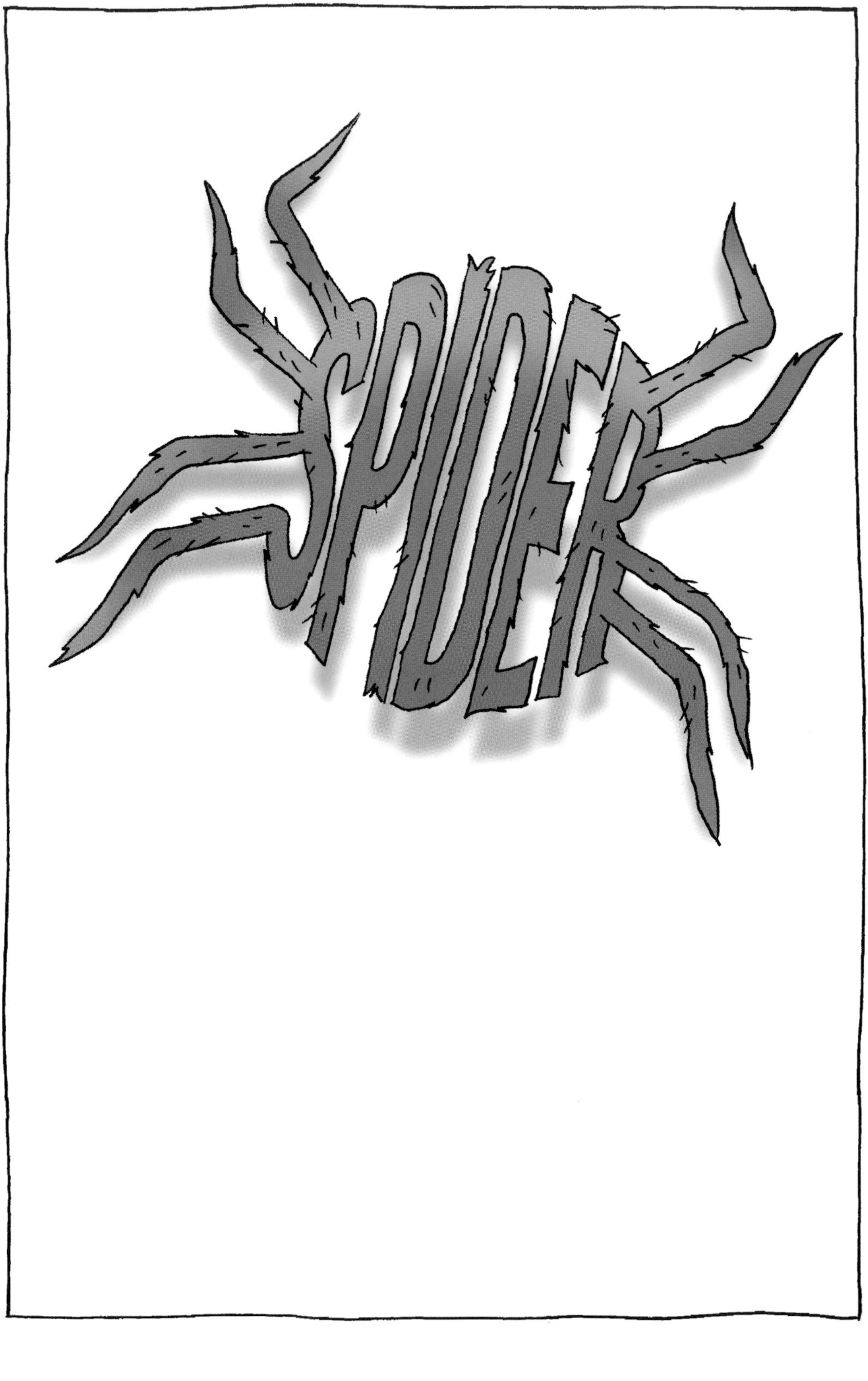
SPIDER

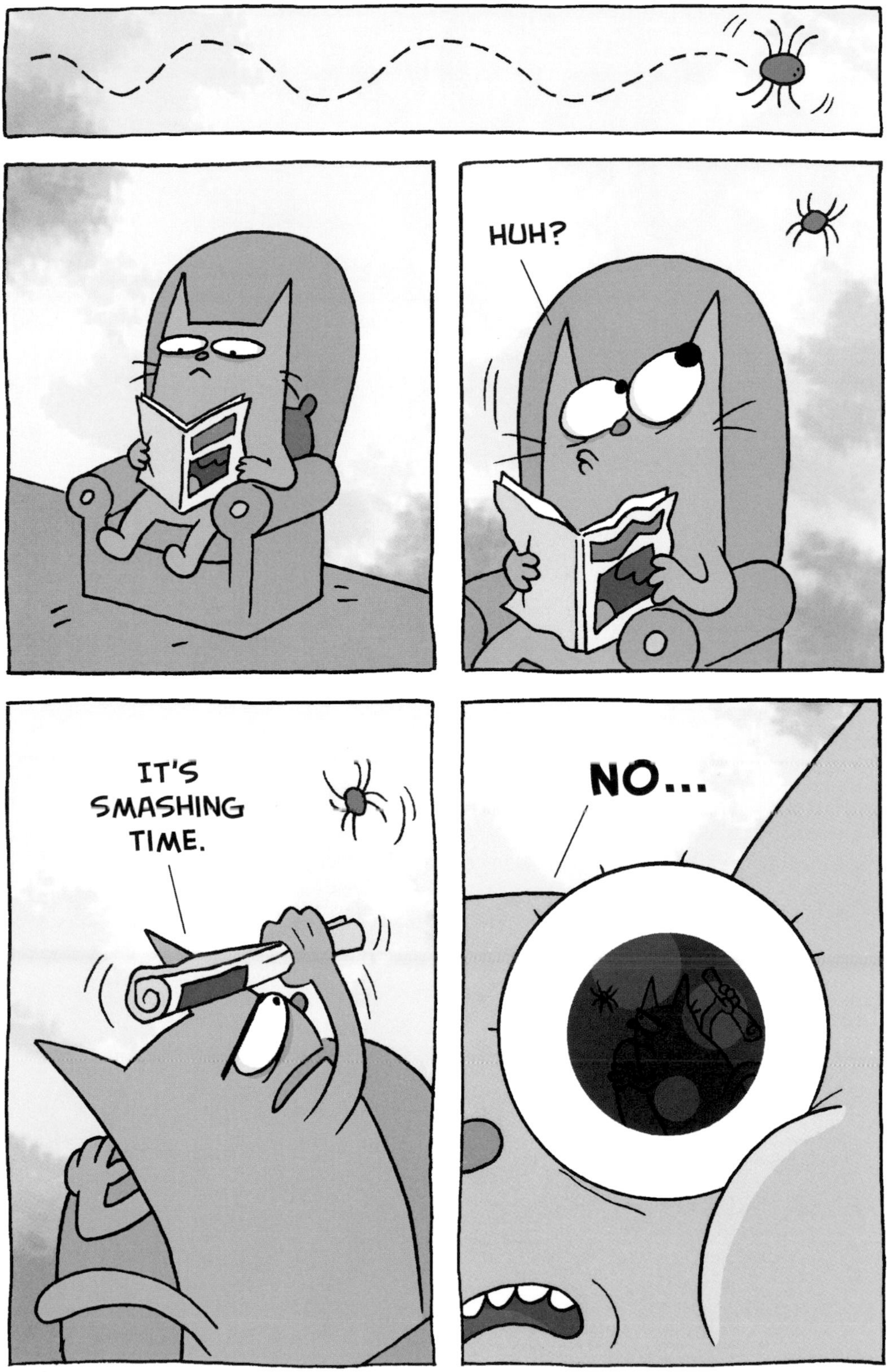
HUH?
IT'S SMASHING TIME.
NO...

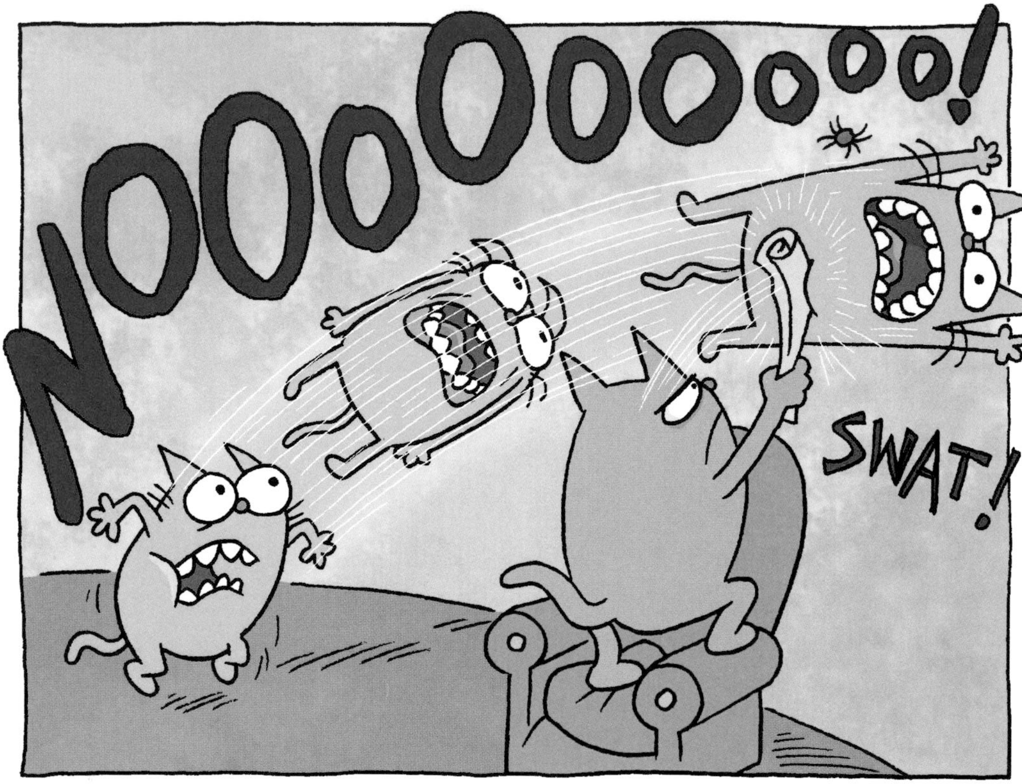
NOOOOOOOOOOOO!
SWAT!

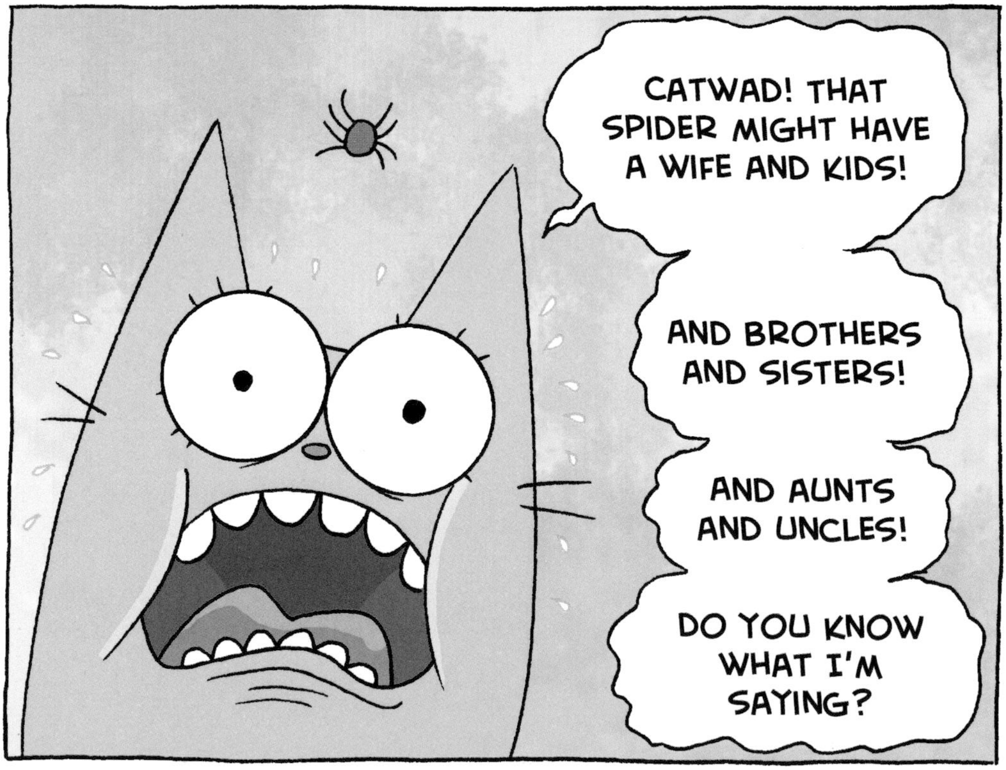
CATWAD! THAT SPIDER MIGHT HAVE A WIFE AND KIDS!
AND BROTHERS AND SISTERS!
AND AUNTS AND UNCLES!
DO YOU KNOW WHAT I'M SAYING?

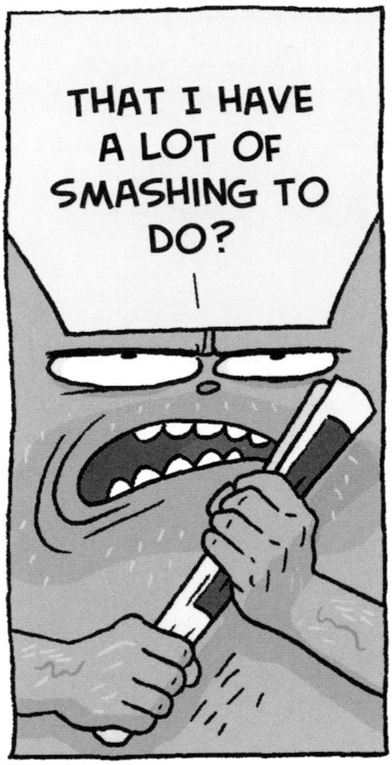
THAT I HAVE A LOT OF SMASHING TO DO?

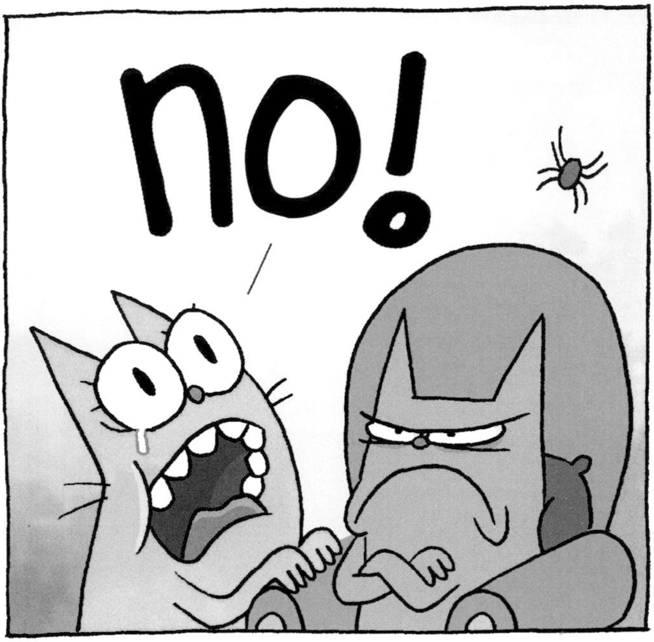
NO!

I'M TELLING YOU THAT SPIDERS ARE AWESOME!

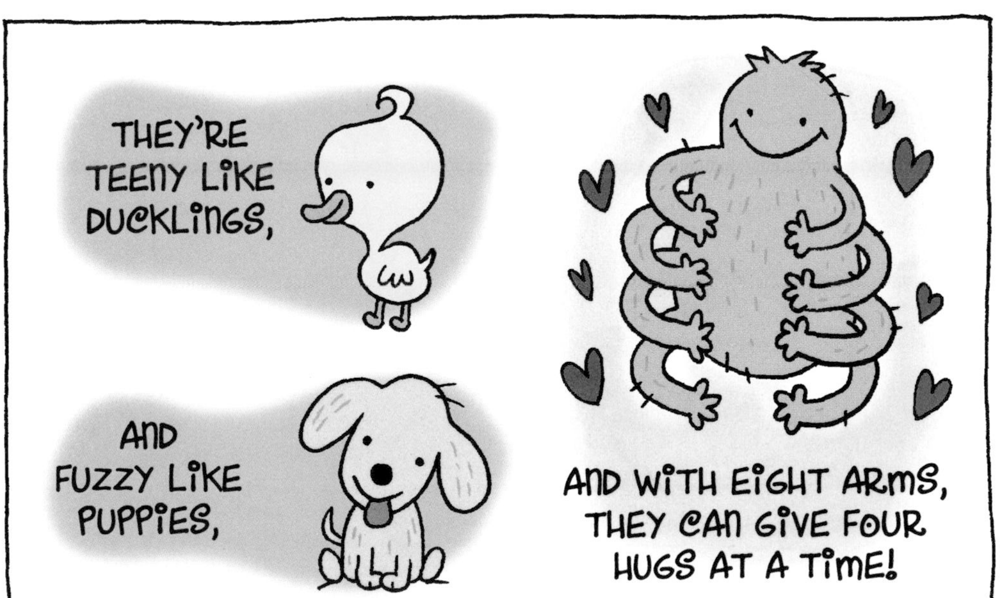
THEY'RE TEENY LIKE DUCKLINGS,
AND FUZZY LIKE PUPPIES,
AND WITH EIGHT ARMS, THEY CAN GIVE FOUR HUGS AT A TIME!

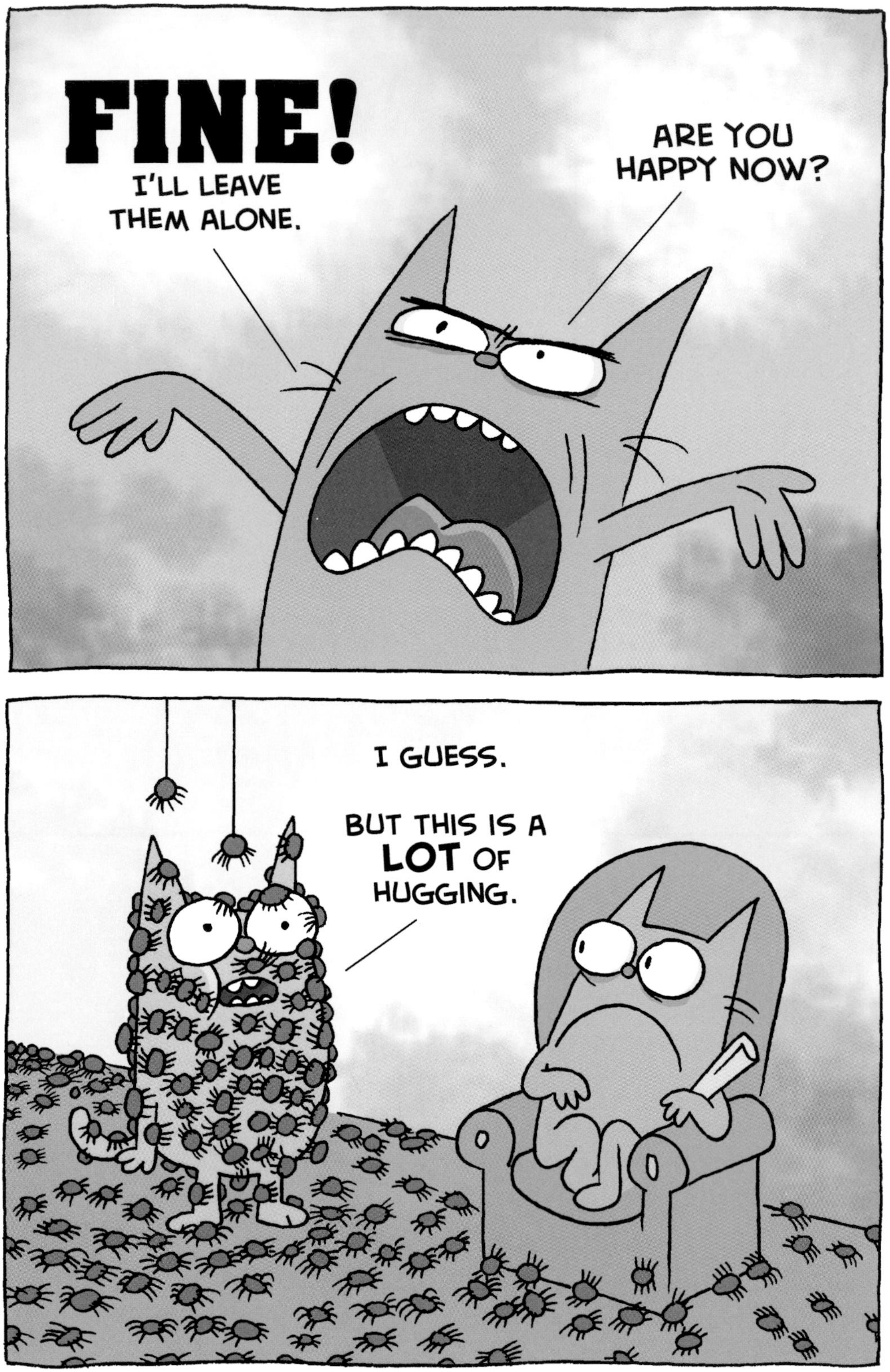
FINE!
I'LL LEAVE THEM ALONE.
ARE YOU HAPPY NOW?
I GUESS.
BUT THIS IS A **LOT** OF HUGGING.

I DON'T THINK
I'VE EVER BEEN
HUGGED ON THE
EYEBALLS BEFORE.

TURN IT UP

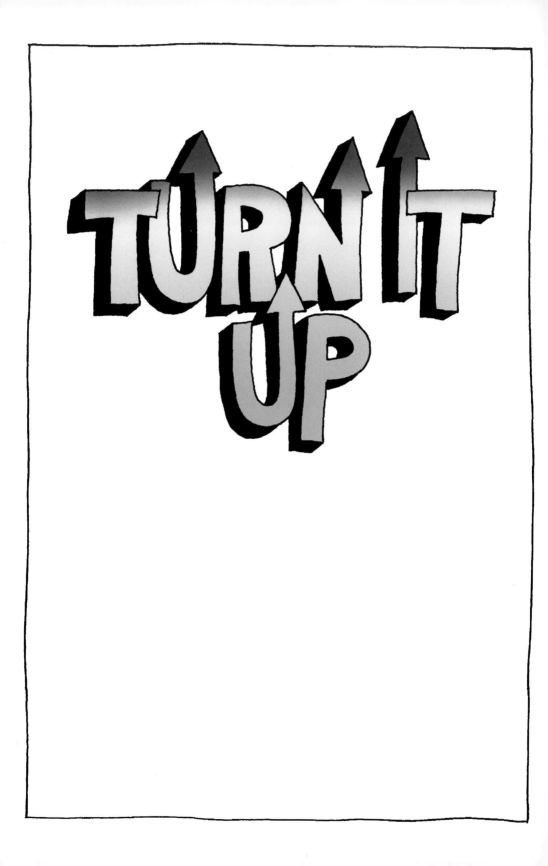

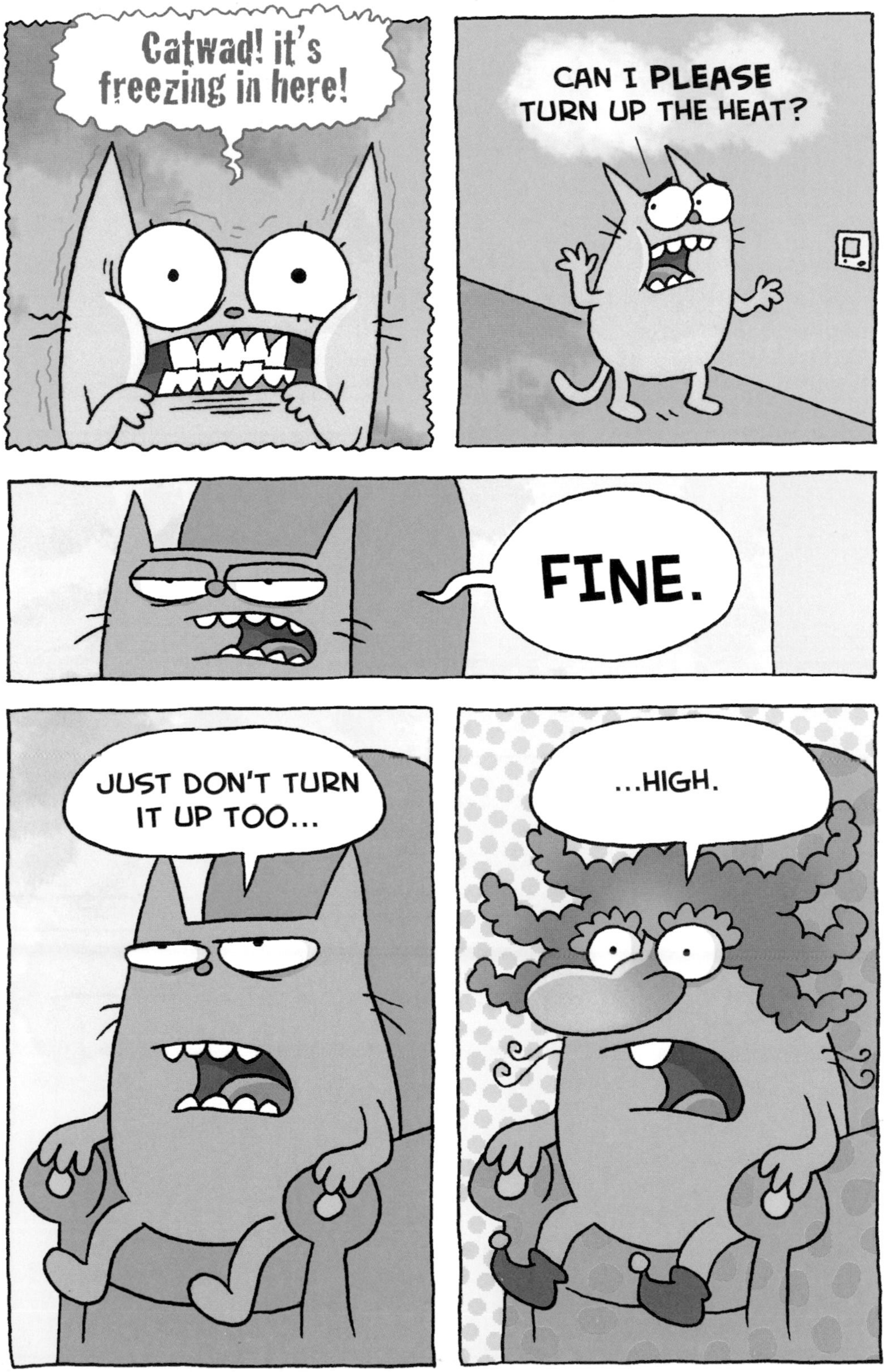
Catwad! it's freezing in here!
CAN I PLEASE TURN UP THE HEAT?
FINE.
JUST DON'T TURN IT UP TOO...
...HIGH.

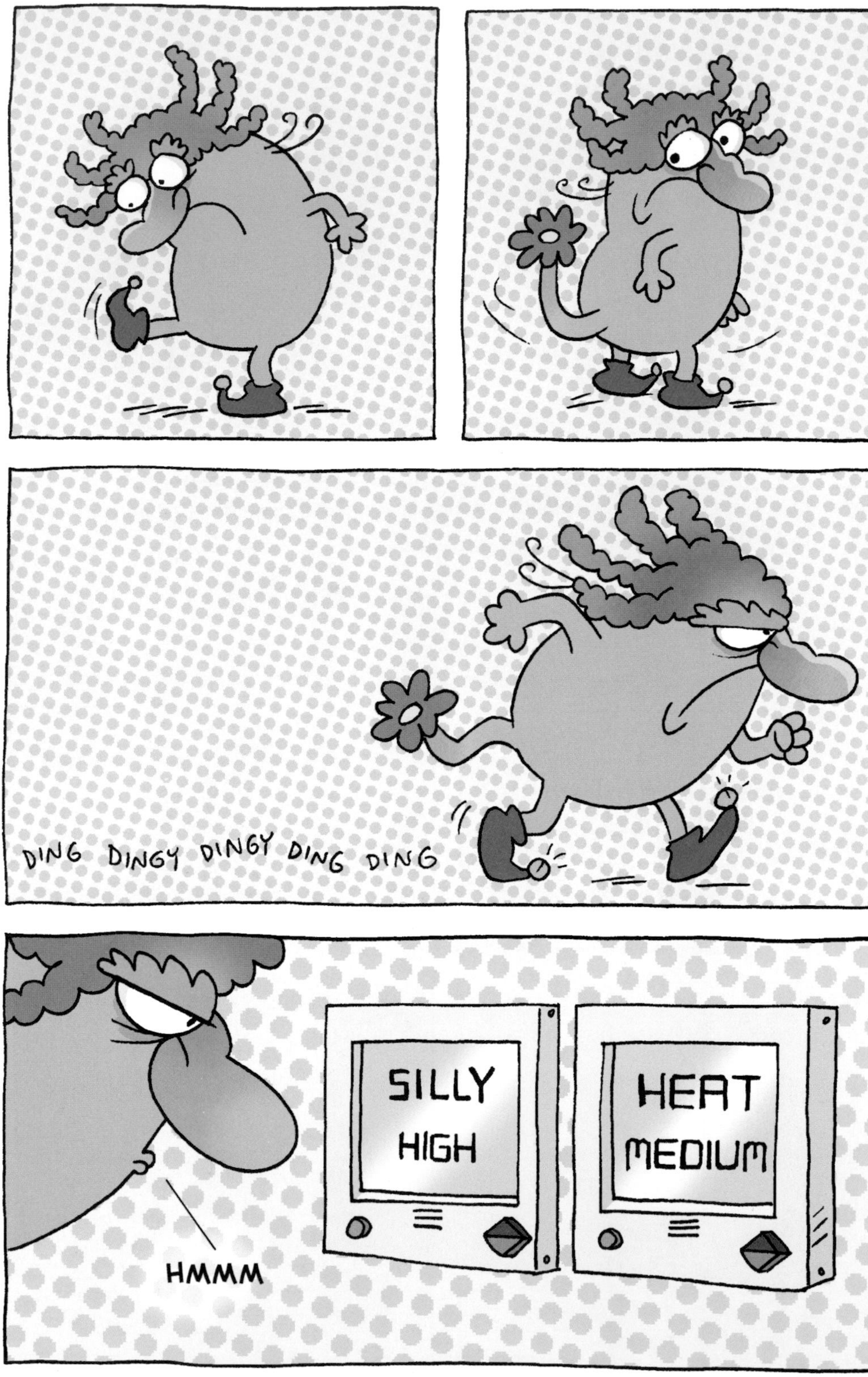
DING DINGY DINGY DING DING
HMMM
SILLY
HIGH
HEAT
MEDIUM

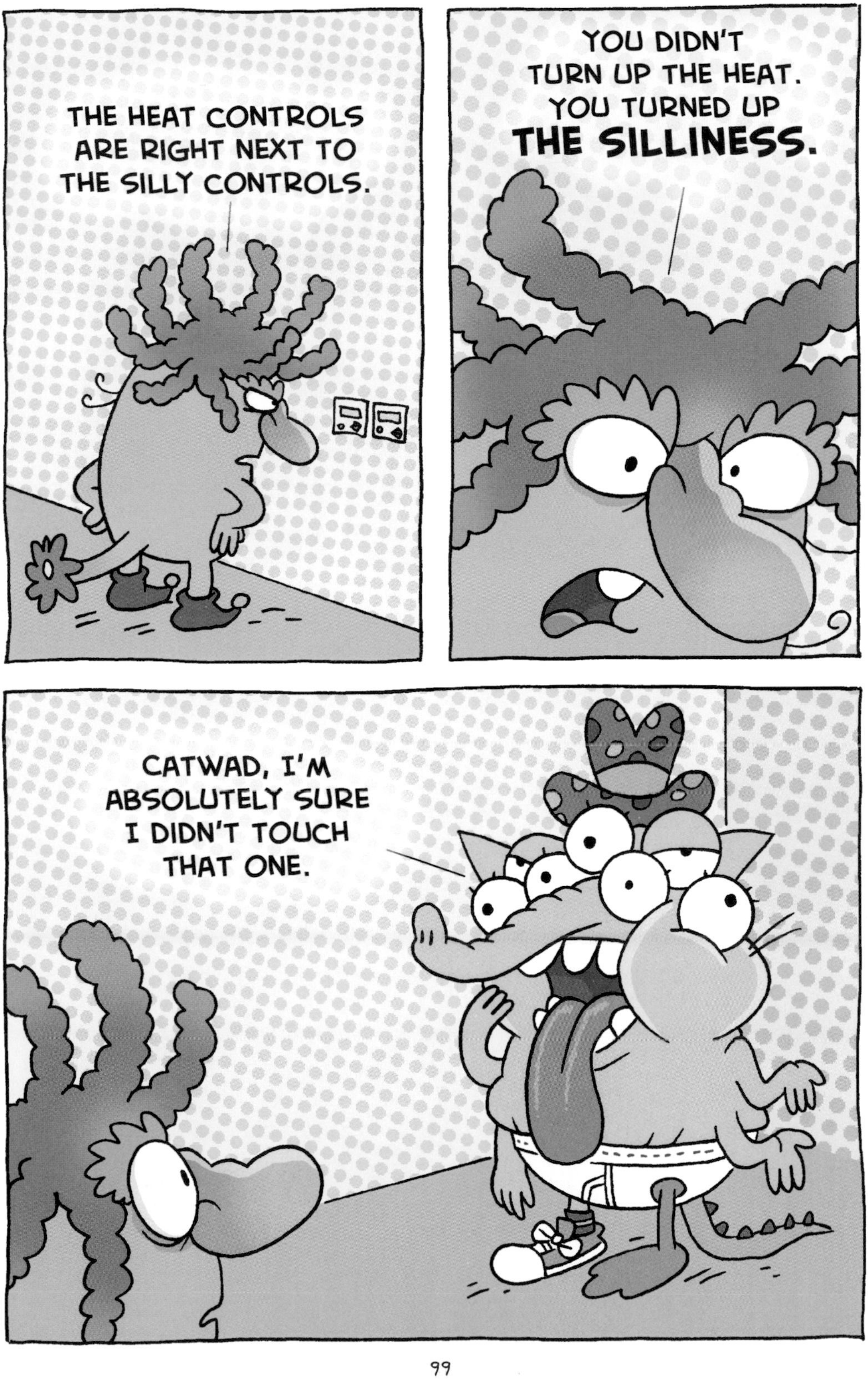
THE HEAT CONTROLS ARE RIGHT NEXT TO THE SILLY CONTROLS.
YOU DIDN'T TURN UP THE HEAT. YOU TURNED UP **THE SILLINESS.**
CATWAD, I'M ABSOLUTELY SURE I DIDN'T TOUCH THAT ONE.

STOMACH

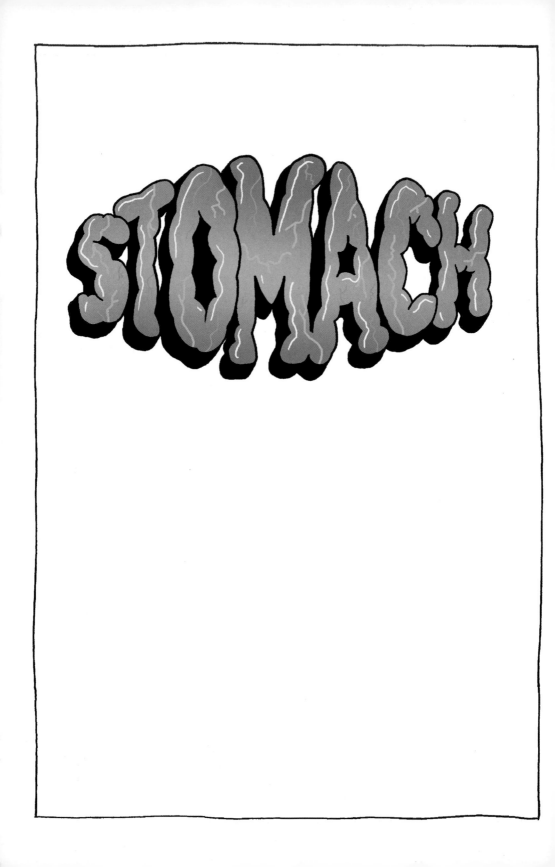

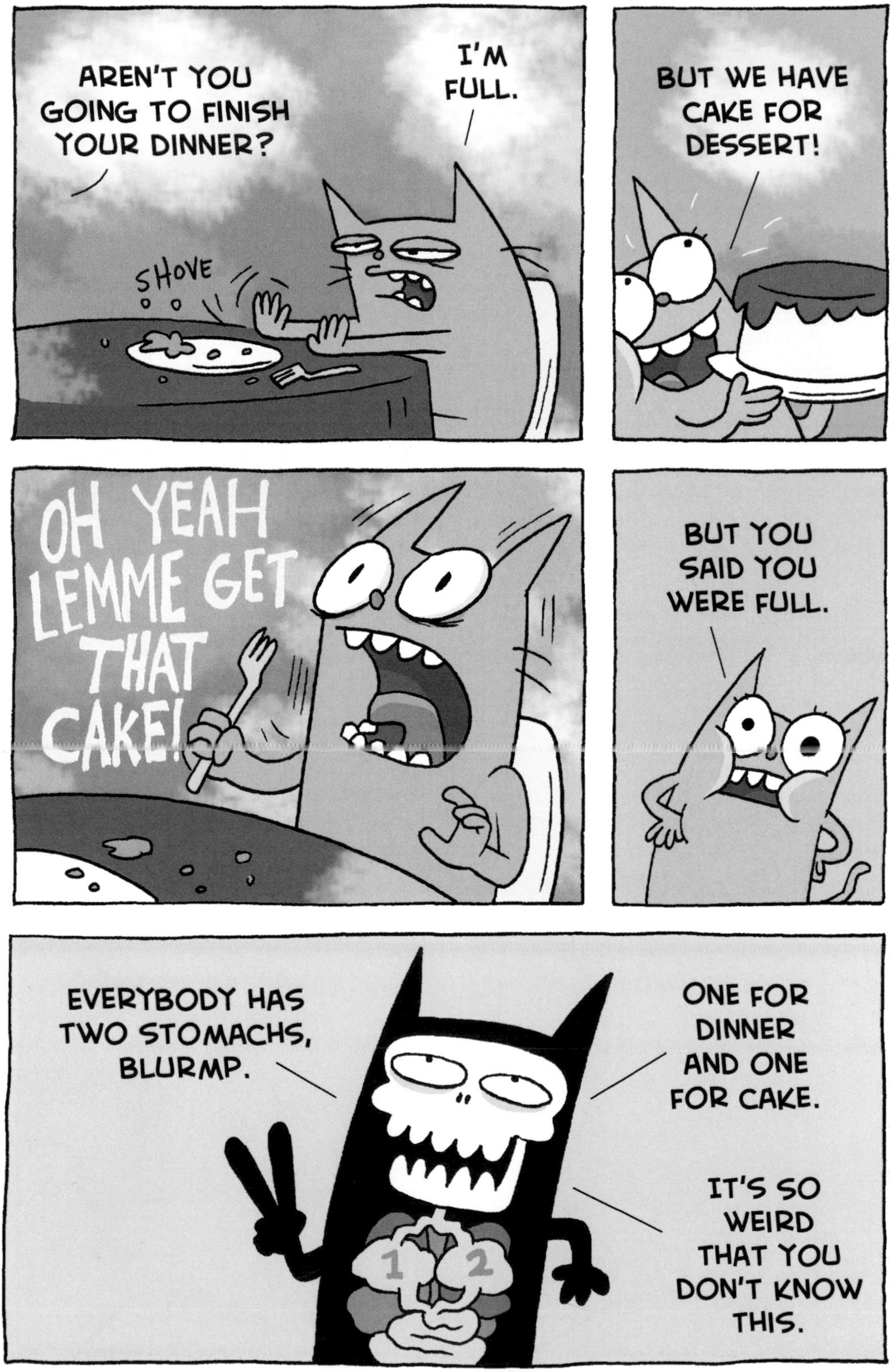
AREN'T YOU GOING TO FINISH YOUR DINNER?
I'M FULL.
SHOVE
BUT WE HAVE CAKE FOR DESSERT!
OH YEAH LEMME GET THAT CAKE!
BUT YOU SAID YOU WERE FULL.
EVERYBODY HAS TWO STOMACHS, BLURMP.
ONE FOR DINNER AND ONE FOR CAKE.
IT'S SO WEIRD THAT YOU DON'T KNOW THIS.
1
2

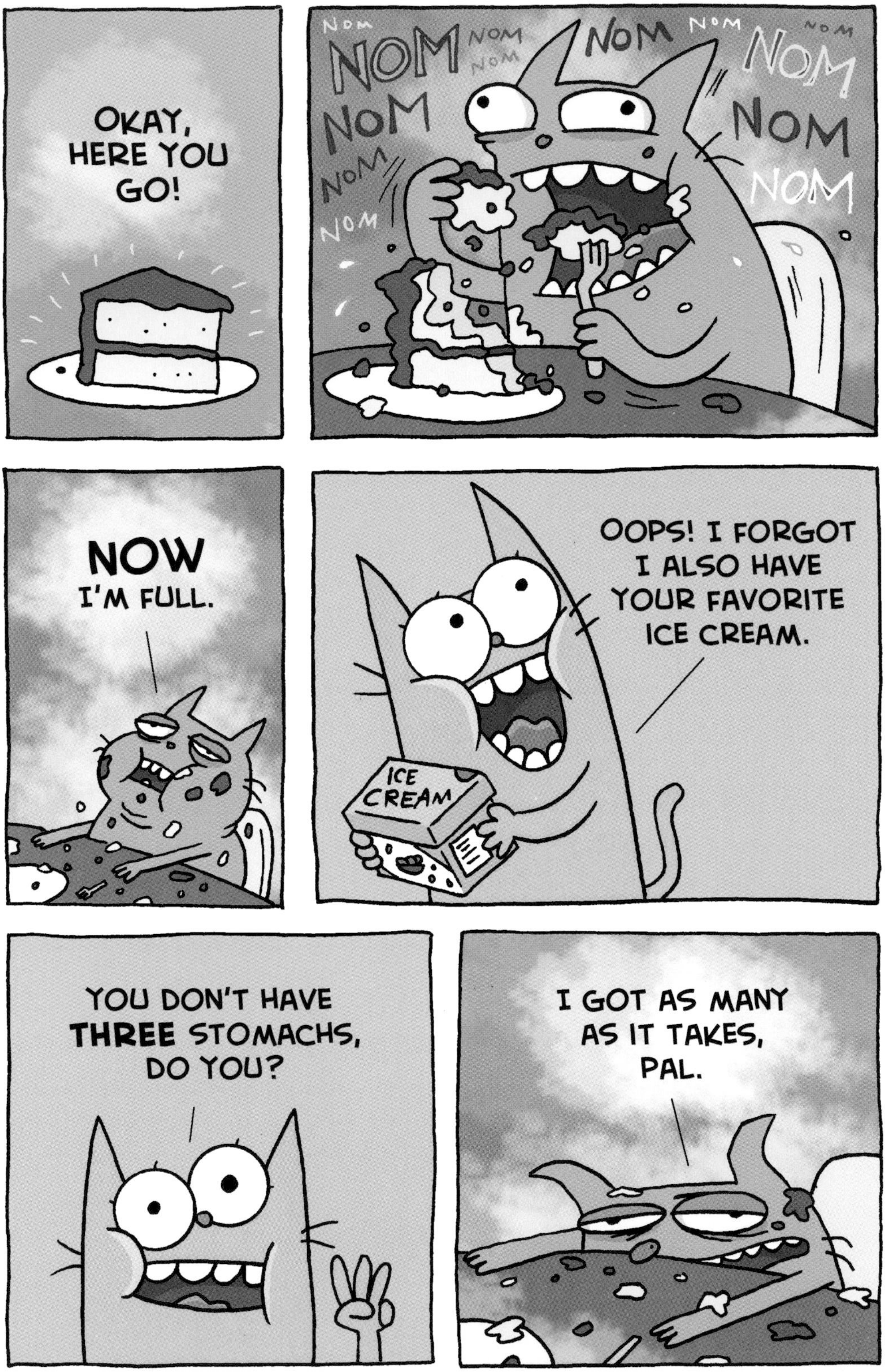
OKAY, HERE YOU GO!
NOM NOM NOM NOM NOM NOM NOM NOM NOM NOM NOM NOM NOM
NOW I'M FULL.
OOPS! I FORGOT I ALSO HAVE YOUR FAVORITE ICE CREAM.
ICE CREAM
YOU DON'T HAVE **THREE** STOMACHS, DO YOU?
I GOT AS MANY AS IT TAKES, PAL.

DON'T BE
JEALOUS
OF MY
ABILITIES.

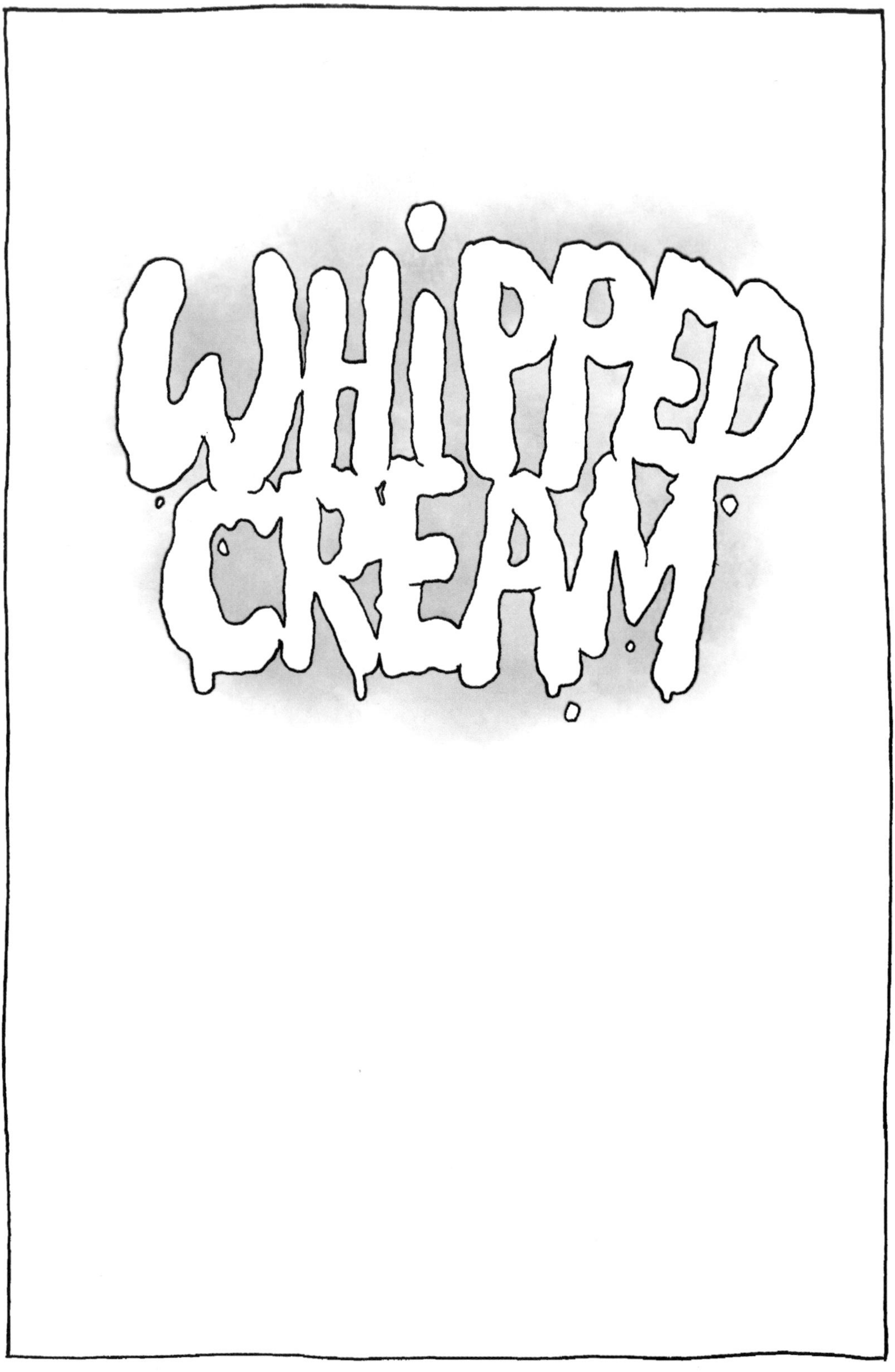
WHIPPED CREAM

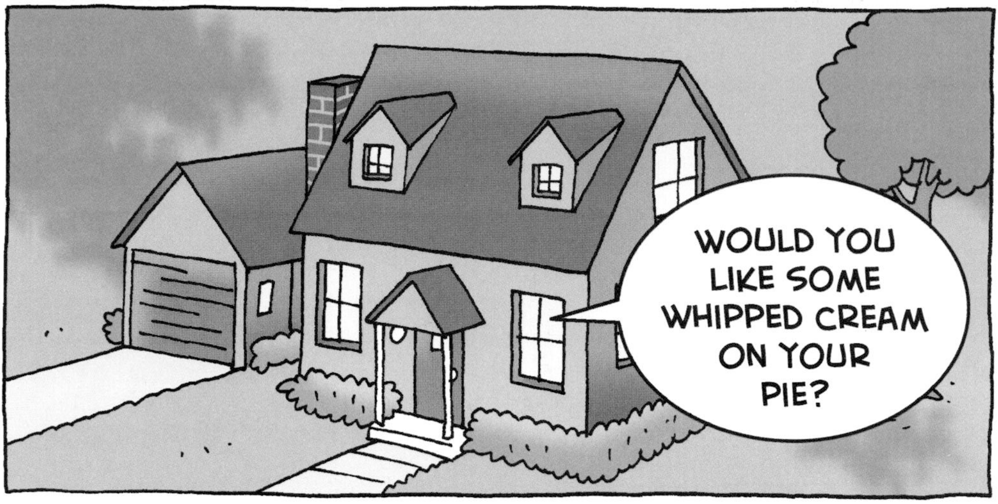
WOULD YOU LIKE SOME WHIPPED CREAM ON YOUR PIE?

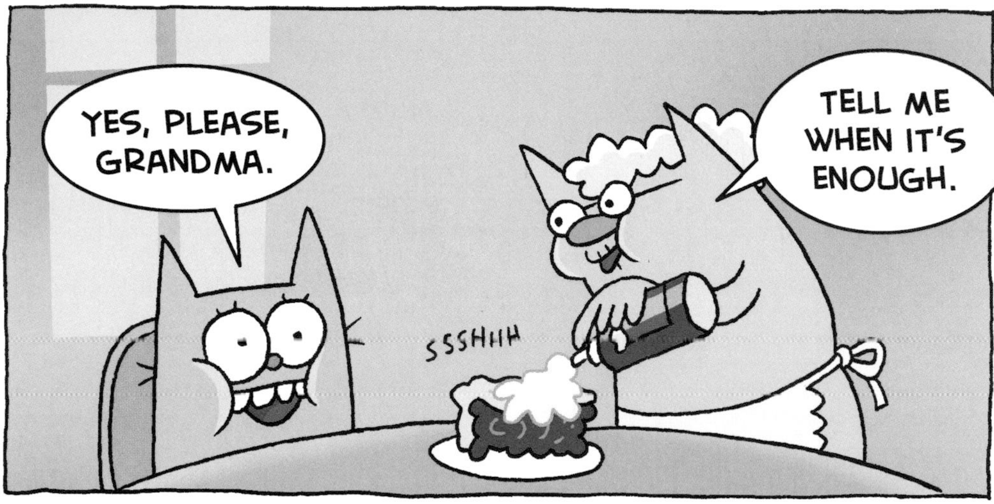
YES, PLEASE, GRANDMA.
TELL ME WHEN IT'S ENOUGH.
SSSHHH

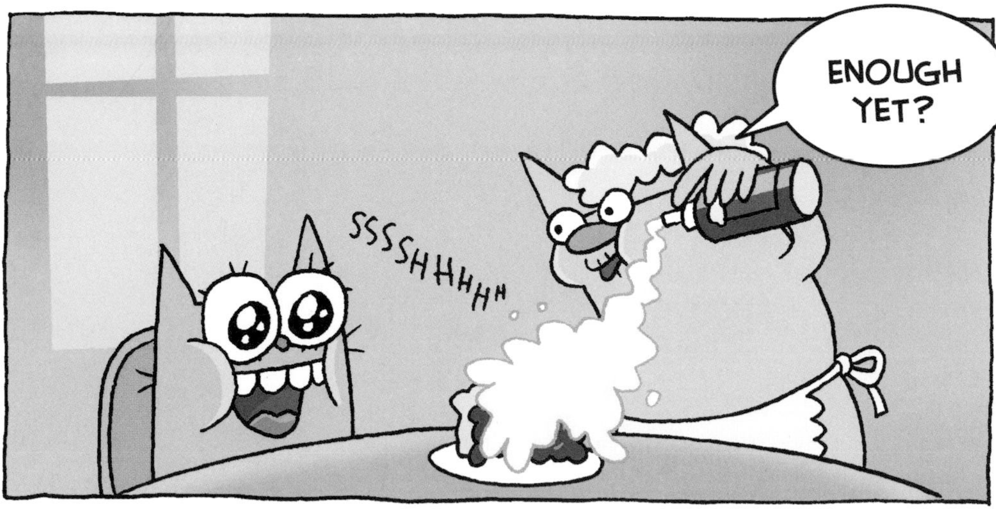
ENOUGH YET?
SSSSHHHHH

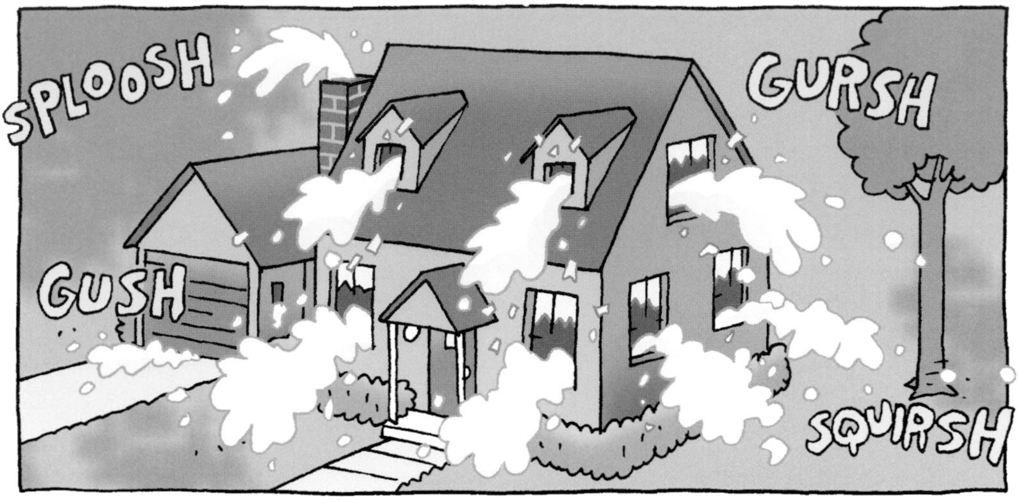
SPLOOSH
GURSH
GUSH
SQUIRSH

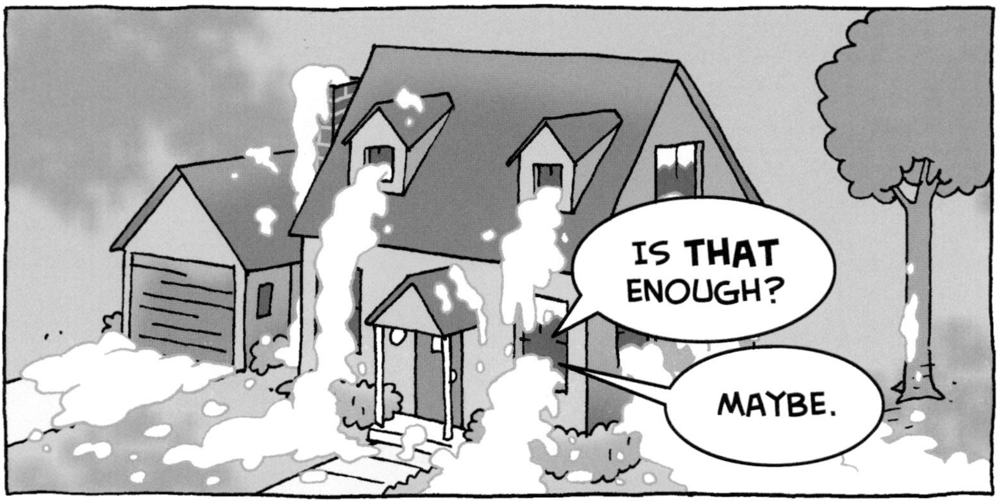
IS THAT ENOUGH?
MAYBE.

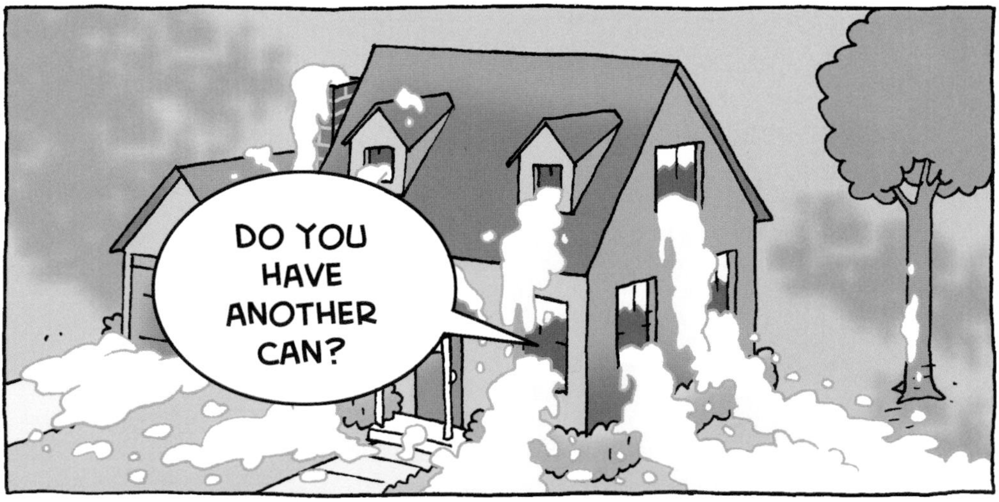
DO YOU HAVE ANOTHER CAN?

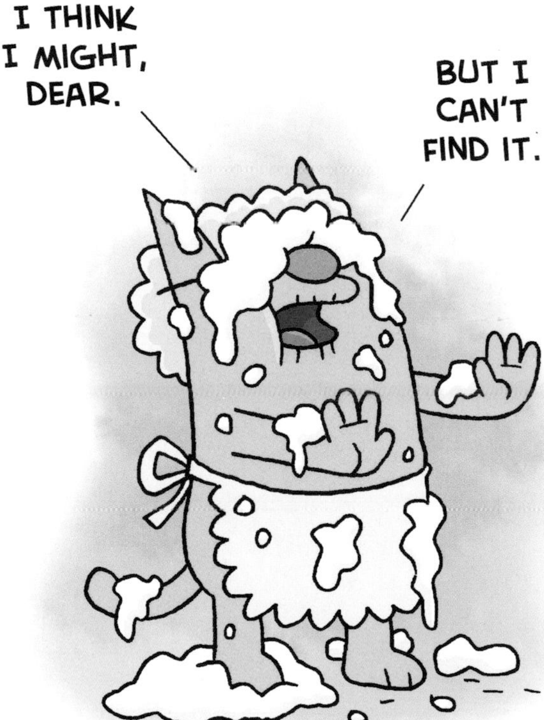
I THINK I MIGHT, DEAR.
BUT I CAN'T FIND IT.

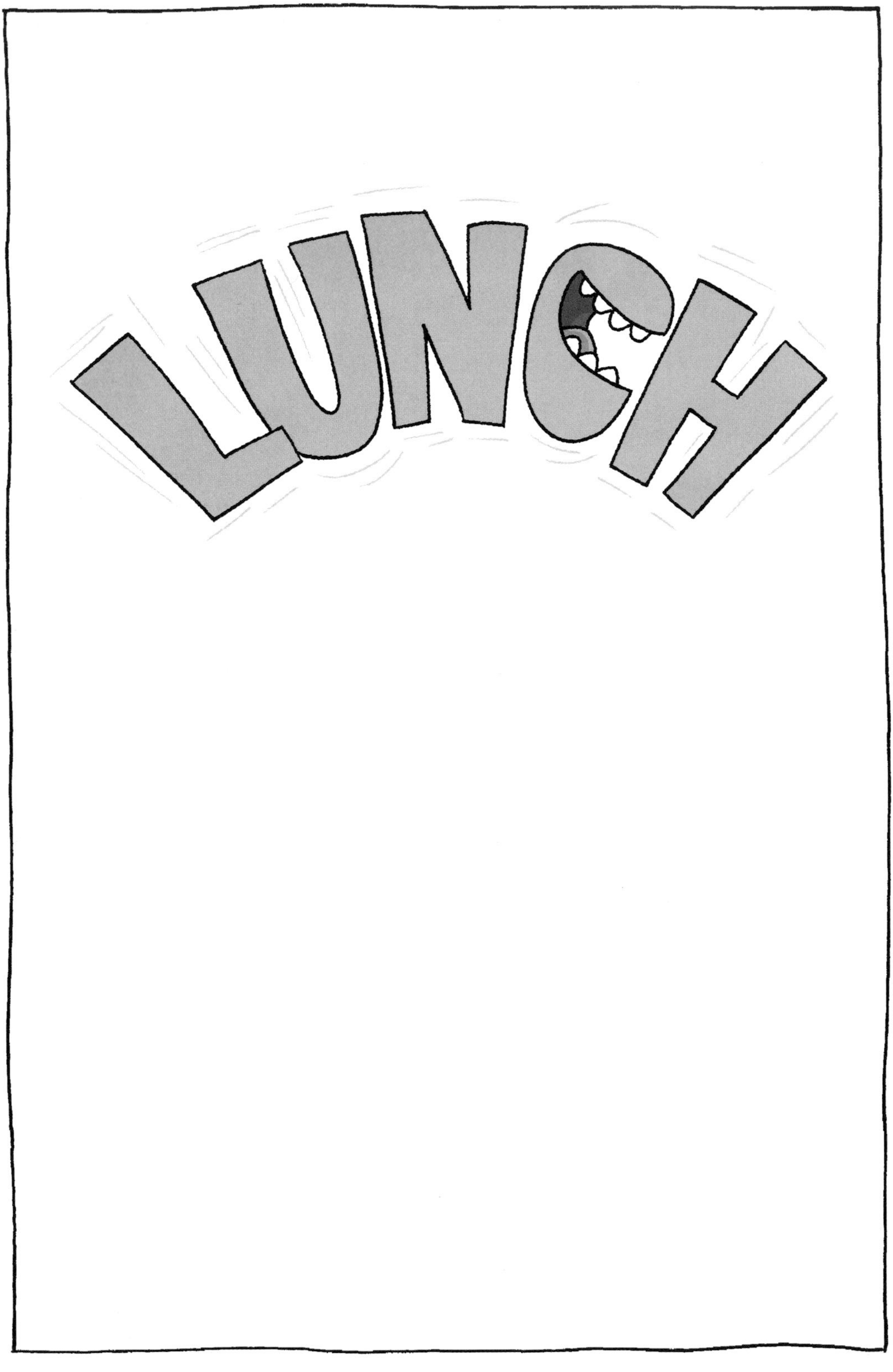
LUNCH

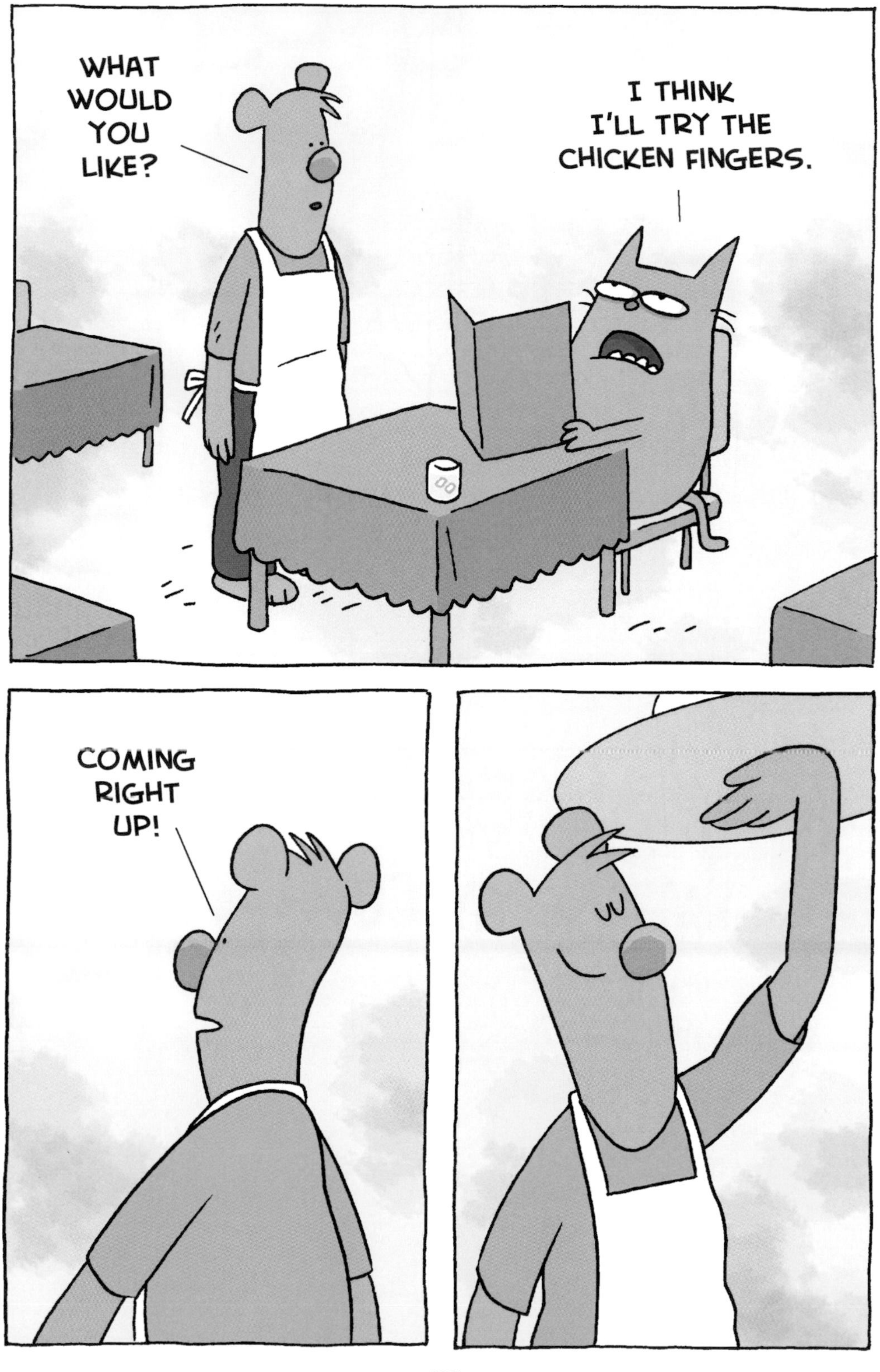
WHAT WOULD YOU LIKE?
I THINK I'LL TRY THE CHICKEN FINGERS.
COMING RIGHT UP!

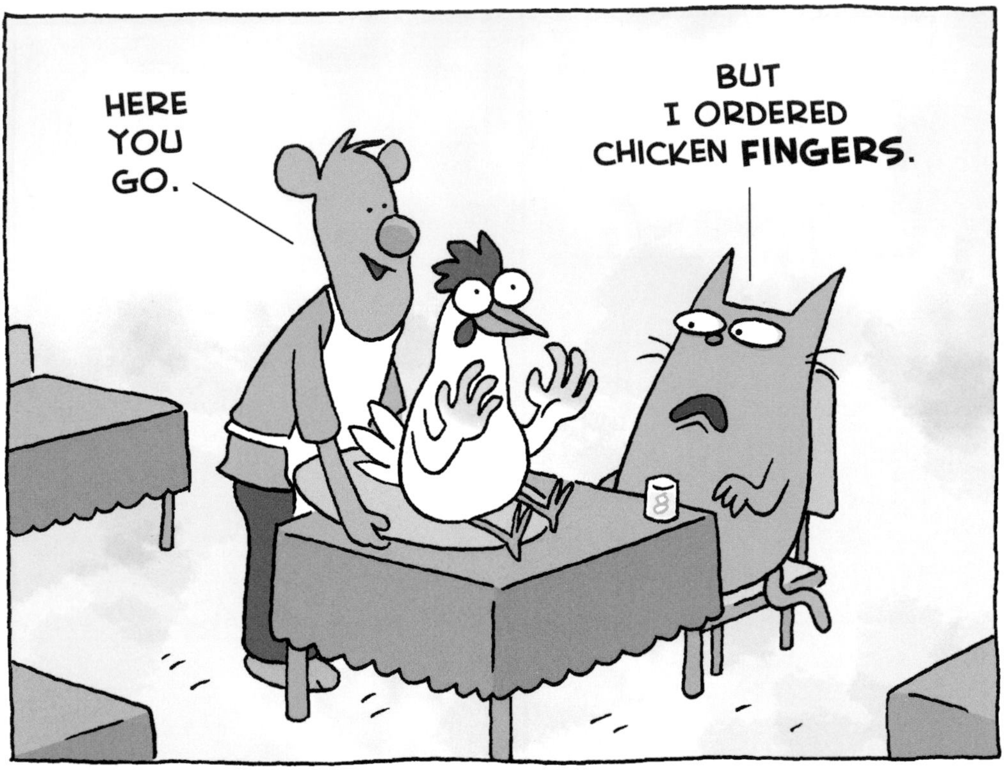
HERE YOU GO.
BUT I ORDERED CHICKEN **FINGERS**.

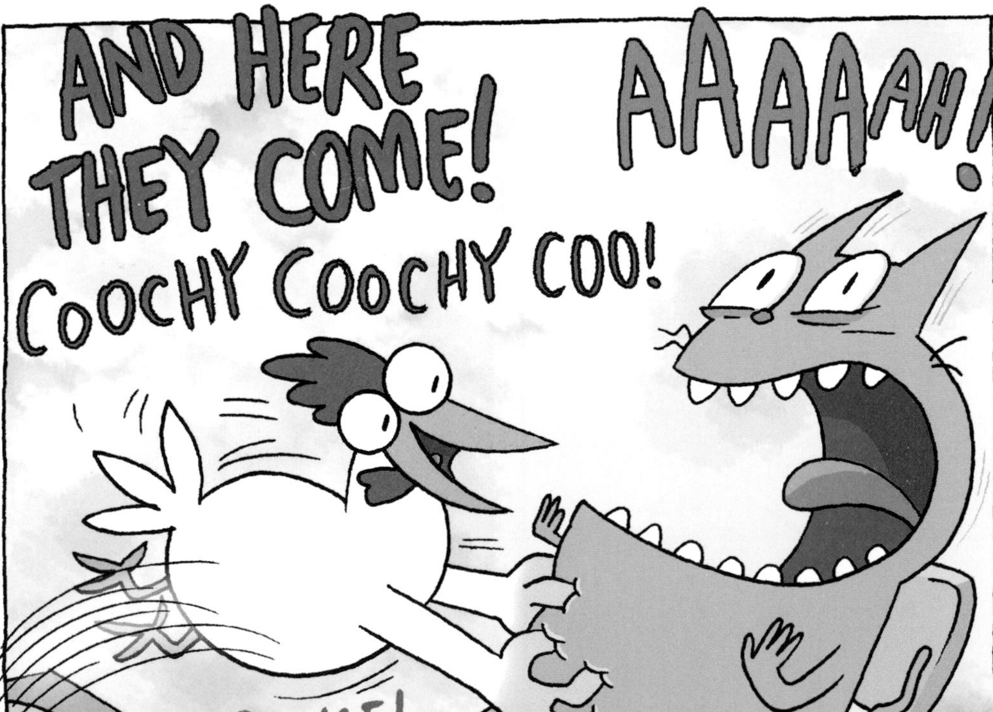
AND HERE THEY COME!
AAAAAH!
COOCHY COOCHY COO!
POUNCE!

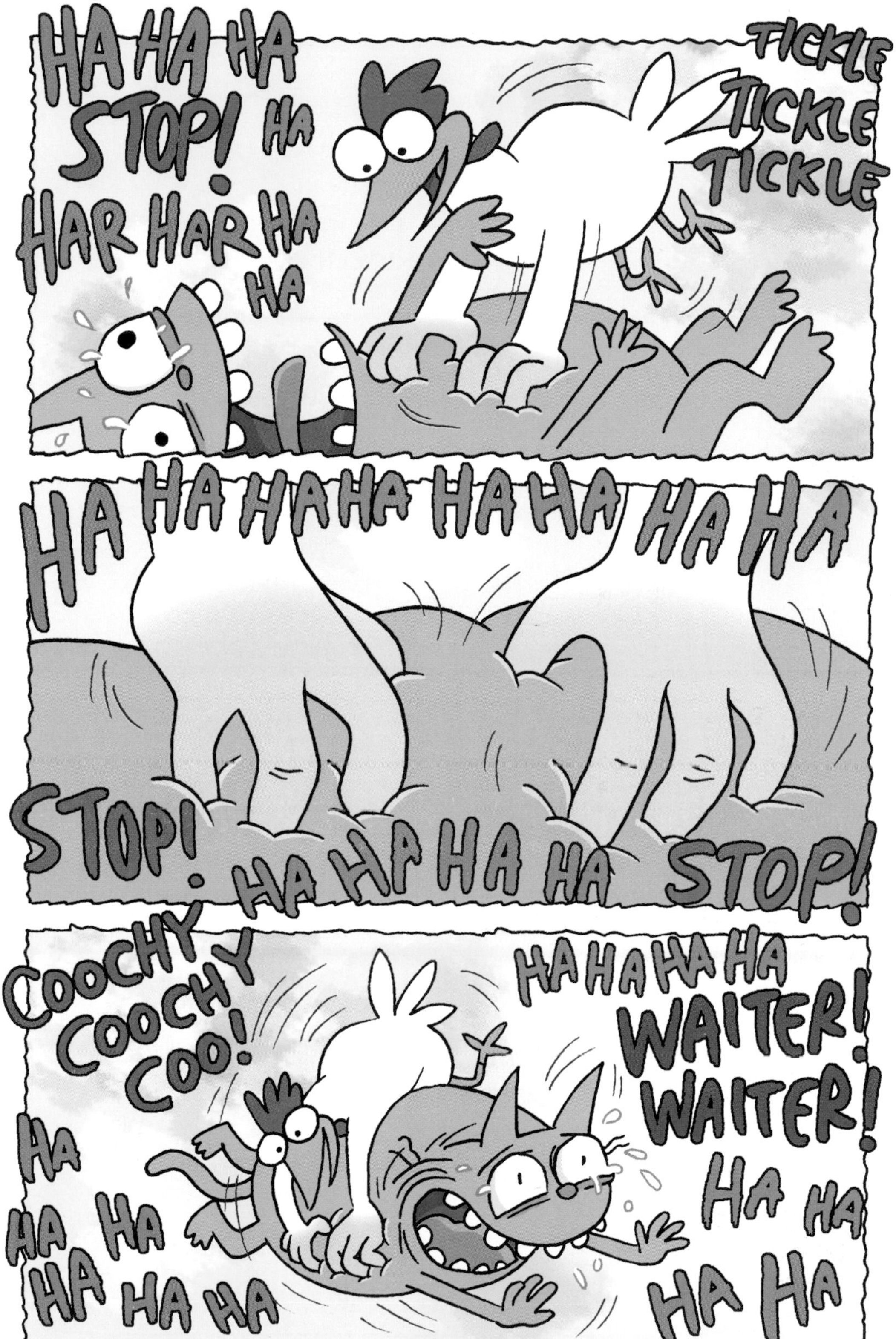
HA HA HA HA
STOP! HA
HAR HAR HA
HA
TICKLE
TICKLE
TICKLE
HA HA HAHA HA HA HA HA HA HA
STOP!
HA HA HA HA
STOP!
COOCHY
COOCHY
COO!
HA HA HA HA HA
WAITER!
WAITER!
HA
HA HA
HA HA HA
HA HA
HA HA

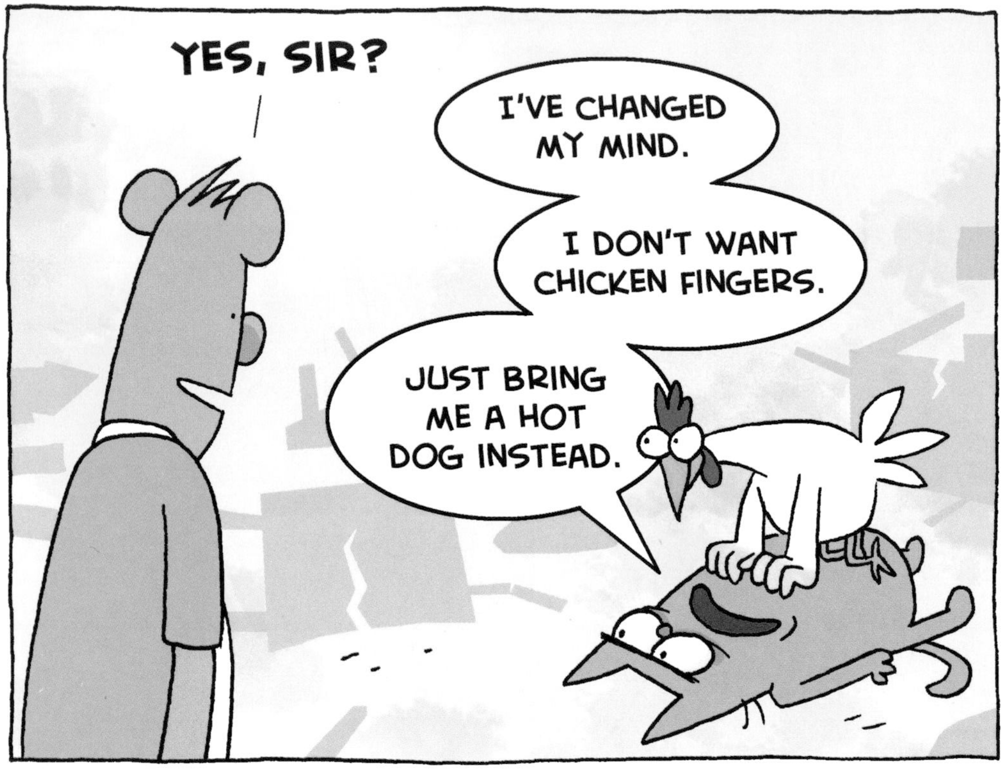
YES, SIR?
I'VE CHANGED MY MIND.
I DON'T WANT CHICKEN FINGERS.
JUST BRING ME A HOT DOG INSTEAD.

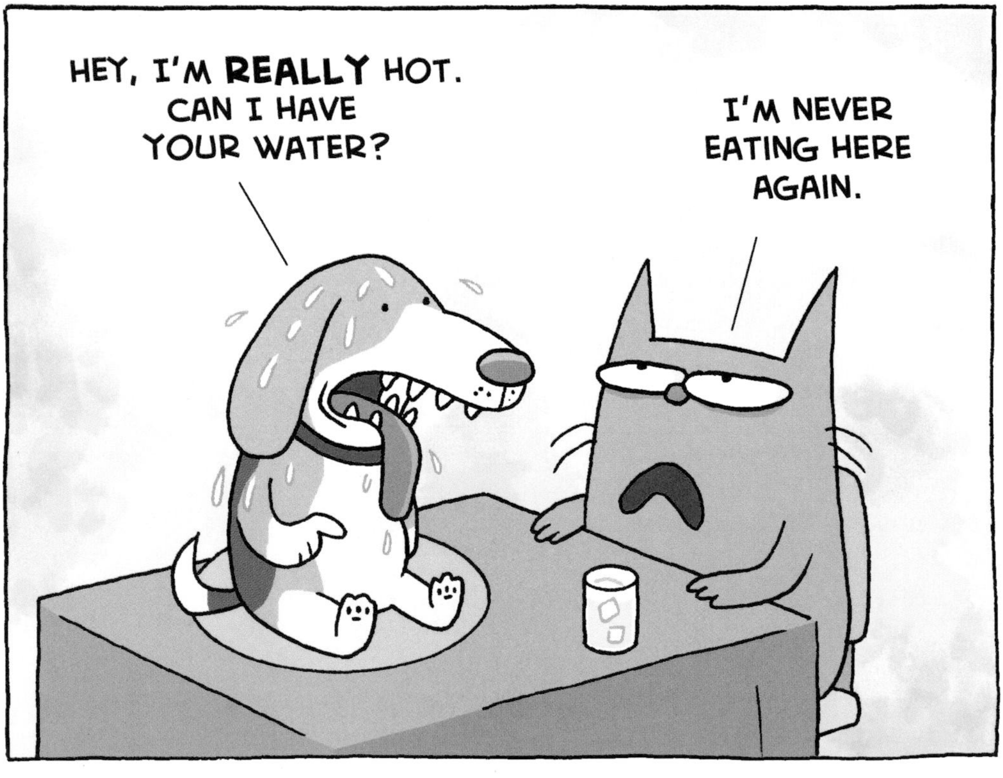
HEY, I'M REALLY HOT. CAN I HAVE YOUR WATER?
I'M NEVER EATING HERE AGAIN.

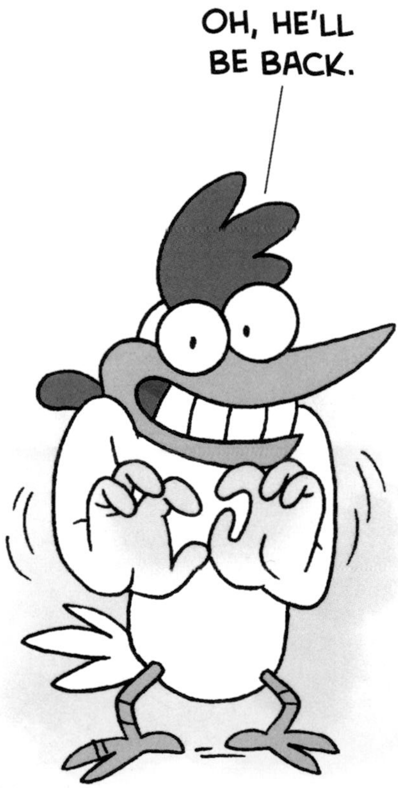
OH, HE'LL
BE BACK.

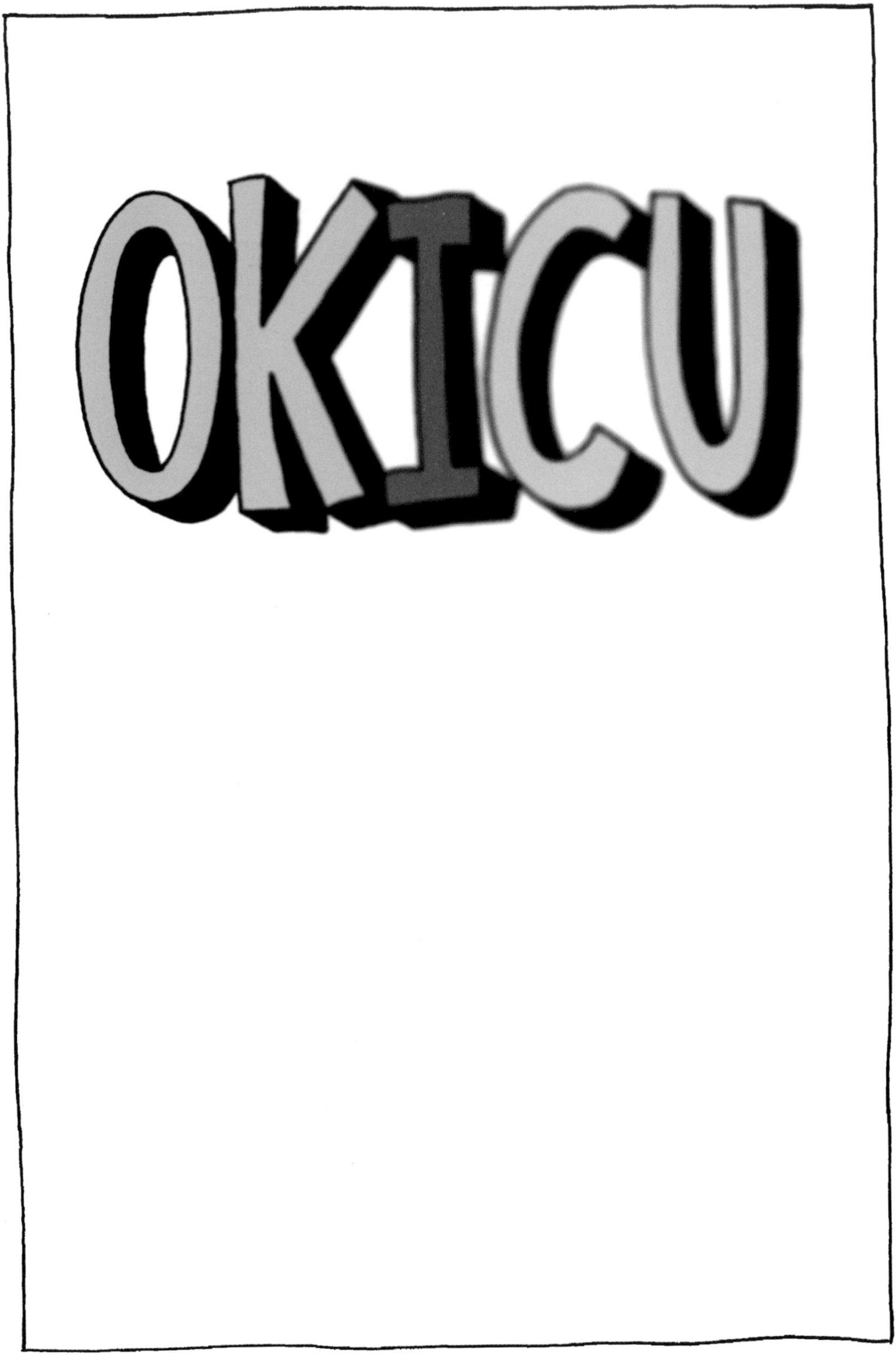
OKICU

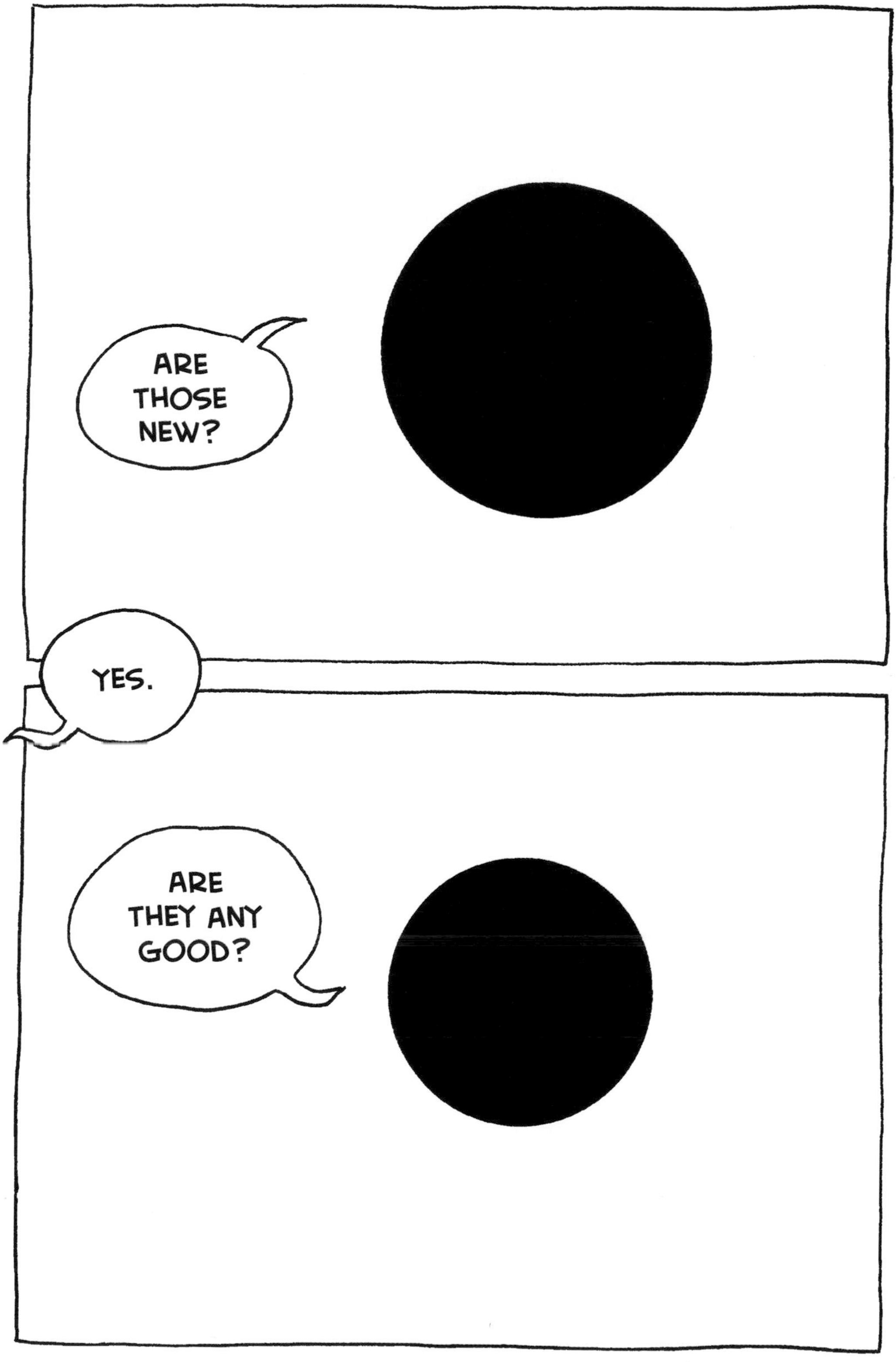
ARE THOSE NEW?
YES.
ARE THEY ANY GOOD?

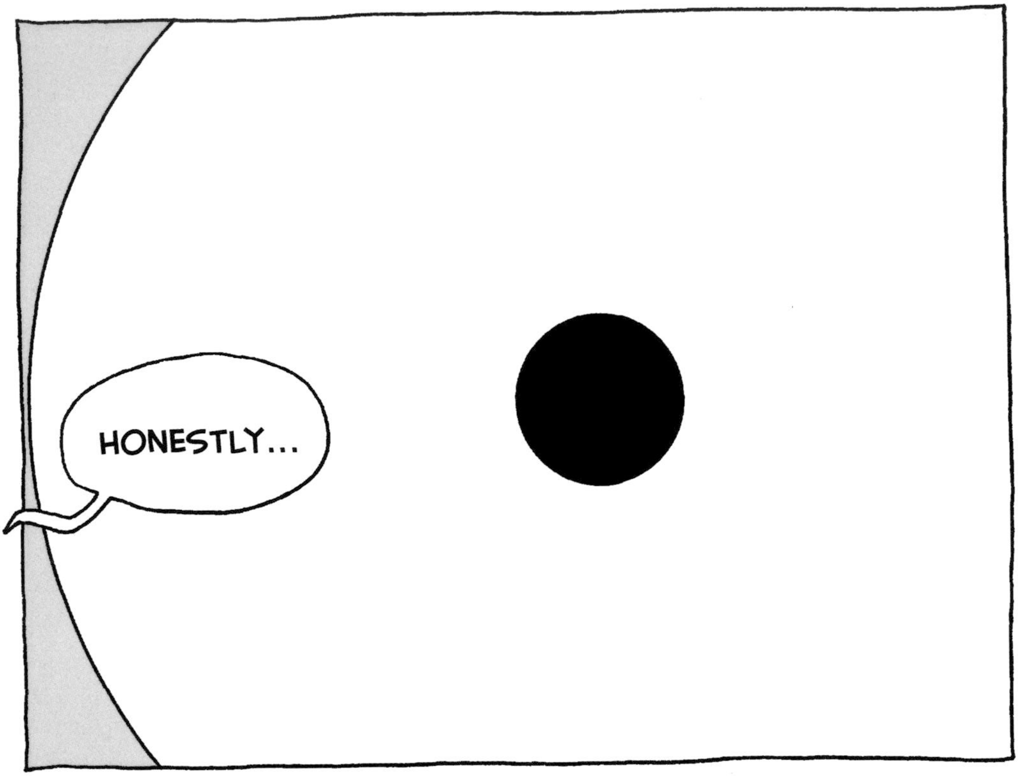
HONESTLY...

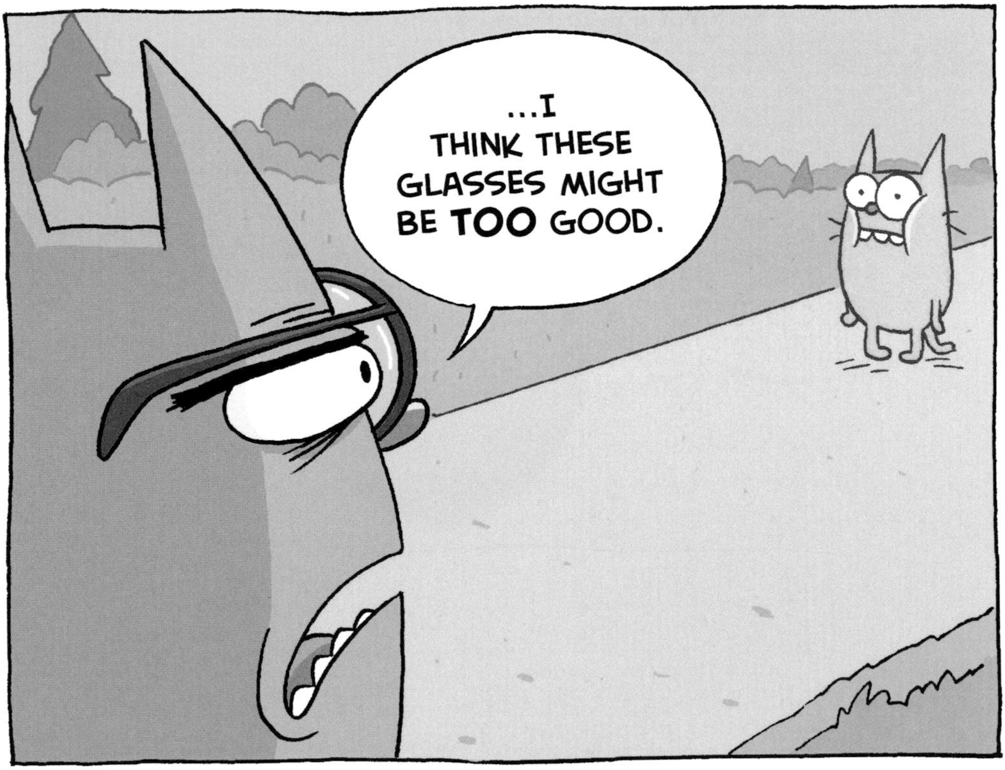
...I THINK THESE GLASSES MIGHT BE TOO GOOD.

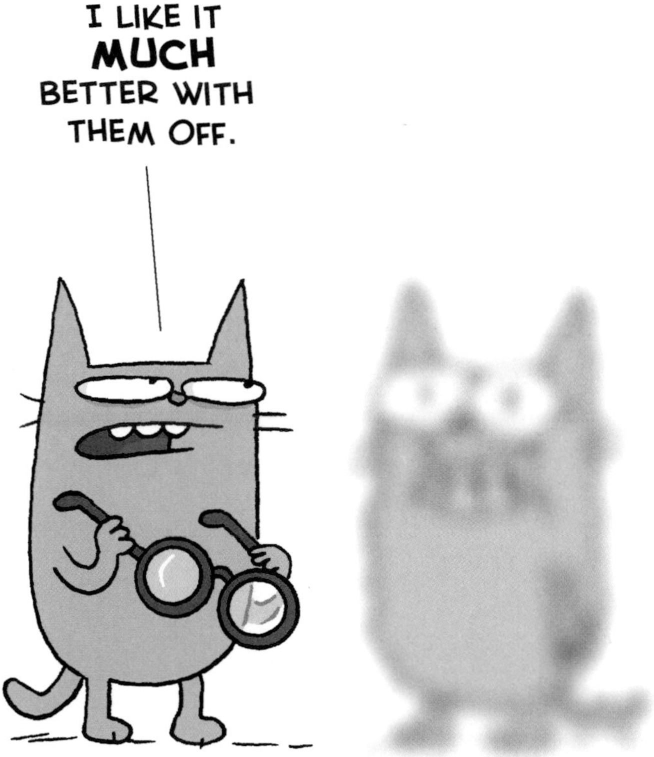
I LIKE IT **MUCH** BETTER WITH THEM OFF.

SIGNS

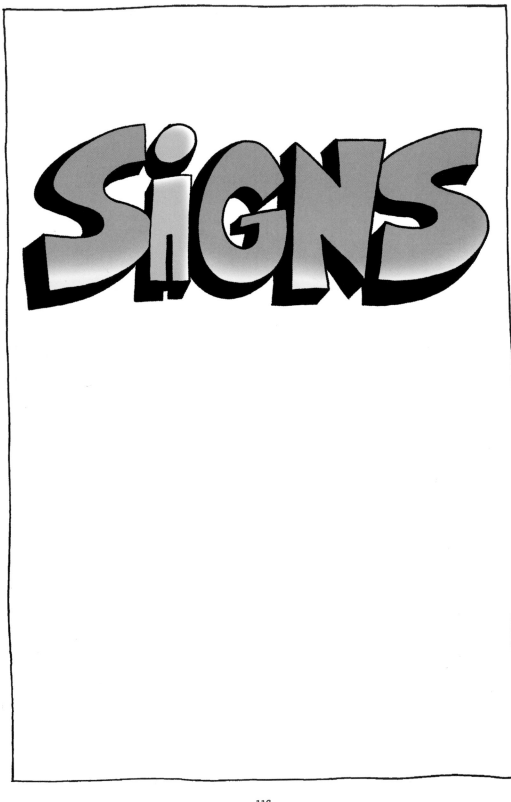

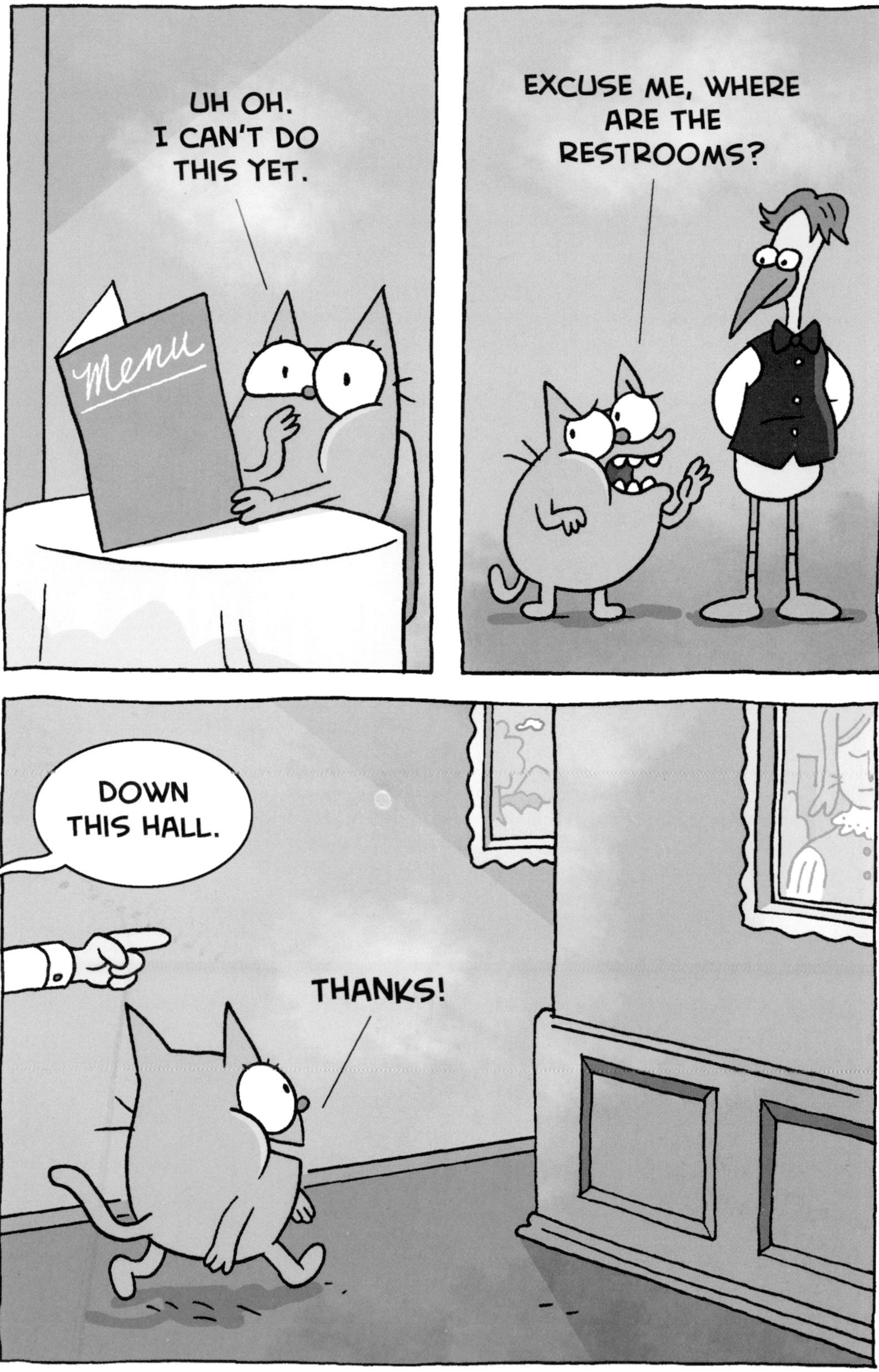
Menu
UH OH. I CAN'T DO THIS YET.
EXCUSE ME, WHERE ARE THE RESTROOMS?
DOWN THIS HALL.
THANKS!

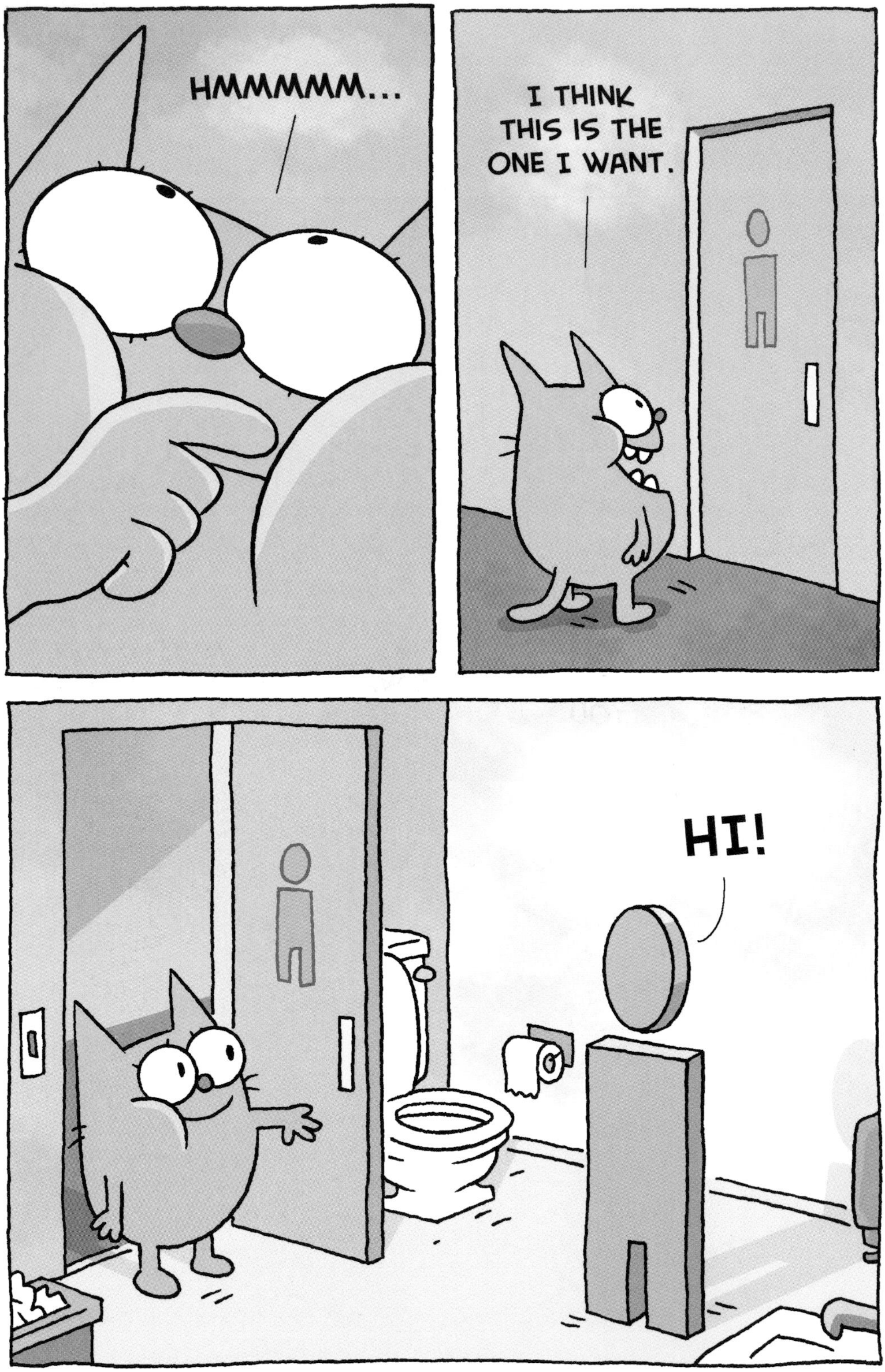
HMMMMM...
I THINK THIS IS THE ONE I WANT.
HI!

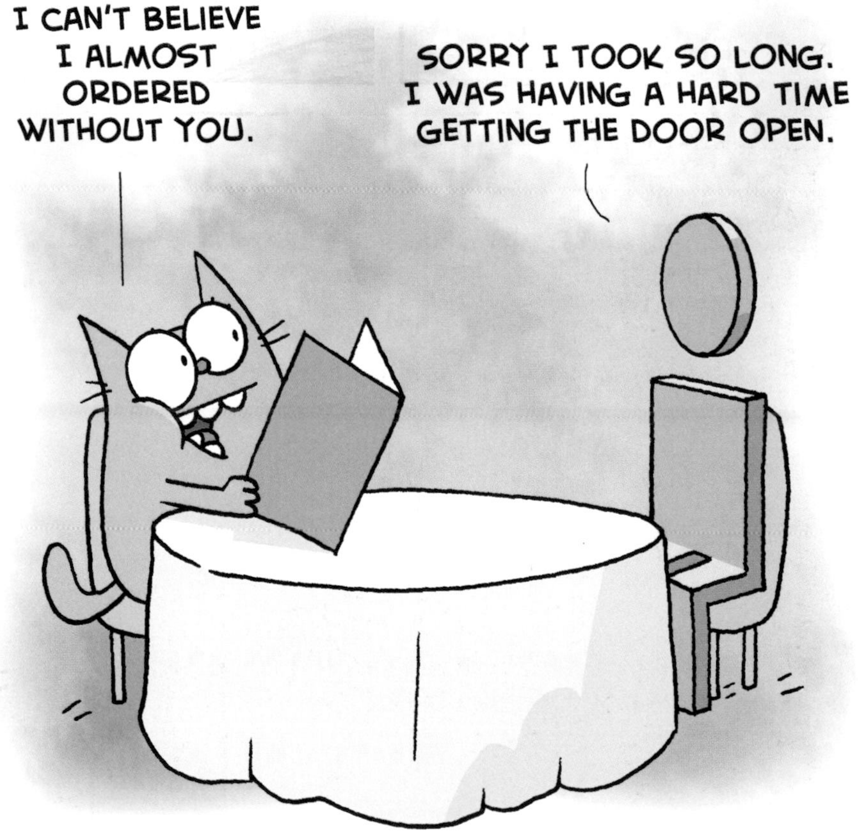
I CAN'T BELIEVE I ALMOST ORDERED WITHOUT YOU.
SORRY I TOOK SO LONG. I WAS HAVING A HARD TIME GETTING THE DOOR OPEN.

THE STAR

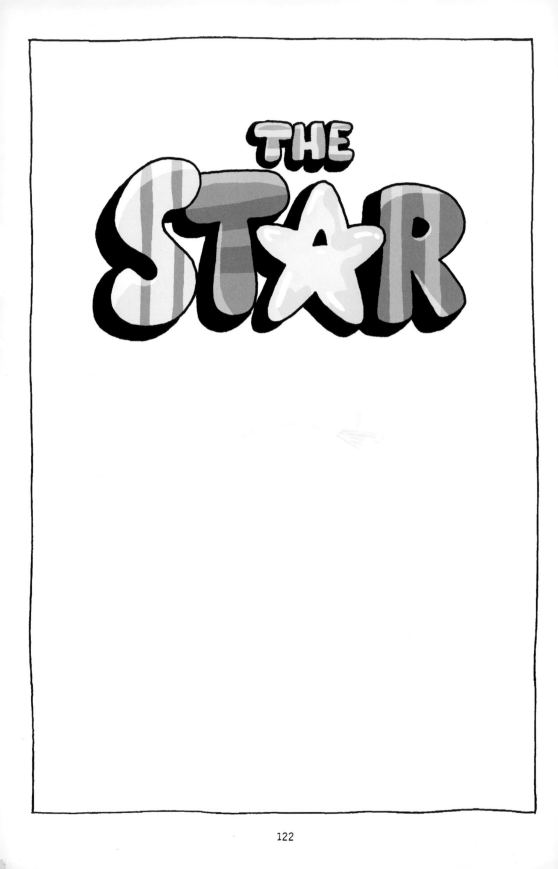

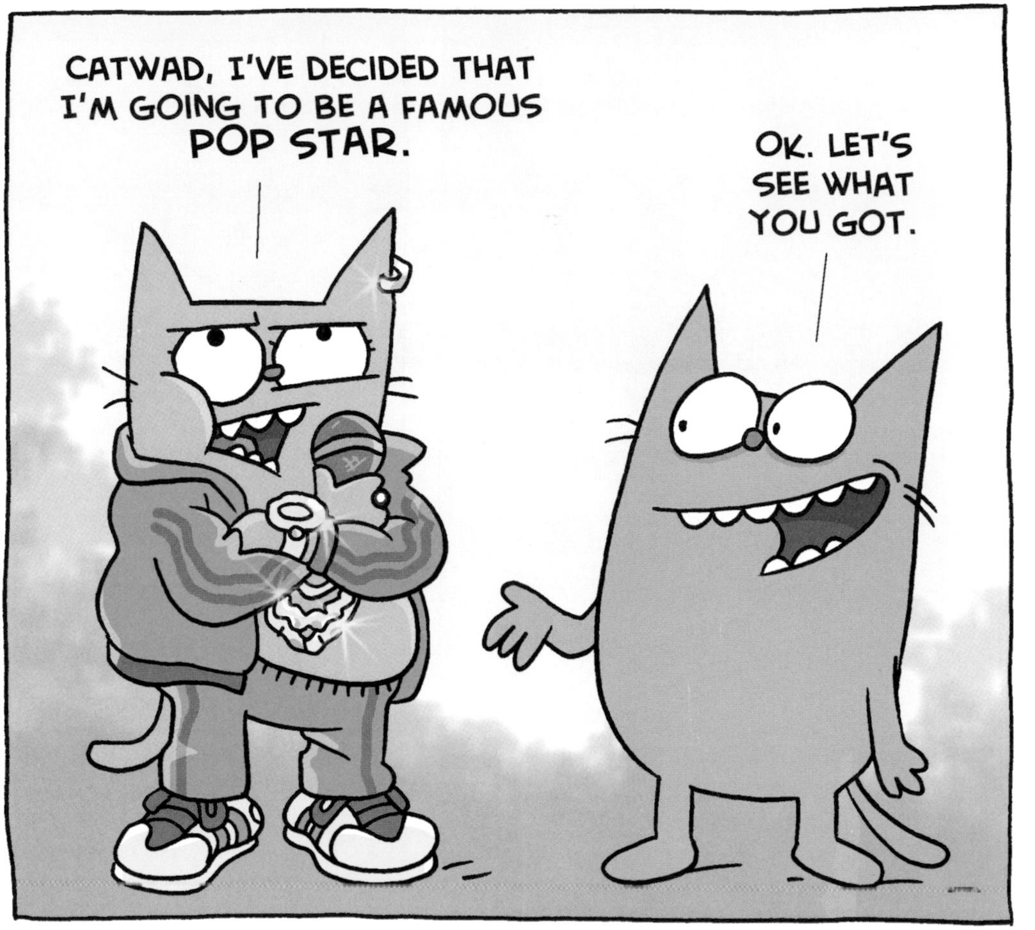
CATWAD, I'VE DECIDED THAT I'M GOING TO BE A FAMOUS POP STAR.
OK. LET'S SEE WHAT YOU GOT.

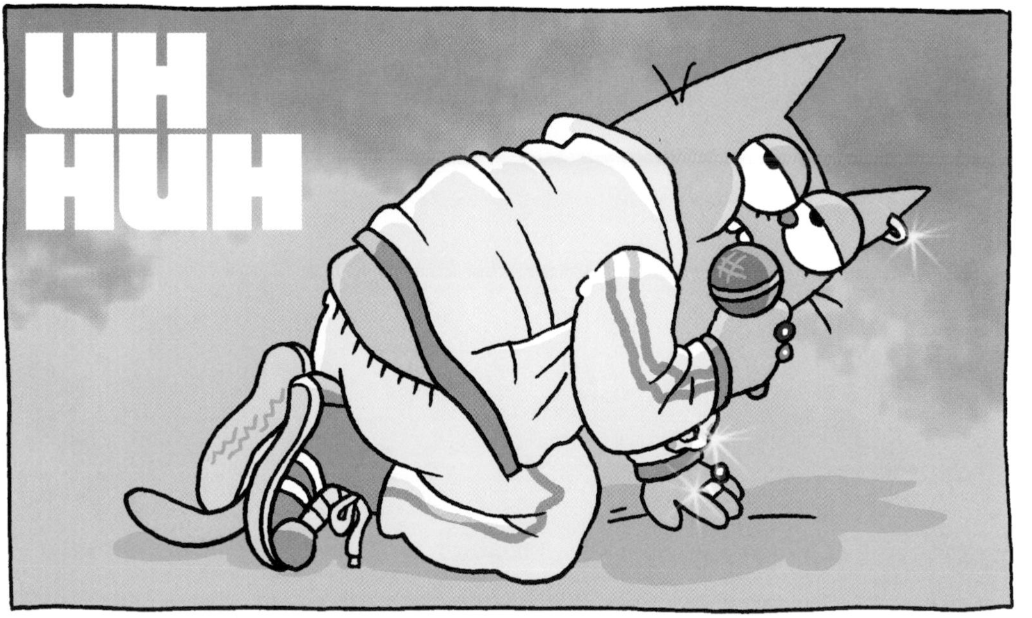
UH HUH

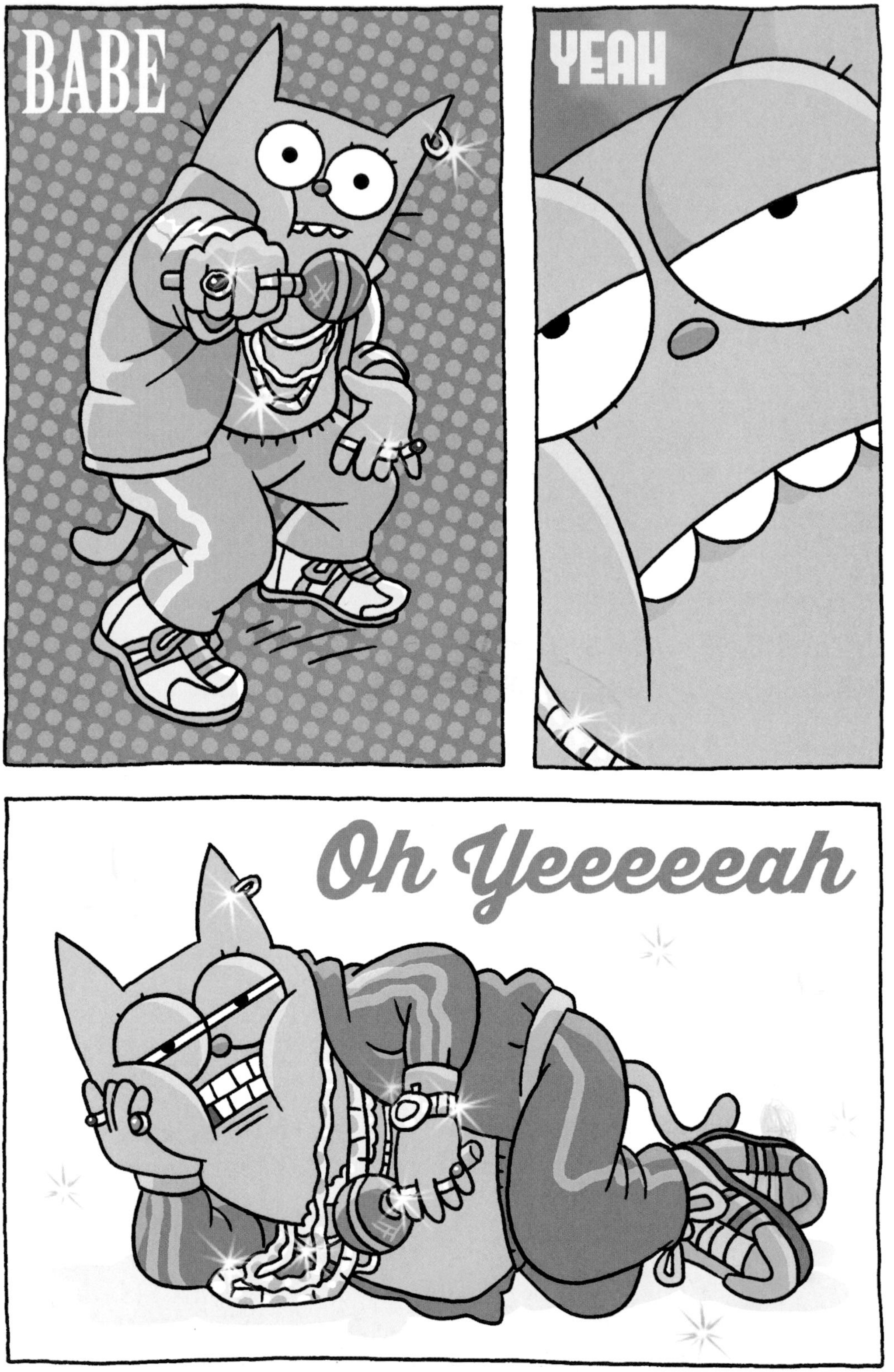
BABE
YEAH
Oh Yeeeeeah

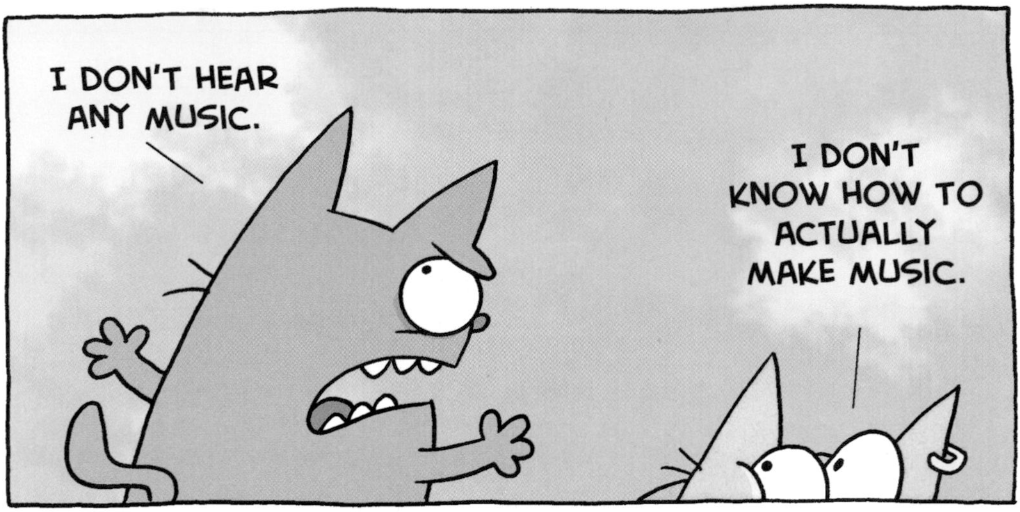
I DON'T HEAR ANY MUSIC.
I DON'T KNOW HOW TO ACTUALLY MAKE MUSIC.

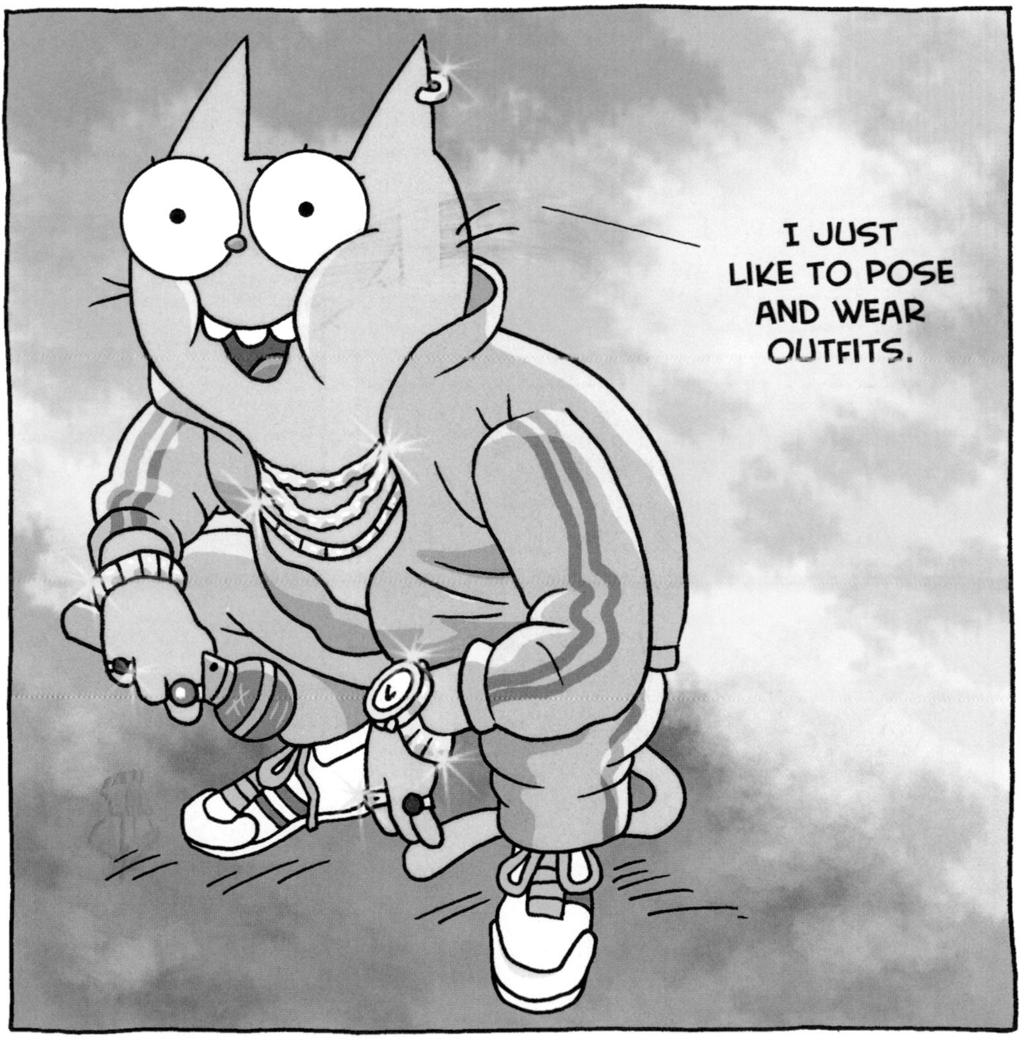
I JUST LIKE TO POSE AND WEAR OUTFITS.

BONUS ACTIVITY!

Maybe a new outfit will cheer up Catwad! Get out some markers or crayons, and add the patterns and colors that he'll like!

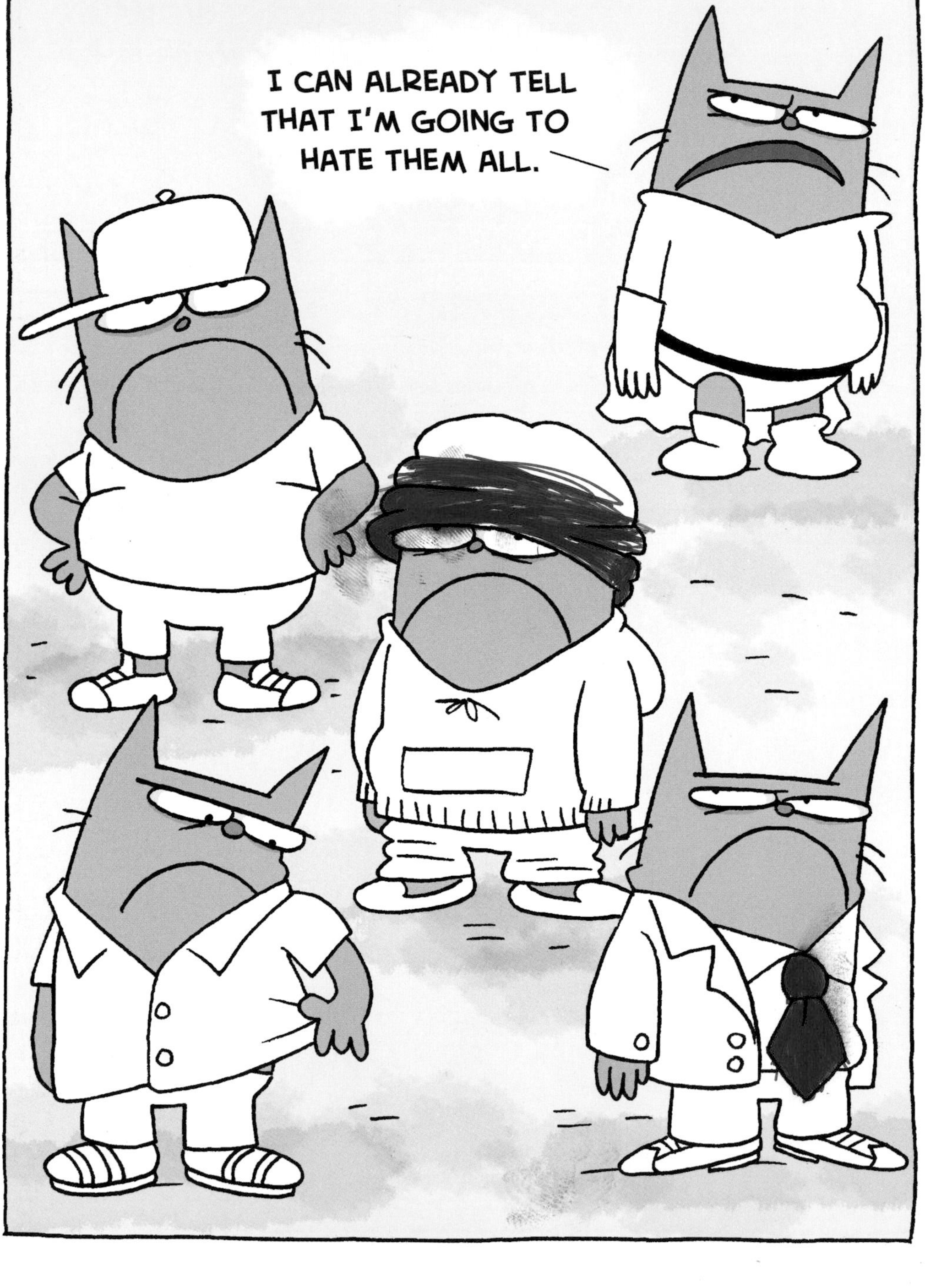
I CAN ALREADY TELL THAT I'M GOING TO HATE THEM ALL.

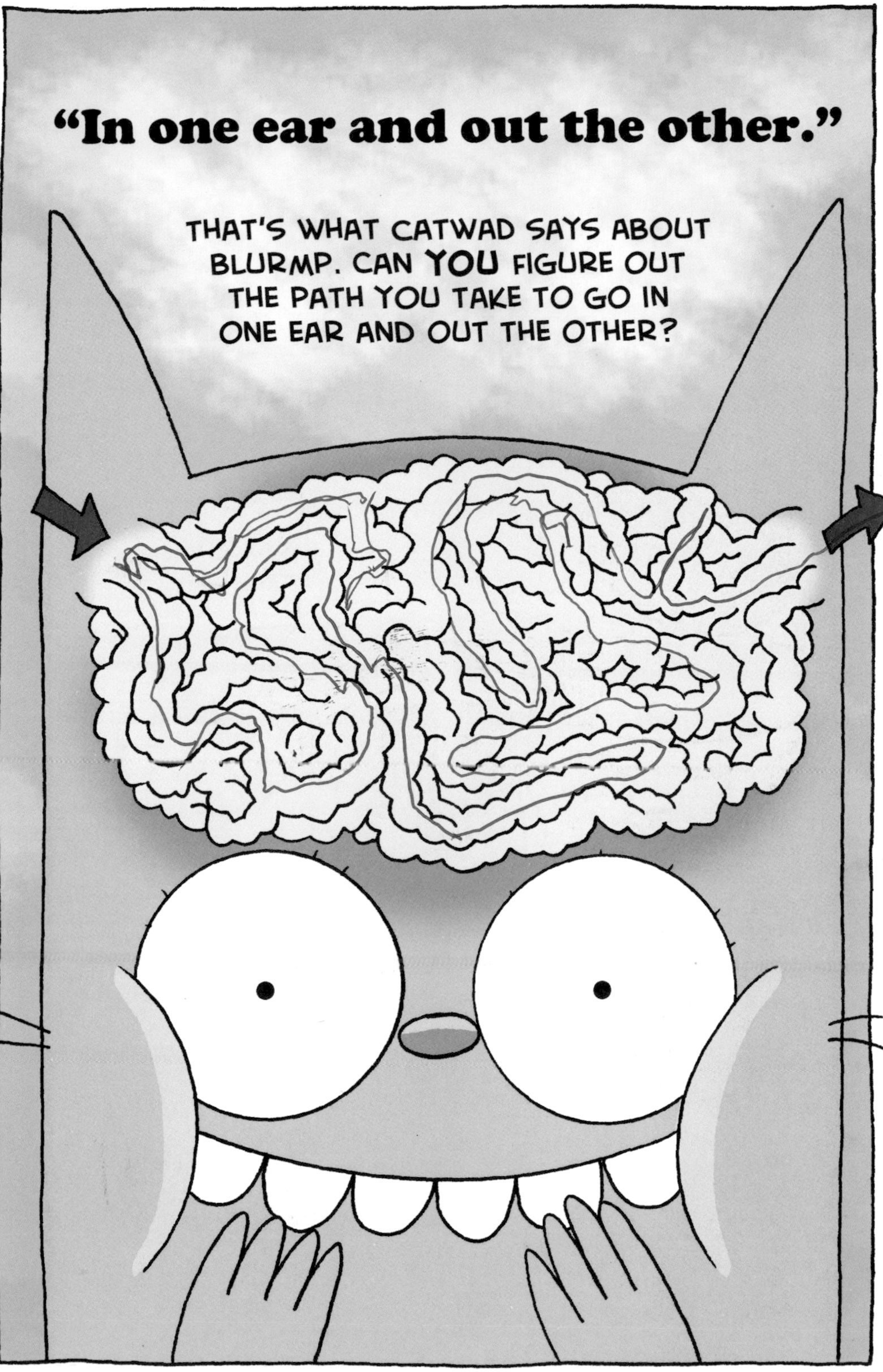
"In one ear and out the other."
THAT'S WHAT CATWAD SAYS ABOUT BLURMP. CAN YOU FIGURE OUT THE PATH YOU TAKE TO GO IN ONE EAR AND OUT THE OTHER?

DON'T MISS THE OTHER BOOKS IN THE SERIES!

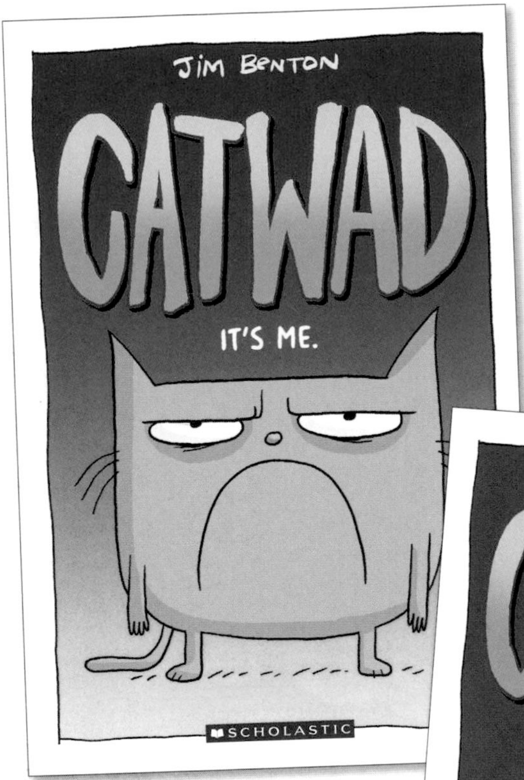
JIM BENTON
CATWAD
IT'S ME.
SCHOLASTIC

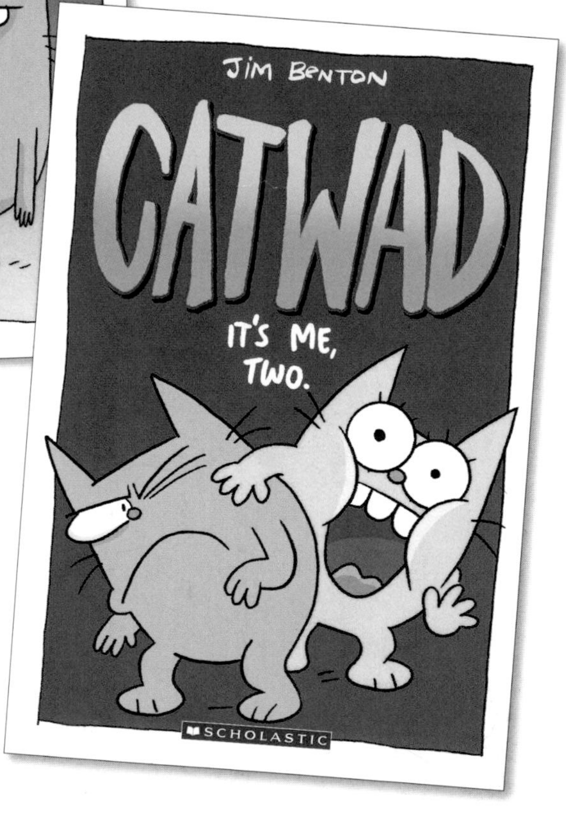
JIM BENTON
CATWAD
IT'S ME, TWO.
SCHOLASTIC